JINXED

Karma Series, Book Two

Donna Augustine

Copyright © Donna Augustine 2014

ISBN-10: 069232528X
ISBN-13: 978-0692325285

Strong Hold Publishing, LLC

For Donna Zink

This is concrete proof.

Edited by Devilinthedetailsediting.com

Express Editing Solutions

I watched as the sun set over the horizon and the world transitioned into soft light. Dusk; not day or night, but some indefinable place in between, a small window of time that doesn't belong to either. I'd never paid much attention to it in my mortal life, but now I anxiously awaited its arrival. I lived in my own sliver of life. Not alive but not dead. I used to think it was a curse. But with so many things in life that seem horrible on the surface, there's often a blessing buried deep within.

Musings from a transfer.

Prologue

"She's uncontrollable and should be eradicated." The woman pounded her fist on the massive, long wooden table she sat at, and a clap of thunder echoed through the air. "At the very least, returned to human status where we can limit the damage she does."

The other woman and man who sat at the table voiced their agreement.

Paddy stood before them, and just shook his head, then looked skyward at the twinkling stars above. He loved this room. It was his favorite place and one of the things he missed most when he returned to Earth. It was hard to understand the beauty of the stars until you were in their very midst, with no Earthly atmosphere to dull their glory.

"She's adding to the danger, not helping." The same woman pounded her fist a second time.

Again, Paddy simply shook his head but kept his

1

gaze star-bound.

"What is it about this soul that you are so attached to? That you think she, this pathetic uncontrolled being, will be our salvation?" the male at the long table asked.

Somebody had been talking.

Paddy pulled his gaze away from the stars to survey the three he'd known before eternity, back when they didn't have individual consciousness. He knew them as well as himself. Or he had, before time and physical distance started to create a divide; as it tended to do to all things, even them.

A long time ago, he'd thought they were immune to what happened to other beings. He too had been foolish in his relative youth. He'd thought that they'd always be in tuned to each other, but here they were, a chasm between them.

"I don't know if she will save us. I don't know anything at all, for sure. Not anymore." The long eons weighed down upon him. This was it. Even if she was the one, and they made it past what was coming, this would be his end.

It had been too long. He'd done all he could. He'd fulfilled his obligations. He was tired. It was time for him to become one with the Universe again. But they needn't know that yet. They'd fight his decision.

If he went back without them, even with their current status it would be painful to them, mentally and even perhaps physically. He understood it, but he only had enough strength for one foe at the moment.

"Then why?" she asked.

He had spent an eternity playing amongst the stars with them, until he'd decided to walk a different path.

Now he was of them but separate, but he still knew them. How could they not see it as clearly as he did? "Because she could be."

The male at the table leaned forward. "You spend too much time with them. It's affecting your thoughts."

"I do, and it's why I know." And why they didn't. They sat removed, peering down from lofty perches that obscured their view.

"Why can't you return to us? You belong here, not with them," Farah said, softening slightly. Once he had thought exactly as she did. They'd been inseparable. He'd changed, but so had she.

Yet, when he saw her now, he saw the sadness that leaked through into the anger. She was trying so hard to mask the pain that it was hard to watch.

"You're wrong. I do belong with them." He knew what those words would do to her.

"We've talked amongst ourselves, and we've decided to end her," Fia, the other woman, said, her first words spoken a death sentence.

"No." Paddy didn't scream but calmly listened.

"It must be done. What if she keeps going against us?" Fith, the other male, asked.

"You end her and you won't need to worry about them any longer. I'll be your biggest problem." It was a lie. Paddy would kill himself before harming them. But even though he still knew them, they no longer knew him well enough to realize it was an idle threat.

Farah jumped from her seat. "You wouldn't."

"I would." That she thought it was possible destroyed him. He needed to leave this beautiful place before more harm was done.

3

He walked out of the chamber. He'd hoped they'd see reason. If not, that they'd trust in his judgment; but the gap was worse than he'd realized.

Chapter One

First step is admitting there's a problem.

I pushed my hair back from my face, took a breath and decided to accept the inevitable. Lady Luck, my closest friend here, had set up this meeting, thinking I still needed help transitioning. Even though I wasn't sure this was the way to go about it, I didn't have the heart to tell her it was a waste of time.

So I stood in front of my mostly bored looking coworkers and decided to get this over with. "My name is Camilla, and I'm a dead girl."

"No!" Luck quickly scanned through the notes in front of her. "You are supposed to say, 'My name is Karma, and I'm a recovering mortal.'"

Was she kidding?

She looked at me and smiled encouragingly. No. Not kidding.

Trying to keep an impartial expression on my face, I stared at the people in front of me, sitting on folding chairs amidst the dingy office that the Universe called its headquarters.

We were in a building operated and run by Unknown Forces of the Universe. The place was a dump and my coworkers weren't exactly awe inspiring, either. The whole place and everything we did was hush hush, but I wasn't sure it mattered. Even if I brought a normal mortal here, to this dated building filled with Formica and employees plucked from every spectrum of the reject rainbow, who in their right mind would buy it? They were more likely to run out of here laughing than scurry up a mob for a witch-hunt.

Luck stared expectantly at me from where she sat next to Murphy's Law, another coworker. I repeated the line and then stood there, waiting for the next order. She's so lucky the ten-year-old coffee maker had held today. If I hadn't had that extra cup, I'm not sure what might have happened.

I didn't know what she wanted next, but she was a tad bossy so I knew I wouldn't have to wait long.

"Now, give us a story of what your normal day would've been, back when you had this horrible problem." Luck checked something off on her notepad, while Kitty, the cat herder in charge of black cats, sat behind her, yawning.

Jockey was a seat over from Kitty, picking his teeth with a piece of hay. I'd heard there was an entire stable of Night Mares around here, but I hadn't found it yet. That was on my to do list, right after I tracked down Santa, who was still on Spring Break.

The Tooth Fairy, who I'd only met recently, smacked Jockey's hand away from his mouth and handed him floss. T, as a lot of people called him, was a nice enough guy, but it was hard to talk to him, with the way he stared at your mouth when you spoke.

Luck cleared her throat, demonstrating her eagerness to continue this little gathering she'd instigated.

The sooner I finished, the better. "Um, well, I'd get up in the morning around seven. Some days, I'd meet with clients or do paperwork. You know, file motions and such. Sometimes I'd have court. Those were the most interesting days, and I think what I was best at, getting up in front of a judge and jury, and trying to sway them over to my way of thinking." My thoughts wandered back to those days. I'd wear one of my classic black suits that lent my girlish looks more of a mature, respectable appearance. "It was invigorating," I said, mostly to myself, as I stared off in space. Some mornings, I still had to remind myself of where I was and that I didn't have clients anymore.

Luck groaned. "That sounds just tragic!" She had a flair for the dramatic.

"It doesn't sound that bad—" Murphy was cut off by Luck's elbow meeting his ribs. He opened his mouth, as if to complain, and then just shut it again. *Good move, Murphy.* He didn't have a chance against her.

Luck either didn't notice his annoyance or, more likely, didn't care, as she covered her heart with her hand. "What a tragedy. It's a blessing it all ended." She looked around the room, giving everyone the evil eye until they started agreeing with her.

Pleased, she moved on to the next thing on her list. "Who's got the one month dead coin?"

"I thought we weren't actually dead?" I asked.

There was a lot of ambiguity surrounding that subject. We weren't mortal anymore, that was for sure. I could swing by my grave and prove that anytime I wanted. But we had bodies with needs and could get hurt or killed. And although I'd been told we didn't age, my hair continued to grow. I still woke up hungry in the morning, and watch out if I didn't get a cup of coffee. It was like we were straddling some invisible fence between immortality and human frailty.

"Seriously? Are we dead or not?" I asked again when I still received no response.

I got several yeses and nos at the same time, confirming my own belief. Somehow, we were neither.

Luck turned to me and her eyes flared. "We are not ruining this wonderful meeting with another dead debate. Now, who has the coin?"

No one spoke. This could go bad and quickly. Please, could someone have the goddam coin so we could be done?

"I thought Jockey was getting it?" Crow said, the black bird on his shoulder cawing in what could've been agreement. If the bird had any sense, he was mocking us all for the fools we were.

"Death said he was getting it!" Jockey, always a little bit defensive to begin with, stood in alarm.

Death, who appeared to be middle-aged man in a sweater vest, looked up from his *How to Help Those of the Recently Deceased* book. "No one told me to get anything. I thought Mother was getting it." Death free-lanced as a grief counselor when he wasn't escorting the newly departed along their way. Really, the guy knew how to work both ends of a situation, and he was excellent at both. He helped kill your loved ones, and then collected a check from teaching you how to cope with it. I could only imagine how bad that would be for his booming business if it got out.

Mother, surrounded by her beefy gardeners, just shrugged in her perfectly petite way. Mother Earth didn't particularly like to get her hands dirty in trivial matters she considered beneath her.

"Fine. I'll get it myself tomorrow, you bunch of lazy good-for-nothings!" Luck was practically frothing at the mouth at her coworker's lack of enthusiasm in making her meeting a rousing success

"Is this almost over?" my boss, Harold, asked. His chair was situated at the very outer limits of the space, where he could still claim participation and yet not have to interact much. Harold didn't particularly care for me, but he wasn't the warm and fuzzy type, so it was very hard to distinguish the difference between his likes and dislikes. I'd yet to find anyone or thing he did like, other than his piles of papers.

Before Luck could address Harold's question, Fate walked in. His eyes immediately landed on me and stayed there. My gaze quickly moved away, but it didn't lessen the effect, or how my senses seemed to attune only to him now.

Everyone else's eyes shot to him. He had a way of doing that, hogging all the attention. This was a meeting about me, not that I wanted it, but he even hogged this. The fact that I didn't think his hogging problem was intentional made it no less annoying.

In truth, it was just something about him. I used to

9

think it was his dark good looks, or maybe his height and build, but the more I got to know him, the more I realized it was none of those things.

Even if his looks were the first thing that drew your attention, there was something else entirely that kept you transfixed. It was something in the way he moved, the way he spoke, and the look in his eyes. It wasn't that the people around him were lacking, it was that he just had more of everything.

To sum it up, Fate was like the Universe's experiment in extra credit. If the rest of us were a scoop of vanilla ice cream, he was a sundae, with extra fudge and a cherry.

Luck stood and pointed a finger at him. "You're late. You said you would be here," she scolded, in no way wilting, even under Fate's full glare, something that caused most people to whither.

I, on the other hand, tried to avoid all direct contact. I'd been dodging Fate for the past few weeks. It wasn't that I disliked him. It was just…complicated.

He'd been letting me, too, up until a couple of days ago. But something had changed in the past forty-eight hours. He'd become a hunter and I the prey. I didn't like the feeling of being a gazelle sprinting away from the lion with about as much cover as the grass on the plains.

No matter where I ducked lately, he showed up. Obviously, I should have expected him to come to this. I just wish he hadn't.

"A job ran late," he said to Luck, unperturbed. He found a chair at the back, slung his arm across the empty one next to him and kicked his feet up on the one in front of him. Only Fate, the space hog, would need three chairs to get comfortable.

The second his eyes turned back on me again, I started squirming in my spot. Wow, look at that interesting dirt mark on the wall near the door. The pretense became more than that as I realized just how dirty the walls really were. You would think they could get a painter in this place. Hell, give me a gallon and I'd do it myself. Someone really needed to get a handle on the housekeeping around here.

There was even shadowing around the doorknob. No wonder they always tried to dim the lights. I'd thought it was Harold being cheap, trying to lower the gas and electric bill. We might be Unknown Forces of the Universe, but Santee Cooper, the local electric company, sure knew how to find us. I'd seen the bills on Harold's desk last time I was snooping.

Somewhere in those stacks, he's got a file on me. I never passed up an opportunity to try and find out what they'd written about me. One of these days, and I had a lot of them coming since I was signed on here for the next thousand years, I'd find it.

The dirty door I'd been staring at opened suddenly, and a blond Adonis stood there, making everything look even shabbier with his elegance. No, not just an Adonis, this was the real deal. Cupid. Decked out in a suit of white silk, from head to toe, he was a sight to behold. Large diamonds in his ears and on his fingers, flashing their value the way only a superb stone could, dimmed in comparison to the person wearing them.

Cupid wasn't just in the building, he was inside our space. Our office radio would've screeched to a stop if it had been playing, and not just because the antenna was broken and someone had walked in just the wrong circumference to disrupt the signal. Just like that, without another word, the meeting adjourned and everyone in the office shot into action. Chairs scraped across the floor, metal clanking into metal, as we all scrambled to get as far away from him as possible.

I wasn't surprised Cupid's appearance had everyone running for cover. I'd found out from Luck, in one of our chitchats, that I hadn't been the only victim of Cupid's love charm. Those who hadn't had firsthand experience still knew enough to avoid him.

But it was worse now. Word had spread that he had a way of transmitting his spells without ingestion, and no one knew how he was doing it. The only case I'd known of was with me, so someone had spilled the beans. Unfortunately, loose lips—also known as Lady Luck—hadn't been discreet enough to omit who had become afflicted.

When confronted about her gossiping ways, she swore she'd only told Murphy. Murphy then swore to her he'd only told Crow. I lost track of the chain of information somewhere around Death, who had even relayed the story to the Tooth Fairy. For all I knew, they'd even told the human accountant—just some run of the mill guy who they'd accidentally rented space to—some jumbled up version of the truth.

That was when I realized that even though it was a small office, filled with beings who weren't quite human, it was still gossip central. And those gossipers were running like hell was on their heels right now.

Cupid was blocking the only exit. Everyone was

aware of what could come from close proximity, and with no other place to retreat, we all bee-lined it for Harold's office.

"Where's everyone going?" Cupid yelled. Nobody looked at him or answered, as if we could all just pretend we hadn't noticed him as we did the fifty-yard dash.

I tripped on a cat toy in my rush to get to the door and Luck, a step a head of me, paused briefly then mouthed the words, *I'm sorry*, as she kept going. I didn't blame her. We all knew the stakes.

Just as I was preparing for the inevitable, two hands went under my arms and lifted me up, propelling me forward.

"Oh no, you're not staying out here when I've got other places to be tonight," Fate said.

Chapter Two

Don't sink my ship.

He practically carried me ahead of him into the already full office. He stepped in front of me and plowed through the group, to grunts of annoyance, until we took up the prime real estate of the northwestern corner, in between the filing cabinet and the trash can.

Harold's office could be described as cozy and not due to the decor. We all barely squeezed in and there was quite a bit of maneuvering to get the door shut.

"This is my office! You can't all be in here!" Harold was pressed against *the* door. The exit that would lead to retirement, with its inch of glowing light that escaped along the bottom, which was currently blocked by all the bodies in the room.

No one answered or bothered to leave, either. Even with his lousy personality, it was hard not to occasionally feel bad for Harold. I'm sure he wanted to be liked. Didn't everyone? Even more so, he wanted to remain in control, but that seemed to be slipping away slowly with each passing day.

"Why are the cats in here? I've got nowhere to stand!" Bernie, the leprechaun, yelled at Kitty, from where he was perched on the desk. He acted like it was an inconvenience, but I noticed he took every opportunity he could to stand on something and attain more vertical leverage.

"He's got a crow in here." Kitty pointed to the bird sitting on Crow's shoulder. "If the crow stays, my cats stay."

And of course, even though my best friend was Lady Luck, I was running on very short supply of it myself. I was up close and personal with Fate, the very person I was avoiding. It was hard to pretend to not see someone who was standing almost on top of you, so I focused my eyes on his chest. Maybe not a good idea, since I became slightly fascinated by the way the shirt mounded and hollowed as it followed the line of his pectorals.

Now here's someone who was naturally lucky in life. No one got to look like that without a little helping hand. He smelled almost better than he looked. It was an indescribable scent that reminded me of walking through a forest on a beautiful fall day, and he threw off a comforting heat like standing next to a toasty fire after you'd spent hours in a blizzard. Everything about him was a lure, and I didn't want to be the catch of the day.

He moved in closer, forcing me further into the corner and shielding me as more people jostled about. I tried to resist the urge to take in a good whiff of him but failed. I wondered if he ever smelled bad. Maybe if he got all sweaty.

No, that wasn't a good thing to think of either; I'd seen him all sweaty, as he covered my body with his. There was good sex, and then there was that night. It had been something different altogether. It hadn't been long, or with any crazy foreplay, or anything else I could put my finger on. And yet, it had been more intense than anything I'd ever experienced. Like he'd fit me perfectly, moved at just the right pace and the most perfect angle. He'd felt so damn good that it must have been Cupid's love spell pitching in. Nothing else made sense.

It made me wonder why we were hiding from Cupid when he could produce those types of results. Shouldn't we be greeting him with tea and cookies? Come on in and hand me over a blissful night of sexcapades?

I knew what my problem was; I couldn't think of that night without remembering the rest. We'd both still been winded when he'd so callously asked about my plans, wanting to know if I'd be hanging around.

I wasn't stupid. I knew why he'd asked, and that perhaps he'd had some noble notion behind it, or thought he did. He was telling himself he was doing the right thing by pushing me out the door, but it wasn't his call. When you truly care about someone, don't you spend even a minute thinking about alternatives? Now, I wasn't saying I wanted to stay, but it was a big insult to get past. No, I'd be remaining right here, in this cramped office, with the rest of them.

"We need to talk." His voice was barely louder than a whisper.

"Sure," I replied, as causally as I could.

16

"After we get out of here, we'll go back to my place."

His place? Oh no, that would *not* be happening.

"No good. I've got a job in about an hour." I needed to stop smelling him.

"Then you have time." His hand came and rested on my back like it belonged there. My spine seemed to agree since it arched as if trying to make his hand more comfortable in its spot. My reflexes and baser self were clearly happy to please. Unfortunately for him, my pride didn't feel as accommodating.

I jutted out the arm closest to him, which dislodged his hand. He retaliated by pushing his hand through the opening my now bent arm made and splaying it on my lower back again and tugging me closer.

"Why do you keep touching me?" My words were stilted. So much for casual.

"Why are you getting so touchy about me touching you? I just didn't want anyone to hear us." His voice was husky and did funny things to my nerve endings.

I was thwarted. If I continued to say anything about him touching me, it would look like I was being overly sensitive. The only thing left to do was act like it wasn't a big deal.

His hand remained where it was, with my begrudging consent, burning a hole into my back. But I wouldn't make it welcome. In an effort to force the arch out of my spine, I ended up hunched over.

No one seemed to notice anything amiss with us, as everyone was shifting around uncomfortably. Elbows were starting to fly and feet were being stepped on as everyone fought for more floor space.

17

"We can talk but it's going to have to be tomorrow. I don't like to run late and I have to stop and get some polish for the guards beforehand." My eyes landed on his bicep. He looked like he worked out but I wasn't sure. No matter what I ate, I didn't gain a pound.

But seriously, who had arms like that and never lifted a weight? And his face somehow always had that perfect amount of stubble, as if it had stopped at the precise length to accent his manliness and never grew a millimeter longer. He'd hit the manly-man jackpot.

"You can get polish for the guards tomorrow." He was getting impatient and I didn't like the bossy tone of his voice. We didn't work together anymore. Everyone else here might think he walked on water, but in my world he looked like a huge iceberg about to sink my ship. I'd struggled enough to get my bearings and I was finally starting to tread water. I had no plans to let him sink me in the middle of the ocean with his perfect stubble and biceps.

"No, I can't. I told them I'd get it today. If we don't get out of here soon, I'm barely going to make it to the shore—I mean the store, before my job." Did he even own a razor?

His hand rubbed over his jaw, drawing my eyes again. I couldn't take it anymore. I had to know. "Do you shave?"

"No."

I *knew* it!

I slipped then and made eye contact. His eyes were strange. Sometimes they seemed darker for being so deep set, and sometimes, like right now, they appeared ridiculously pale, with specks of light green in them.

18

One thing stayed constant though, they looked at me as if they knew me on the most basic level. In truth, he did.

No matter how much I wanted to deny it, I couldn't. It was as if time stood still when it came to him. It was a month ago, and I was lying next to him after a short but intense bout of sex when he dumped a cold bucket of water on my orgasm afterglow, asking when I planned to leave.

Even still, when we locked stares there was still something between us that made my breathing labored and my heart kick up a beat. I knew it and so did he. Of all the men in the world, why did I have to have this connection to him? Maybe we weren't special though. What if he had this connection with every female he came into contact with? It was more likely the case.

I remembered what he'd said to me. *I don't do doe eyes.* He was probably used to girls acting like fools. And this was the problem; I couldn't look at him and not remember what had happened. When I'd slept with him, besides Cupid's spell urging me on, I'd thought I wouldn't remember any of it in a week. I was going to be out of this office and this crazy life. There weren't supposed to be awkward moments, or hurt feelings, because I wasn't supposed to still be here. If I'd only known.

"You keep trying to dodge me and it's not going to work," he said. His fingers pulled me closer to him but I wasn't sure he knew he was doing it.

"Oh, but I think it has." My voice had a snarky edge that I knew would aggravate him. *See? I'm not one of your little doe eyed girls.*

19

"When did you start running from things?" His tone dropped slightly, and there was a taunting edge in it that hadn't been there a minute ago.

Even now, his hand on me heightened my awareness of him. I knew what he wanted, for me to join his crew of men. Couldn't happen. Too much exposure and I *might* be doe eyed.

"When the person nagging me wouldn't stop beating a dead cat." My voice rose enough that Kitty, who was a couple of bodies over, turned her head in our direction.

"Hey!" Kitty said, clearly alarmed and only hearing the tail end of the sentence when I'd raised my voice.

"Sorry, Kitty. I didn't mean that literally. No one is beating a cat."

With Kitty seemingly appeased, I turned back to Fate and concentrated on keeping my voice lower. "You want me to be up front with you? I don't want to have this conversation because we've already had it. Weeks ago. What I said then still stands."

I'd told him I wasn't going to work with him and I didn't see why it would be a good plan now. I didn't care if there were more bad guys out there like Suit, the thug I had killed. Unless forced, I wanted nothing to do with the situation. Back in another life, I used to tell my clients that if they wanted to live a clean life, they needed to stop walking around in mud piles. It was time to follow my own advice.

I tried to infuse my voice with a confidence that left no room for argument. "*Nothing* has changed."

His head bent until his forehead was almost

touching mine. "Exactly my point as well. Nothing has changed," he hissed.

Our whispered conversation was disturbed by Cupid yelling outside the door. "Hey! Can you let me in? I'll be good. I promise!"

We all froze as eyes shifted from one to another, trying to determine who would be our spokesperson. The least likely candidate took the bait.

"No!" Bernie yelled back. The small statured leprechaun had a disproportionately deep voice but a bluntness and lack of tact that was exactly what you'd expect when you saw his permanent grimace.

"But I just want to visit." Cupid's voice sounded childlike.

Eyebrows rose across the room like a Mexican wave going around a baseball stadium; we all were at a loss for what to do. His entreaty tugged at my emotions, as well as everyone else's, but I had to remind myself that he played dirty.

"He won't leave. Someone is going to have to go out there," Crow said. "*Someone* is going to have to sacrifice themselves and take one for the team."

"Literally," Luck said, as she buffed her red nails against her low cut blouse.

"I say we send you out." Bernie was looking directly at Luck. "You'll sleep with anyone. No harm done."

"I will not!" Her hand shot to smooth down bed head hair.

"Even now you stink of cologne, and you've got a hicky on your neck."

Luck threw some of her dark hair in front of her

21

shoulder. "No, I don't."

"Yes, you do!" Bernie, quite a bit shorter than Luck—even standing on the table—started to wave his arms at her, trying to shove her hair out of the way. She pushed him away and that set off another round of shoving throughout the room.

Harold tried to jump over Death, who was between him and his desk. "My papers! You're scrunching my papers!"

This shoved Kitty toward the Tooth Fairy. One of her cats, which had been sitting on her shoulders, screeched and lunged toward the Tooth Fairy, who started shrieking.

"People!" Murphy held up his hands and shouted over everyone, interrupting the squabble. "I will do this. *I* will go out there."

All movement ceased and every pair of eyes in the room swung to Murphy.

"No, Murphy, you can't!" Luck started into action and clung to his arm as if he were about to throw himself into Mount Vesuvius.

"Don't fret, my dear Luck. I'll be okay." His chin held high, he was playing the stoic hero to perfection.

"Murphy," she cried.

It was very hard not to mock this overly dramatic demonstration, but I held back. It wasn't from kindness, though. If Murphy was willing to fall on his sword— quite literally—I certainly didn't want to draw attention to myself. I was still recouping from the damage the last curse had created.

Maybe if that hadn't happened, I wouldn't be so acutely aware of Fate on every fundamental level.

Banging started on the other side of the door, and then we heard Bobby, one of the three Jinxes, yell, "What's going on in there? Let us in!"

"Who's with you?" Crow asked.

"It's just us, you dirty bird man. We told Cupid to take a hike. Now let us in before we pluck all the feathers off your crows!" This was followed by a youthful chorus of laughter from the other side of the door. If anyone could scare off Cupid, it would be them.

Another small fist hit the door.

The Jinxes; it warmed my public defender heart a bit to hear their foul little voices kick in to a rant of curses.

Bernie hopped off the desk and wrestled his way in between legs. He opened the door a sliver and Billy and Buddy yanked it the rest of the way open, causing Bernie to sprawl out into the larger room. He got to his feet and the small and stout leprechaun waved a fist in their direction.

"Whatever, greenie, take your best shot," Bobby said.

Bernie made a grunting noise and waved his fist again but stomped off.

"He's really gone?" Luck asked as the office cleared out with no sight of Cupid.

"Yes, you big bunch of sissies." Bobby looked over to Fate and added, "Of course, I'm not talking about you. Just the rest of them." Bobby leaned on the wall, mimicking the way Fate often did, as we walked past him.

"Fate! You going to golf with Death this

weekend?" Billy asked as him and Buddy trailed Fate, who was shadowing me as I headed for the door.

"No. Have plans," Fate responded and I wondered if I'd end up waist deep in whatever it was they were.

"Yeah, we don't have time either," Buddy said.

Fate stopped briefly and grabbed my arm, forcing me to do the same.

"Guys, if you don't mind, I need a minute." He didn't look at them when he spoke, just me.

The Jinxes' eyes hopped back and forth between the two of us, and then their little faces lit up with smirks.

"We got it, bro," Buddy said.

"We know the score," Bobby, who had caught up to us, added. Something similar to a leer appeared on his face. A leer on a prepubescent face was just too creepy for words.

"Oh my god." I yanked my arm free and turned to continue on my way. Fate followed on my heels, stalking me out of the office. Even the Jinxes knew? I didn't care how old they were; they looked like they were twelve, tops.

I didn't say anything until we got into the hallway, which provided the thinnest veneer of privacy. Still, it was better than the middle of the office.

"I told you, I don't have time for this." I wrapped my arms around my body to prevent any dangling temptation, since he seemed to keep trying to touch me. It was probably his weird controlling manner.

He stepped in front of me, blocking my way. "If you had such an issue with people knowing then maybe you shouldn't have said something." His eyebrows rose accusingly.

I just wished I could be more like him about it. He didn't seem fazed at all that the whole office knew. He also hadn't been the rejected one, either.

I felt a blush spread on my cheeks. I wanted to kill Luck right now. She hadn't meant to spread it—I knew she'd just gotten nervous and wanted to warn Murphy—but it didn't make it any less embarrassing. But ultimately it was my own fault. Why did I tell her in the first place?

Either way, the reminder did nothing for my desire to talk to him about anything.

"I told you, I'm not doing this now," I said and stepped around him.

Despite my preventive measures, he managed to force his fingers through my locked arms, forcing me to stop and look at him. "This isn't going away."

"You know what? For me it is. I don't want to play your games. I don't know what's going on and I don't want to. It has nothing to do with me, and I want to keep it that way." At least I hoped I could. I knew Suit had been searching for me, but that didn't mean his colleagues would continue to do so. Who knew how many there even were? Maybe it had been a lie. Maybe he'd been a lone wolf. And even if there were more of them, as long as they left me alone, I was perfectly content to leave them hiding wherever they were. I'd had enough drama in the past few months to last me a long time.

"You're not listening to what I'm telling you. You can't walk away."

"Everything about my life has been hijacked. I've

had no say in where I live, where I work, what I do—"

"No say in what you do?" The words were staggered, each pronounced with emphasis. His eyebrows couldn't have lifted higher on his forehead.

"Fine, perhaps I've had a little say in what I do. My point is, I'm maxed out on being dictated to. I'm not putting up with it." I shrugged and waited for him to do his worst.

"I told you this was non-negotiable."

"I remember what you said, and I've decided it is." I yanked my arm back again and crossed my arms in front of me, tighter this time. If he wanted a limb, he was going to have to seriously fight for it. No more easy conquests.

"Come with me." He started taking off in the direction of the elevator, but I didn't follow.

He looked back to see I hadn't budged and walked back. He reached out for an arm and I turned my back on him. When he moved with me, I wouldn't let him budge it away from my body to get a firm grip.

It was a good thing the hall was empty. We must have looked ridiculous, but I didn't care. He wasn't getting a hold. I'd beat him at his game.

He wrapped an arm around my waist and just lifted me entirely.

"That's cheating!" I yelled, my feet dangling as he started walking.

"It's not cheating, because there are no rules." His voice was smug. "There is no legal system for us."

I was torn. If I undid my arms to hit him, he'd just grab one of those. If I didn't, he'd just keep carrying me. Without another clear-cut plan of action, I figured a verbal assault would be the most prudent. "Why do you insist on physically forcing me to go where you want? Have you no couth?"

"No. I don't. Why do you refuse to do what I want you to?"

"Because I don't have to do what you want."

"Looks like you do." He wasn't laughing but he was definitely close to it.

I made the mistake of looking back at the office door down the hall. Someone had opened it and they were all hovering nearby. Every head swiveled guiltily away the second I saw them.

"Do you know what this looks like? They all think we slept together now."

He leaned his head closer to mine. "No, they all *know* we slept together, remember?"

"Now that you've done even more damage, would you mind putting me down?"

"Sure," he said as we strode through the hallway. "In one minute."

We left the building and I thought he was going to try and make me go somewhere with him, but he stopped at his car.

"Do you plan on putting me down?" I asked. My legs were still dangling a foot off the ground and I was surrounded by his body heat.

"Are you going to listen?" he asked.

"Yes, I'll hear you out."

"Why do you sound so winded when I'm the one that carried you?"

"You were squeezing my lungs." That sounded a lot better than the truth.

27

He set me on my feet and looked around to make sure no one was listening. My arms were still wrapped tightly around me, just out of principle.

"You aren't going to be able to walk away from this."

"Why? Because I know about your men? If the paltry amount I know is too much, you guys are in worse shape than I gave you credit for. And as far as catching your objective, I'd say you're chasing your tails more than your target. Maybe it's time to pack up and call it quits."

"You can ID my guys," he said, but I couldn't help feeling like he was just throwing out excuses.

"But I haven't."

"But you can, and they don't feel comfortable with someone that isn't with us knowing who they are."

"Then they can come talk to me." I remembered the night it had all gone down. I really thought they would try and kill me after I'd stabbed Suit. But I'd had time to adjust and take stock since then. I wasn't going to live out the next thousand years being bullied.

"I'm talking. For now."

I didn't like the implied threat and it made my hackles rise. "What would you like? Do you want me to come and sit in your warehouse, drink a couple of beers and ponder the mysterious bad guys? Fine, I cave, pencil me in." I whipped out the cell phone from my pocket. I'd finally pestered Harold into an upgrade with a calendar option. "I'm free for ten minutes next Saturday. That should be enough time to cover all the leads you guys have and squeeze in a beer, too."

"This isn't a joke." His hand ran through his dark

hair as he shook his head, looking more frustrated than anything else, like I was wearing his patience down to the nub. "Don't act like everything is just some game that you have no part in. I know better."

I smiled. "It is a game, and in case you don't realize, I'm winning."

He leaned against his car with a look that made me nervous, but didn't stop me from walking away.

I felt his eyes on me as I crossed the lot to my Honda and got in. I'd thought he knew me, but maybe not as well as I'd imagined.

Nothing about this was a game. I was running scared.

Chapter Three

I'm currently away from my table right now.

After ditching Fate in the parking lot, I'd barely had time to get the polishing compound for the guards before my job. As it was, I'd have to cut the explanation of the directions down to a minimum, which could be a problem. They took polishing very seriously, and did not appreciate being rushed.

"Now, you need to wait for this stuff to turn white before you rub it off." The medieval looking armored guards of the doors nodded their heads as I handed them both a bag. "If this one still doesn't make you as shiny as you want, we're going to have to start doing mail order. This is the last brand sold locally."

They nodded again. They weren't known for their great communication skills. I often wondered what was under those suits. When I'd tried to peer into the eye slits, I never saw anything but pitch black. I'd stopped looking after that. It was a notch creepier than I preferred to know.

As it was, I could barely see past the reflection they were throwing off, but if it made them happy, I'd keep finding new polish.

The guard on the right started making circling motions with his left hand. I knew what he wanted but tried to ignore it. The guard on the left joined in and did it in larger motions until it was impossible to pretend.

"You couldn't have gone through all of them, already. I just bought you a new pack two days ago." I was on a first name basis with half the staff at the hardware store these days.

They both nodded vigorously.

"What are you doing with all the rags?" They didn't look like much, but they weren't free and I was on a fixed budget. I hadn't been out to Vegas with Luck in a while, and my paycheck was barely over minimum wage. If I'd had to pay rent at the condo, I would've gone under for sure.

They dropped their heads but didn't answer. Then they both slumped their shoulders.

I'd never done well under the force of a guilt trip, and they had me reacting true to form. "Okay, I'll get more rags, but that's it for the rest of the month."

When they nodded eagerly, I felt bad about giving them a hard time. The polish made them so happy that I hadn't waded into a lake or pond in weeks.

My watch ticked to three p.m. "Time for work. I'll see you boys in a bit."

The doors shimmered into existence and swung open to a street in historic Montreal. The crowds swelled past as I walked into their midst, sending my senses on a roller coaster of awareness. Ever since that night on the beach with Lars and Fate, I could feel each individual's karma hit me right in my core, as if it were magnified by a thousand.

At first, I'd had trouble even walking through a small group of three or four people. But I'd adjusted. It's amazing what people can live with when given no other option.

The only ones who didn't affect me at all were the people who were in perfect alignment. It didn't mean they were good or bad; just whatever they'd done had caught up with them. They'd either reaped the benefits or paid the piper for their misdeeds.

Looking around, it appeared like the Universe was behind, since there were so few of them. When I really thought about it, shockingly few. Is this how it had always been? I mean, there was only one of me. I could only get to so many people, and my workload was supposed to be dedicated to those who had an immunity of sorts to being balanced out.

Appraising the busy streets right now, there was probably only one in ten who looked like they were in balance. It just didn't seem like it should be this off kilter. But at least one more would be, by time I was done today.

I walked along the cobblestoned street, lined with shops that had signs hanging from wrought iron posts above their doors, until I spotted the name I'd been looking for. *Vintage Reads.*

No one saw me as I entered, blind to my form walking in and deaf to the chime of the door opening. The store was a front—one of many—to launder money from illegal sex trafficking. And there, behind the register right now, was the man in charge. Everyone thought he was a pillar of the community. A criminal of the worst type, he was hiding in plain sight.

He sat behind the small counter, probably looking like an average man to most, in his plaid button-down shirt and khakis. They couldn't see the deathly pallor of his skin, or the cracks along his cheeks that oozed the sickness of his soul. That was my special gift, if you wanted to call it that; being able to see him for what he was.

An officer of the Sûreté du Québec, the Montreal Police Force, walked in the store behind me, and then past, equally oblivious to my presence. He wasn't dark or bright, just perfectly aligned with his karma.

"Hey, Tim," the officer said, greeting the owner.

"Nick, how is everything?" His cracked skin erupted into a smile, forcing pus from the cracks in his cheeks.

"Pretty good. How's the wife?"

"Same old. Complaining about my hours." Tim stood and moved toward the back stock room. "Hang on, I'll go get that book from the back I was telling you about."

Their entire conversation had been in French and I'd understood it. Wow, that was a neat new trick. Could I speak it, too? I didn't have time to ponder it now; I had a job to do.

I grabbed the passport that had appeared in my hand this morning when I'd had the vision of the job. I still hadn't opened it. I didn't want to see the face of the young girl staring back at me again. It was too late for her. She was already dead but her passport would hopefully save many others from the same fate.

The store's walls were packed with shelves of antique books. I tossed the passport at the police officer's feet, and he immediately looked upward, assuming it had fallen.

He scooped the passport up, probably out of reflex, and looked at the picture. It was the same image as the one posted in his station earlier today, right before his shift.

His face transformed and then he looked at the door leading to the back, where Tim had gone. He pocketed the passport and called out to him, "Hey, I gotta run. I'll be back in a few hours."

"Sure," Tim yelled from the other room.

Tim didn't realize Nick would be returning en masse.

**

The leather-bound notebook had cost twenty-five dollars, but I'd wanted something that would hold up over the years. Harold wouldn't pay to have copies made for something that was against the rules, so this was it. It had a ringed binder inside, so I could add pages as needed.

Flipping to the first page, I wrote the title.

A Transfer's Guide to Forces of the Universe

Skipping a couple of lines, I jotted down a brief introduction.

First of all, if you are reading this, you're a new transfer to the agency. I'm sure you've looked around and felt as if the world has turned upside down. That you are the one who's gone crazy. Don't be alarmed. It's them, not you. This place is odd. The people are even odder. The whole situation is reminiscent of a bad acid trip.

Second, flip to the page of your new occupation. This manual will give you a description of the position and a run-down of all your new responsibilities.

It's very important to do this, as no one else will tell you. I'm not sure if it's from unwillingness or inability, but don't kill yourself trying to get answers out of them—please don't be offended by that last statement if you actually got here by killing yourself. Answers are few and far between. If you do get them, they tend to not be worth the time and energy you invested.

Hopefully, this book will get you through the initial confusion. But keep in mind, it's written by a transfer, just like you.

I flipped to the next page and titled it *Harold*. In charge of...reading papers? I'd leave him for later, I decided, and flipped to the next page.

"What are you doing?" Murphy asked as he sat down at my favorite table with me.

"Writing up a manual for transfers."

"What's going to be in it?" He lifted his chin, trying to glimpse over my hand at what was written on the page.

I tilted up the edge of the book. "A description of

35

all the positions."

His eyes opened up just a smidge wider. "Is that allowed?" he asked, intrigued.

My lips parted in a smile I couldn't seem to stop. "I haven't been told it isn't, exactly...yet. I'm sure that will come as soon as Harold finds out."

Murphy dragged his seat a little closer to me, the glimmer of a coconspirator shining in his eyes. "Can I help?"

I didn't try and stop smiling now. "Sure."

Turning to a fresh page, I put in big fat letters, *Murphy's Law*.

A car door shutting caught his easily distracted attention. Murphy had a rather bad case of ADD.

"Fate's here," Murphy said, looking out the window we were seated by.

I ripped out his paper from the notebook. "Take this and just write down anything you think is pertinent to your position and don't tell anyone."

Then I ripped out another sheet and scrawled out a quick note.

Look at that, I managed to dodge you again. See? It is working.

I folded the paper and handed it to him as well. "Give this to Fate for me? I've got to run."

He nodded and I thanked him. Slinging my purse onto my shoulder, I grabbed my notebook and high-tailed it out of there.

Chapter Four

A past that won't stay dead.

The electronic doors of the local Wal-Mart swung open. It was the only place that carried this particular brand of polish, so it was here or pay for shipping.

This place was always so busy that it had taken me a while to build up enough karma stamina. Even now, a gentleman paused his cart at the opening of an aisle to allow me to pass first, and I had to focus on not throwing up from the stench of him. I used to think people who did that would always have good karma. Not even close.

The people with the worst karma often had a foul smell, which lingered around them. But the people with really good karma smelled like a spring day in a garden full of roses. In the beginning, I'd actually found myself following a few of them unintentionally.

Between the pretty glow and the sweet scent, I just sort of got sucked in. I'd follow a couple of people home by accident, but after a few calls to the police, I was more careful. Now, I made sure I concentrated when I walked down the aisles. It was really embarrassing to be called out as a stalker and the Universe didn't always shield me from things like that. Somebody in charge definitely had a warped sense of humor.

Surrounded by the overwhelming smell of cleaning supplies on either side, I wasn't prepared for what I suddenly sensed. I almost choked on the smell of a bad karma so strong that it radiated outward, even when the person wasn't in clear view. It wasn't just the smell, either. There was a feeling of spiders crawling all over my skin.

I'd felt it a week ago, but I hadn't been able to find the source. I'd been driving down the road when it had hit. I'd tried to turn around, but it was gone by time I did. I'd driven up and down different streets for hours with no lead. I wasn't losing it again.

The smell and feeling were so strong, I feared I wouldn't be able to handle it up close, but that didn't stop me. I dashed down the aisle, and made a right. No, not that way. I backtracked toward the toys.

Then it was there at the end of the bike aisle. He couldn't have been more than fourteen. I stood there, frozen in my spot by the atrocity I saw before me. He wore shorts and a t-shirt, and everywhere I looked, his skin was blackened as if it had been burnt. Cracks ran up and down his exposed skin, oozing a constant drain of pus.

He turned and looked at me. At first I thought it was because he'd caught me staring, and it was retaliatory glare, but then he smiled like he knew me.

He was human; he couldn't possibly know me.

He was with two other friends and I heard him telling them he'd be right back. He walked toward me, dripping ooze as he came. Someone would trip on that ooze later and never have any idea why they fell.

Flashes of what he'd already done in this life hit me; animals mutilated, smaller children beaten. I wasn't surprised by anything I saw. You weren't oozing like that as a teenager unless you had some *horrible* acts on your resume already.

What shocked me and made my breath catch was when images from another century came slamming into me. How could this be? Was I sensing what he'd done in a past life? This had never happened before.

Bodies bloodied everywhere. Images of the worst part of war, people in agony, loss on a level rarely seen.

A swastika.

He kept walking toward me and I took a step back. I caught myself before I took another. It was hard; the pure evil of what was heading my way instinctively repelled every cell in my body.

He stopped a foot away from where I stood. "I was wondering when we'd meet."

"You know me?" No way.

He smiled then nodded. "I know you and I know myself."

He knew who he used to be. Maybe that was why I could pick up on it?

I'd heard of something similar to this recently, in the office. Death and Jockey were having a discussion about it last week. Jockey was saying how sometimes a person's past life would leak into their dreams.

When I asked how this could happen, Death explained that when people crossed, strong emotions and images were harder to shed with their mortal skin. They leaked into their new body's subconscious. Neither of them had any idea what happened after they crossed completely. Everything that happened after retirement was a mystery to everyone I'd spoken to.

But still? This wasn't just glimpses from a dream. He knew. No one would believe me, but here was living proof it could happen. He knew it, and reveled in the glory of what he'd been, and what he still was.

I wanted to kill him. It must have been there in my eyes, because he said as much in his next words.

His lips curled upward as he spat out the words. "Try it."

I couldn't remember the last time I'd wanted to accept a challenge more in my life, or death. Right there, in the middle of Wal-Mart, I lifted my hands to snap his neck but stopped. If I killed him, he'd be reborn and I'd lose him into the Universe, maybe not find him again until it was too late. If I let him live, I could watch him and possibly contain him. My arms dropped but my fists were still clenched.

"Yeah, I thought so." He made a half laugh that held no joy whatsoever.

"What's your name?" It was a dare of my own, and I hoped he had the balls to tell me.

"Henry Starcher." He said it proudly without a flinch, goading me to do my worst.

"We'll see who wins this." I'd have to skin this cat in a different way. But in the end, he'd be just as bald.

"Do your best." He turned, heading back to his

friends like just another cocky kid of fourteen and not the monster I knew him to be.

He was halfway down the aisle when the bike rack collapsed on him. His wails immediately filled the store. The two broken legs he'd have should put him out of commission for the next six weeks. After that, I'd figure something else out.

"I'm going to get you for this," he yelled in my direction.

"If you can't handle this, you certainly can't handle my best. You shouldn't fuck with Karma." I didn't realize what I'd said until I stepped away. There was no denying it; every day I lost more of who I'd been, the human attorney, and became more of what they wanted. Karma. Now I just had to decide if it was a good thing or not.

People were running toward the aisle to find the source of agonizing screams as I walked away, back toward the cleaning aisle. Not really in the mood to browse, after meeting one of the worst souls to have ever walked the Earth, I grabbed the polish and headed to the checkout.

That's when I saw her. I immediately wished I were back in the toy aisle, because here was someone who scared me worse than the leader of the Third Reich.

She was standing in line, putting some items on the conveyor belt. Home items, dish detergent, garbage bags, etc. Every time she lifted another item from her cart, the light caught the diamond on her left hand.

It was huge, probably twice the size mine had been. It wasn't just the ring; she *looked* happy. No one looks like that buying cleaning supplies, unless they're stupid or in love. I'd been dead less than two months. Sixty days! And he'd already proposed?

Then her head poked up. She scanned the store until she settled on a spot behind me. She yelled, "Hurry up!" It wasn't a nagging yell, but a playful, *where've you been and come back to my side*, type.

I knew it was him; Charlie, my fiancé. The way her face lit up told me everything. Polish leaked onto my fingers from squeezing the container in my hand.

Walk away. Put down the polish and just walk away without looking. Seeing this would do me no good whatsoever. If I walked away, if I didn't see it, it's like it didn't happen. Just like all those dead trees that fell in the forest, right?

Sure, like I could do it. No one I'd ever met in my life, or death, would've been capable of looking away from their ex with a new person. I had to look, and I knew even before I did it was going to kill me a little.

Charlie, my former fiancé—now hers—ran through the store with a bag of chips in one hand and a DVD in the other. He was the picture of domestic bliss and looked healthier and happier than ever.

"They had one copy left." He put the items on the conveyer belt, wrapped his left arm around her waist and kissed the top of her head. It wasn't a fatherly kiss; it was the type you give to someone who is precious to you.

In all the time we'd been together, he'd never kissed me like that, not once. I would've remembered it.

She lifted her face to him, like a flower soaking in every ounce of sun it could get. In return, the adoration beamed from him. A look passed between them that said without words, *you are my everything.*

She lowered her head and caught sight of me, standing not even ten feet away, silently inserting myself into their moment by my awkward and unwanted attention. I watched as she nudged him and motioned toward me, the interloper.

He looked my way and recognition flickered across his face. He remembered me, but not the woman he used to be with; the crazy woman from his parking lot. I was the whacko who used to watch him at the luncheonette. He got that look, the one people get when dealing with someone mentally unbalanced and they aren't sure how to proceed or extricate themselves from an uncomfortable situation.

They turned away, obviously deciding that the best course of action was to pretend I wasn't there. I put the polish on an empty shelf and headed for the door. I shouldn't have turned back again, but I did.

My retreat making them more comfortable, they watched me leave. And as I did, I could make out the word "crazy" when he spoke. They threw their heads back in laughter, before returning their attention back to their items.

I left the store but not the parking lot. Instead, I sat in my Honda as they came out. They got into his car looking truly happy, not a care in the world, the crazy woman already forgotten.

Chapter Five

Whiskers of wisdom

There was a pounding at my condo door.

"Who is it?" I yelled from my position, lounging on the couch, the manual on my lap.

"Luck."

I moaned aloud. She wasn't going to be easy to get rid of, and I really wanted some space. "It's open."

She strolled in wearing a bright red dress, which clung just the right amount and in just the right places.

"When did you start knocking?"

"I don't know. Just figured in case... You know, you could've been busy." She bit one of her long red nails as she tilted her head.

Sometimes—quite often, actually—I hated that office. At least when you worked with humans, they knew you were supposed to gossip *behind* the person's back. These people were killing me.

I decided to shut this down right away. "I'm not sleeping with him."

"Then where've you been the last two days?" She tossed her tiny sequin purse down on my table.

"Had some stuff to catch up on." I knew I should've just gone into the office. It would've been easier, but then the Fate problem would arise. Although, why he didn't come and pound down my door here was something of a mystery.

"You don't answer the phone? Something's wrong with you." She tapped her red nails on my counter as she paced about.

"It's dead. The phone, that is." Since I couldn't get clarity on my own state of mortality, I couldn't help but clarify everything else's.

"Something's obviously very wrong. Tell me." She slammed her fist on the counter, trying to act with authority. It was a hard thing for her to pull off, when those same fingers reached up to twirl a lock of hair a second later.

"I'm on a little bit of overload, but I'm fine. Just needed to lie low a couple of days." I stuffed a salt and vinegar chip in my mouth from the bag of comfort sitting next to me. I was going to have to run out for more. My comfort was running dangerously low.

"Why are you on overload?"

I sat up and debated whether to come clean or not. I didn't want to make a big deal of it, but Luck wasn't going to leave me alone. I was going to have to tell her something, and I didn't have the energy to make up a lie.

"I met Hitler." It was partially the truth and maybe enough to get her to back off. Then I realized how sad it was that I'd been more rattled by Charlie's new fiancée than Hitler.

"You did?" Her eyes went huge and she squeezed next to me on the couch, grabbing my arm. "What was it like? Was he scary?"

"Not actually scary. More distasteful."

"What does he look like now?"

"Awkward looking fourteen year old." As I said it, I realized I wasn't giving the subject enough weight to make it believable.

She tilted her head and got that look in her eyes, which I knew meant trouble for me. "And that was *all* that happened?"

"Yes. Why? You don't think that meeting the reincarnated Hitler in the body of a teen—who aren't usually pleasant to begin with—isn't enough?" I tried to infuse more drama into my words, but it was probably too late.

"I think you're lying." She leaned back on the seat of the couch, crossed her arms and nailed me with a stare.

"I'm not." I turned on the TV and feigned interest in a show I normally liked. Luck kept staring. I'd never noticed before that she really didn't blink much. It was a very disconcerting trait. I shivered.

It took about ten minutes and the rest of my chips but I cracked. Who knew how easy I'd be to break, given a non-blinking stare and empty bag. I had some rice cakes on the counter, but that wasn't nearly enough to get me through this. "Are you going to sit here like this all night?"

She crossed her arms in front of her chest. "Nope. Only until you talk."

If I told her, the whole office might find out. If I didn't, she wouldn't leave. "Fine. I saw Charlie. And don't go telling everyone about this, either."

"You've seen him before. What's the big deal?" She shrugged.

"He was with *her*."

"Oooh." Luck's "oh" lasted almost a minute as she looked down and to the side.

My lips opened of their own accord as another detail slipped out. "She had an engagement ring on."

"You knew it was going to happen. Fate warned you Charlie wasn't your soul mate." Luck was quickly slipping into damage control mode, as any good girlfriend would.

Nothing she could say would fix my next revelation. "It was bigger."

"What was bigger?"

Suddenly I couldn't hold back anymore and it all came spewing out. "The stone! He gave her a bigger diamond! And she looked at him all..." I tilted my face upward and tried to glaze my eyes over. "And then he looked at her like..." Not being able to, or simply unwilling to put it into words, my hands flew into a tizzy as I tried to mimic the look I'd seen.

Luck started to fidget and was blinking rapidly now. "I understand."

"No, I'm not sure you do." I leaned back on the couch, somehow feeling worse, now that I'd gotten it out. Wasn't it supposed to work in reverse? "This is not helping," I said to Luck, wishing I'd never said a word.

She stood up quickly and started to nervously fumble through her oh so teeny purse.

47

"Who are you calling?"

She plastered on the fakest smile I'd ever seen and held her hand up, motioning for me to give her a minute.

"Need you at Karma's, ASAP. DEFCON one." The entire time she spoke, the smile never slipped and her voice sounded like she could have been congratulating someone on a recent promotion.

I stood and went to grab the phone from her hand but it was already too late. "Who was that? I just told you not to tell everyone."

"I didn't tell everyone. I only told Kitty. She doesn't count." Problem with Luck was no one actually counted, and everyone was in the loop. She had a *very* large loop.

"Kitty?" She was a nice lady and all but not the one I'd call for something like this.

"I'm sorry, but it's too big for just me to handle." She shifted her weight to one hip.

"I wasn't asking you to handle it." I was on the verge of pulling my hair out as she dug her red lipstick out and puckered her lips. No one was too trivial to not get fresh lips in Luck's opinion.

"Clearly, this needs to be handled. Would you have rather have had Murphy? Crow would stink us out of this place. It's way too small. Or worse, Fate? Now *that* would've been awkward, considering you slept with him, too." She finished her lips and made a popping sound with them.

Kitty wasn't the knocking type and strolled right in ten minutes later. Luck blurted out the whole story while Kitty poured herself some iced tea she'd fetched from the fridge.

"Any lime in this place? I like a slice of lime in my tea," she yelled, louder than necessary, across the condo to me.

"Nope. No lime," I said as I watched her finish off my iced tea. Why did they always finish off my tea on the worst days?

Luck came and sat with me on the couch while Kitty opened every drawer in the fridge. Apparently, she needed to confirm there was no lime herself. After she eventually gave up, she stood in front of where Luck and I were sitting on the couch.

She looked around for a minute before she began to speak. "Obviously you don't care that much for material things, or you wouldn't be living in this dump."

"That's true," Luck added, talking mostly to Kitty. "One night with me could get her a better place, and then there's that car she drives."

"I've seen it." Kitty shuddered. "So this is the problem. You view the larger ring as him putting more value upon his new fiancée than he did you." She shifted her weight from her right leg to her left. "And he does."

"This is supposed to be helpful?" I looked at both of them.

Kitty paced around my small living space, a cat trailing her feet. "Because he's supposed to be with her. She was better for him. It has nothing to do with you. In Charlie's existence, you were rawhide when he wanted catnip.

"The problem with all you young kittens is you

think it's all about you. It isn't." Kitty waved her finger toward the two of us, now sitting side by side. "There is no better or worse, inferior or superior. It's figuring out where you're meant to be and then getting there. This is true in every aspect of your life. If you fight to stay somewhere you don't belong, it will never be good and never get better.

"That has always been your problem." She made sure to stop and point an accusing finger in my direction, so there would be no confusion which one of us she meant. "You try and squeeze into the wrong spots. And don't tell me you didn't know. You did. When you find the place you belong, it feels right, even on the worst day ever." Kitty leaned down and looked at me. "You, missy, know exactly what I'm talking about."

I hated to admit it, but I had really started to enjoy something about being Karma. Maybe she had a point. Did I really belong here with these people? Then images of Fate flashed through my mind. He'd felt so right, even in that short time. Nah, she was talking about the job. That night was Cupid's doing.

Kitty grabbed her crocheted bag and headed out the door without even saying goodbye, her cat right beside her.

I looked at Luck, not sure how to describe the kick in the ass I'd just received. "Wow. That was..."

"She's good, right?"

"Honestly, I do feel a bit better."

Chapter Six

Wrinkled and liking it.

My old Honda pulled into the usual parking spot the next night. I scanned the condo complex parking lot for Fate's Porsche before I got out. When I didn't see him, I guessed he'd taken some time off, maybe had a job to do or something. Another twenty-four hours I'd managed to avoid him checked off.

Grabbing my take out, I got out and walked to the condo. I'd left the lights off as I walked in, the dark not bothering me as much now that my eyesight had improved somewhat. I was about to head into the kitchen and pour myself an iced tea when I saw a figure sitting on my couch.

"Lars, what are you doing here?" The only panic I felt was that I might not make it to my bed in the next hour.

He remained seated as he said, "We need to talk."

Another one who wanted to talk? He sounded just like Fate had the other day. I dropped my food and purse on the counter and went over to where he was sitting. Even with better eyesight, it was more like looking at an impressionistic version of him. I could still see his dark hair hanging down around his broad shoulders, and feel his eyes on my body, but couldn't make out the more subtle features, like the tattoo that ran up the side of his neck.

"I realize you might have missed the finer points of humanity, since you skipped over that grade, but breaking into my condo isn't a great conversation starter." My lesson in human manners didn't appear to faze him. "Are you just going to sit there?" Even most burglars, who I'd say hung on the very bottom rung of the politeness ladder, would show enough respect to try and run when they're caught.

I looked upward, a habit I'd started to form and said, "I realize he is a past employee, but did you people just hire anyone? Have you no standards?" I brought my gaze back to Lars. "You can't just break in to people's homes. Even if I'm not technically a person anymore, that rule should still apply."

Lars's head, shifting slightly to the right, caught my attention and that was all the warning I had before Fate slipped an arm around my waist.

He leaned down slightly, just enough to make my skin tingle where his stubble grazed my cheek. "You're not giving us much choice, now are you?"

I quickly stepped away from him and he didn't attempt to stop me.

"Were you in my bedroom?" It was the only place he could've been.

"Just taking a look around." He strolled over to the

dinette set, leaned a hip on the table and smiled.

"How many times do we have to have this conversation? I can't be the only one getting bored of hearing myself turn you down."

"You know about us," Lars said.

"Yes. I do." I shrugged. "So what?"

"So, we've got a problem. That means it's your problem, too."

I watched as Fate took a silent back seat. I guessed he was waiting to see how this would play out?

"Sorry, but it's not." I walked back to the kitchen area where I'd left my food." My problem, that is."

Lars stood and walked past Fate, who was still leaning in the same spot. It shouldn't have bugged me so much but it did. Then I realized; it wasn't so much the leaning, it was that he seemed to always own the space. This was my apartment, not his. Who was he to nonverbally own it?

Lars stepped closer, blocking my view of Fate and his leaning compulsion. "You knew the deal. And if you had a problem, maybe you should've voiced it *before* you took out our best lead."

I went and grabbed the iced tea from the fridge and finally poured myself the glass I meant to earlier, before I answered. "I figured that subject was dead and buried by now. Seriously, didn't you throw him in a ditch somewhere? I don't know, maybe in the field out back?" Sometimes, I really cracked myself up. A giggle welled up as I unwrapped my food and took out a fork. They were uninvited guests. Why should I not eat in front of them when I was starving?

"This isn't a joke." Lars leaned over the counter

between us. Lars was a nice male specimen, but I could handle him. He didn't make me nervous like some others.

My fork pierced through a particularly nice piece of grilled chicken and grabbed a piece of romaine to go with it and then paused halfway to my mouth. "I'm sorry, I'd offer you some but there's only enough for me." I bit into the crunchy lettuce and hummed in satisfaction. It was a good thing my mother thought I was dead, or she'd kill me for how bad my manners had become. The speed of the decline was shocking. "Really sorry, because this is a great dressing." I took another bite and made an exaggerated moan.

"Lars." Fate stood and motioned to the door.

Lars straightened up and then looked at him. "All yours."

"Antonio's Pizzeria on Ocean Drive," I yelled as Lars walked toward the front door. "You know you want it!"

And then there were two. The chicken didn't go down as easily now, as I watched Fate close the distance between us.

"You know, they all think we should just off you. Eliminate any possible future problem. If it weren't for me, you'd have to watch your every step."

He walked around the counter and just as I was preparing to take another bite. He stopped right beside me and wrapped his hand around mine, directing the bite into his mouth instead. I didn't even try and stop him. There was something incredibly intimate about the act and I was too frozen in my spot to think of stopping him.

54

"Seriously? This is what you think is fantastic dressing?" He made a face. "It's okay at best."

I didn't argue with him over the salad. I knew I'd oversold it.

"For all your intimidation, Lars didn't look too worse for wear. Am I supposed to be prostrate in gratitude for you telling them not to try and kill me? For people who are supposed to be on the right side of this situation, it's a bit questionable that this is even a problem."

He took a sip of the iced tea I'd poured myself.

"I'm glad you switched brands. I hated that other stuff," he said as he placed my now empty glass back down and walked into the living area. He dropped onto the couch where Lars had been and kicked up his feet onto my couch, shoes and all.

He looked around, scanning the room and the exits. I'd noticed recently that he did that everywhere he went. For as much as he always looked relaxed, I was starting to doubt that he ever really was. "I think it would be better for you if you came into the fold."

"I don't need to be in the fold. I'd prefer to stay wrinkled." The salad in front of me didn't look so good anymore. The last piece went down about as tastily as a piece of cardboard.

Leaving the kitchen, I walked over and perched myself on the dining room table. I only had one couch and I wasn't sharing it with him.

My feet planted on the seat of the chair in front of me, I rested my forearms on my knees. I tilted my head forward and my hair fell in front of my face. I was tired of the cat and mouse game of the last couple weeks. He wasn't going to leave easily, so I resigned myself to hashing this out; to a point, anyway.

"You know I won't say a word about your guys and how they aren't really retired, or that you know how to cheat the system, so to speak. I would've done it already. And I've got zero interest in the invisible boogeyman you are secretly hunting. I've had plenty of opportunity to spill the beans and haven't, so why don't you tell me what this is really about?"

"I'm trying to do this the nice way." His jaw tensed. He was still reclined on my couch, but not one part of him appeared relaxed.

"Can't you just forget that night and leave me out of this?"

He sat up but wasn't looking at me as he started to speak. "You're strong and you aren't even finished transitioning completely. The mortal that a lot of us sense is still there. And yet..." His eyes finally landed on me across the dark room. "They want you. No one in that room the night you killed Suit believed anything but that. You *let* him out of that cage."

It was the first time he'd asked about why I'd killed Suit since it had happened. I felt myself looking at the wall instead of meeting his eyes and then forced myself to look at him.

All those years I'd wondered why some of my clients couldn't stop themselves from showing their guilt. Being adept at lying wasn't as simple as I'd imagined it to be. And just like with them, I would still lie. I wasn't ever going to admit Suit had been after me. Not to him or anyone else.

"I was trying to be nice to him, so I could get

information for you, since you believe he's part of some big conspiracy theory. You're so intent on finding this disruption you believe exists that I felt compelled to help."

"Stop lying. I don't want to hear it anymore. I'd rather you joined us willingly, but if it comes to it…"

There was a threat left unsaid but instead of scaring me, it drove me to anger. "You don't even know who *they* are."

He stood, and as he did, every last shred of his relaxed demeanor fell from him. For the first time ever, I realized I was seeing the real Fate. He wasn't holding anything back and the energy he put out rippled off him so strongly that I knew he wasn't someone I wanted as an enemy. This was why he commanded a room and everyone in it. This was that thing everyone sensed. I still couldn't put a name to it, but it was scary as hell. I had no doubt that if he chose, he could indeed force me to be whatever he wanted.

"What are you?"

He didn't answer but crossed the room and I felt myself leaning backward. He didn't stop until I was resting my hands on the table behind me and he was leaning over me.

"I know you're hiding things. Keep your secrets. I don't care. But this is going to happen."

I had to consciously force myself to breathe, as I could feel the heat from his chest. My lips parted and his eyes shifted to them and paused there a minute before he abruptly straightened up and put some distance between us.

Once I could think clearly again, I knew he was

right. Whatever they were after did want me. And joining with him and his men would put me in closer proximity to something that could jeopardize my situation. I didn't say that to him, though. I said nothing.

He walked out of the condo without saying anything else. It was the second bad departure from my condo in less than fifteen minutes. I really knew how to make friends, I thought to myself sarcastically.

My head dropped a little lower until it was finally resting in my palms. It didn't matter who I pissed off, my gut instinct was screaming that I needed to steer clear of what they were after.

Chapter Seven

Employment Opportunities

A glass of red wine was placed in front of me and I turned to the bartender.

"I didn't order this."

"It was sent by the gentleman over there." He pointed to a man sitting at the other end of the bar.

"Thanks."

After Fate and Lars left my condo, I hadn't been able to sit there another minute. Problem was, I didn't want to speak to anyone, either. My aversion to having company spurred my exit and I grabbed my purse from the seat next me to leave. By time I grabbed it, the man was already standing there next to me.

He was in his late forties and aged to perfection in a Clooney kind of way. Everything about him was well manicured, like he had all the time and money in the world. He was the type of guy that wouldn't have noticed me in my old body.

My human form had been attractive, but my appeal

never kicked in to full force until I spoke to someone and my wit won them over. I hadn't had the looks that would bring unknown men to my side. It was flattering, but I still didn't want to talk to him.

"Just a moment?" he asked. His impeccable manners encouraged my own to resurface from where I'd buried them alongside my human body.

"Of course." I settled in my chair as I tried to get a read on him. I couldn't figure out if he was human, or if his karma was in perfect balance. He had to be human. Wouldn't I know him otherwise?

He pulled out the stool and settled in with more elegance than should have been possible.

"My name is Malokin. I'd like to offer you a job." Hands in front of him, fingers knit, he waited for my reply.

"I'm already employed, but thank you." He didn't even know who I was. He could at least ask a few questions before using a line like that, to make it a bit more believable.

"Yes, Camilla, I know you do. And you could be so much more."

I'd gone from figuring out how to get rid of him to giving him my full attention. "Who are you?"

"I'm someone who *could* help you."

There was a threat in the way he said could. As if he could do other things that wouldn't be as appreciated.

I looked into his nearly black eyes and saw the menace and intent there. This man, whatever he was, got his way no matter what it took.

He smiled. "Or not. It's your choice."

"What exactly are you saying?" There wasn't a doubt in my mind anymore that this person wasn't human, and he wasn't from the agency. That didn't leave any good options left.

"I'd like you to come and work for me."

"I'm not interested." Whoever Suit had been, like he'd warned, he hadn't been alone. All this time dodging Fate just to keep my distance from this—to avoid this moment—had been futile.

Paddy appearing right next to us threw us both off guard. The stranger looked alarmed, but I was one hundred percent grateful.

"Didn't know we were having drinks tonight?" Paddy said, already with a beer in hand.

"Who is this?" Malokin asked.

He looked alarmed. And why did nobody know who the hell Paddy was?

"Name's Paddy." He held out his free hand to Malokin, who still looked ill at ease.

Malokin shook his hand and I saw a flash of apprehension shoot across his face. Malokin relinquished his grip and pulled his hand away a little too quickly.

"What are you doing here?" Malokin asked. That was an odd question for someone he didn't know. Did he *know* him, or not? What was going on here?

"Can't an old guy enjoy a beer out?" Paddy replied, but I had the strangest feeling that wasn't what Malokin had meant at all. I was pretty sure Paddy knew that as well.

"I'll be going." Malokin smiled stiffly and then reached into his pocket and laid a business card on the bar before me. "Call me. Soon." He looked at Paddy one last time before he stood and left.

Paddy took his vacated stool as I looked down at the card. The only thing on it was his first name and a phone number.

"Now that's a bad sort you might want to watch your step around."

I took a sip of the wine I'd initially wanted to decline. "What's that say about you then? If you're scaring off the bad element?" Malokin had taken off pretty quickly after Paddy's arrival.

"Oh no, lassie, we aren't going to go down that path again today, are we?"

"You mean the one where I ask who you are and you ignore me or give me some lame recruiter explanation? Nah, I'm done getting stuck on that dead end myself. Keep your secrets. Just know that they come at a price." I had a bigger issue. I pocketed the card, hoping I wouldn't ever need to look at it again.

He sighed in agreement. "When do they not?" He took a swig of his beer. "So, how've you been settling in?"

"Cliff jumping is starting to lose its appeal." I spun my cell phone on the wooden bar top.

"I'll take that as a good sign."

"I thought so." I took another sip of wine. "Hard to get cell service up there, anyway."

"You know, you're a lot like me." Paddy plunked his draft down on the bar, causing the beer inside to splash over the rim, but somehow not get the bar wet. When he lifted it, I waited to see if there'd be a puddle left behind, but there was nothing.

"That statement might mean something to me if I knew exactly who you were. As it is..." I shrugged and then pushed the wine to the edge of the bar and asked for a Maker's Mark on the rocks. Wine felt too refined for the life I led now. My existence was definitely more in line with bourbon. I was even contemplating switching to straight up.

I turned my head back to Paddy, just in time to see him smile before he vanished. There wasn't really a point to looking around the room for him. He was an old hat at the vanishing act, and I'd become almost as experienced at ignoring the oddities that surrounded him. Still, it was a nifty trick I wished I could pull off.

I'd have to settle or my own less impressive skills for now. A guy with bad karma was sitting a few stools down. I blew out a gentle breath and watched as his money flew off the bar and into the bartender's tip cup. It was enough to entertain me while I worked on a nice bourbon buzz.

Chapter Eight

Some things stick.

"Why are we here? Do you have a drinking problem? I can set up another intervention," Luck said, looking down at the glass in her hand, the cleanliness of it slightly in question. Her eyes scanned the bar room next, as something close to a cringe started to appear.

"I don't have a drinking problem." What I had was a stalking problem; as in too many people were following me around lately.

Ever since I'd met Malokin at my usual haunt, it hadn't felt as comfortable as it once had. When I went to the office, I felt Fate's presence more than ever, just waiting for that ticking time bomb to blow. I now had two options: sit in my condo all day, and wait for either Fate or Malokin to show up there, or hide.

I could only walk the store aisles for so long and the parents at the park were starting to give me weird looks. O'Henry's was an old corner bar, low on tourists; well, technically, low on customers altogether. It was the ideal place to hide.

I heard the creaky door open and Luck's attention was diverted not even a second later. "Ooooh, I like him!"

Turning, I saw exactly what I had expected. A young twenty-something guy walked in the bar. His biceps were so well developed they forced his t-shirt sleeves to wrinkle into the crease under his shoulders.

Just like a tiger squats, as it gets ready to pounce, she pulled out her compact and lipstick, freshening up before she made her move.

"Good?" she asked, toying with a couple of stray locks of hair. She shifted her neckline so low she was in danger of one of her breasts breaking free.

"Perfection. He's yours, at least for the evening."

She smiled, immune to my sarcastic delivery by now. Her white teeth gleamed brightly against her red lips. "You don't mind, do you?" she asked as an afterthought.

"Not at all. Do your thing." We'd barely sipped our first drink, but I knew the drill and was fine with it. Luck liked shiny new toys that came in the form of muscle bound men in their late twenties. Once she spotted one, you lost all of her attention. If you couldn't deal with that, you probably weren't going to be friends.

"You know, you could come play." She slipped her lipstick back in one of the teeny-tiny purses she preferred.

I looked over at where her Ken doll was. He had a fairly healthy glow about him, but his friends were quite dull in appearance. "The guys he's with have bad karma. If I played, I'd ruin the evening." Having to take your buddy to the emergency room for a broken leg had that kind of effect on an evening.

She looked over at them and back at me, serious for a change. "What do you see when you look at them?"

"Some are beautiful and bright, like a summer's day, some are dark and dull with sores and cracking skin. What do you see?" I looked at her and wondered why we'd never had this conversation before.

"I don't see anything. It's more of a feel, like I'm a magnet being drawn to a huge chunk of metal. Someone will walk in and I just want to be near them. Sometimes, there's no pull at all. I just like people for no reason other than it strikes my fancy at the moment."

"And that one?" I moved my head in the direction of the guy she'd picked out for tonight.

"He's a big chunk of hard metal I want to stick myself all over." Her voice was breathy as she said it.

She didn't mean to be funny but I laughed anyway. "Have fun."

Luck grabbed her purse and walked over to her target. She had a way of sashaying that encouraged attention, and the target pulled out a chair for her before she even reached him.

Luck was smiling adoringly at the luckiest man in the world tonight. Wonderful things would be set in motion for him after this, possibly life changing things.

Grabbing my glass off the bar, I took a sip of Maker's Mark, but then pushed it to the edge, half full. I'd rather be home, working on my manual. Sitting here hiding was ridiculous. I had a deadbolt, and I knew how to use it.

By time the door swung closed, and I was walking out of the bar, Luck was already on the guy's lap, fully engrossed.

I hadn't made it more than a couple of steps when I spotted Murphy. He had just parked his car, an Audi. I liked my little Honda—I really did—but it burned.

Did everyone have a new car except me? Was it because I was a transfer?

"Is Luck in there?" he asked, as he crossed the pavement to talk to me.

"Yes, but she just found some amusement for the evening." I didn't add *good luck separating her from this target. It's definitely going to be an all-nighter.*

His face scrunched for a second, knowing her well enough to read between the lines. "Damn. I'll never get her to the casino tonight."

Luck was Murphy's virtual ATM. She was occasionally mine as well, so I wasn't going to cast any aspersions on the man for taking advantage. Harold was as cheap as they came. Half the building relied on the Lady Luck cash machine.

I motioned him over to the side to let a young couple past us into the bar. He stepped aside but as soon as he saw them, his eyes lit up. Uh oh, I'd seen that glint before. Something was coming. I wasn't sure exactly what that something would be, but I'd find out shortly.

They were barely legal drinking age, younger than even I had been at my death. The girl, eyes watery and red, reached forward and grabbed at the guy's arm as he tried to keep moving away from her.

"Kenny, you can't mean that!"

"I do. I want to see other people. I'm sick of your

67

shit." He yanked his arm away and she grabbed the banister to steady herself.

I wanted to turn away but I watched anyway. The banister broke loose from what looked like a solid support of cement, and the girl tumbled the five steps to the ground. It wasn't that much of a fall, and if there hadn't been a helping hand by the name of Murphy, she probably would have ended up with a couple of bruises.

But Murphy *was* around. She started wailing and the guy cringed. I'd like to think it was distaste from seeing her get hurt. Unfortunately, there was a certain edge to his expression that made me think it had more to do with the fact that he couldn't just walk away. There was a second's hesitation, but in the end, he headed down the stairs and knelt by her side.

Grabbing Murphy's wrist, I tugged him over toward my car.

"Did you have to do that? She was already having a bad day."

He raised one shoulder up and tilted his head toward it. "It's who I am. Can't help it. The worse the day someone's had, the more it draws me in. Can't seem to resist." He looked at my Honda and cringed. "This thing really *is* as bad as they say."

"Who said that?"

"No one. I just thought I heard something but maybe I didn't." Murphy was also the worst liar in the office.

"Forget it; I know it's bad. I'll see you tomorrow, Murphy."

"Night, Karma."

He walked past the couple into the bar, and of

course the guy's phone fell out of his pocket and smashed on the cement steps. Poor schmucks.

I dropped my purse on the passenger seat and almost missed the note.

52 Maple Lane Road
9:30 P.M.
Come or else.

Or else? I crumpled up the note and threw it in the back.

It wasn't a job. I would've had a vision or a dream if it were. The ripped edge from a spiral notebook confirmed it. The Universe had better taste in stationary than that. The Universe also didn't bother with *or else*. The creepy feeling you got shooting up your spine when you stepped out of line already implied it.

Definitely wasn't Fate. He didn't need an *or else*, either. Most people just did what he wanted, except me. I wasn't sure if he knew what an ultimatum even was, but I was pretty sure he might be trying to figure it out now.

No, this was one of Fate's guys. They'd been hanging out with enough humans over at Lars's tattoo shop to pick up on our—their—ways. I kept forgetting I wasn't human anymore.

I swung my car left—away from home—instead of right, hoping I'd have enough gas to make it there. The Honda's gas seemed to constantly disappear somehow, and I wanted to make this meeting. It was time to have a chat with the boys. This stalker business was getting on my nerves. The longer I hung around, the more I was fairly sure no one was going to try and kill me. Bully me, harass me and who knew what else, yes.

It was just after nine thirty when I spotted the stucco building at the given address. It had a dingy sign hanging sideways that read *Zombieplex*. I pulled into the empty lot of the closed down arcade, weeds sprouting up between the cracks of cement, and turned off the engine.

Feeling underneath my seat, I grabbed the can of pepper spray hidden there. I'd feel bad nailing Lars in the eyes, but if he got too annoying, I would. He had threatened me with death at one point. Pepper spray wasn't an overreaction. Retired or not, when Death threatens you with dying, you needed to come prepared, no matter what your instincts told you. Who knew what kind of mojo he still had going on?

The Honda's muffler had warned all of my arrival, so I wasn't surprised when the door was pushed open by Cutty. So, did that mean all the boys had decided to come out and play?

I'd found out that Cutty was named thusly for his favorite drink, Cutty Sark. They had all adopted weird names since they had never been human and given one by parents. Once they retired, they needed to call themselves something that was totally disassociated with the agency.

It's not like Lars could walk around being called Death. Then I thought of his long dark hair and habit of wearing black. Actually, he might be able to pull it off.

I wondered if all four of them would be here. Bic, named in honor of his bald head, and Angus, who had an affinity for red meat. I'd find out soon, I thought as I stepped into the building.

The lights were dimmed but my eyesight adjusted fairly quickly. A lot of things were better since my death. The Tooth Fairy had once described mortality as being covered in bubble wrap, everything around you muffled slightly.

It seemed plausible, since as time slowly crept by, my eyes became sharper, my hearing more acute and my limbs more nimble. The only thing that hadn't changed was my sense of taste. That was pretty much same ole'.

I took in my surroundings with my new and improved senses as I followed Cutty. An old Pac-Man video game was standing in the corner, with Donkey Kong right beside it. We skirted around an air hockey table.

I used to be great at air hockey. It was all about the angles. Just when your opponent got into a habit of blocking the sides, you shot the puck straight down the center, lightning fast.

"Hey, Cutty," it was the first words either of us had uttered. "How about we settle this like civilized people, with an air hockey duel?" I wanted to add, *because I'm going to kick your ass*, but it was best to leave the trash talking off until he accepted.

Even in life, I'd loved a good trash talking. It was truly part of any healthy competition, if you thought about it. Well, maybe not, but it was a ton of fun if you were good at it.

He stopped and turned to look at me. "You really are one strange girl," he said, then kept walking.

I took that for a *no*.

I followed him away from the table. It was probably for the best anyway. Those games were part of a past I didn't like to think about.

The smaller front room opened up into a larger back area that had been used for laser tag. I'd guess it was probably a transition from the arcade to something fresher, when the trend turned toward home units. Didn't look like it had turned out so well.

An empty chair sat in the center of the abandoned room with chipping paint and missing carpet. A light hung overhead, creating harsh shadows in the corners of the room, where I could see the barest outline of the others.

Now I really knew Fate wasn't here. He wasn't this dramatic; not on purpose, anyway. His was more of a natural gift, effortlessly stealing the show.

"Oooh, so spooky," I mocked, and wasn't surprised when I was the only one laughing. These guys had no sense of humor. "Should I presume this is my seat?" I didn't wait for an answer but sat down.

"It's time for answers. Are you with us or not?" Cutty leaned over me, placing a hand on the back of my chair. "Think before you speak."

These guys weren't a laughing matter; I knew this. And yet, I couldn't seem to work up any respectable level of anxiety for the situation. I didn't know what exactly Fate and I were to each other, but somehow I knew he wouldn't hurt me. And because of him, neither would his guys.

Maybe, like so many things in life, it's a matter of perspective. I'd recently gained some, by the name of Malokin. Him, I was worried about, and I had a really bad feeling he wasn't going away.

These guys might be bad news, but they weren't on the same scale. They'd threaten and scream but wouldn't actually do anything to me.

Malokin was different. If Paddy was nervous about him, he was bad. He wouldn't scream or threaten; he'd just kill me.

But threat or not, I really couldn't afford to piss more people off. Perhaps I should try and pretend I *was* scared, to plump up their egos.

"Did you hear me?" Cutty screamed.

Oh no. I'd been so focused on my concern over Malokin I'd already blown the whole fear charade. I'd been drifting off as Cutty had been mid-scream. Now they certainly weren't going to want to be friends with me.

"No, I'm sorry. I didn't." It was a tad ridiculous to admit I'd been distracted when he'd been bellowing an inch from my face.

"Give me the duct tape," Cutty yelled to one of the other guys.

"Are you going to tape me to the chair?" I asked, still not overly concerned.

"Yes. You going to listen now?" he asked mistaking the reason for my squirming.

"Actually, I need to use the rest room first, if this is going to be a while." That Maker's Mark was flying through my system at an alarming rate.

"Tape her up," Cutty said.

"But she's got to pee?" Bic said. "If she pees in the chair, I'm not cleaning it."

"If she pees in the chair, she sits in it," Cutty

replied.

"Do you know what that'll smell like? She smells pretty now. I don't want her to be smelly," Bic said.

"I don't want to be smelly either," I added to the argument.

"Give me the goddamn tape!" Cutty ripped the roll from Bic's hand.

A noise drew our attention to the door where Lars stepped into the room. His hair was flowing free around his shoulders as he came to stop a few feet from me

"You're late," Cutty said.

Lars didn't argue, but instead motioned for Cutty to go over to the side with him and then walked away.

"Don't. Move," Cutty said before following Lars.

"Okie dokie, smokie." I crossed my legs, trying to buy my bladder another few minutes and dug the nail file out of my purse. I'd chipped a nail earlier today and it was driving me absolutely crazy.

Cutty threw me his best evil eye and then walked over to Lars. They must have underestimated my senses, me being a transfer and all, since I could hear everything they said.

"I'm not sure that's a good idea," Lars said.

"Why? We can't kill her or beat her, but he said nothing about scaring her. The tape is all we've got left."

I glanced up quick enough to see Lars make a face.

"He never said anything about scaring, and this needs to be done. She's either with us or against us," Cutty continued.

"He's going to care," Lars shot back. "Just don't do the tape thing, and maybe we should let her use the bathroom, too."

"Why are you acting like such a wuss? It's not like she's his. They aren't together."

"Not technically, no. But if you saw the way he looks at her..." Lars eyes widened a bit. "I've been with them. There's something there."

The way he looked at me? I'd never noticed Fate looking at me weird. Intense maybe but that was just how Fate was normally. What was Lars talking about? He was making it sound like I was dating the guy!

"If he wanted her, he'd be with her. He's not," Cutty replied.

"I'm not sure what they are."

Cutty took a moment to ponder it over before he replied. "He slept with her?" Cutty's tone had quickly switched gears from arguing to gossipy.

"I've got reason to believe so. Plus, I've heard some things." Lars was nodding like, can you believe they're doing it?

Keeping my face as neutral as possible, I forced myself to sit there. Bic and Angus had taken a few steps away from me, and closer to them, clearly enjoying the gossip as well.

Lars looked over at me and I tried to pretend I couldn't hear every word he said. I couldn't decide if it was better to stop the gossip or pretend I didn't know. Either way was equally humiliating, so it was a tough call.

"The story is they slept together and then he dissed her," Lars said. The other three all made gasping noises at this new tidbit.

Holy shit, this could not be happening. The second

75

I left here, I was going to track Luck down and beat her with every last ounce of energy I had.

"So he dissed her?" Cutty asked, completely engrossed in the intimate details of my life.

Lars shot another look my way and then lowered his voice a notch before continuing. "From what my source said, it wasn't an *I'm not interested in you* rejection as much as *it's better for you if we're apart* type."

"What did she do?" Bic asked, he and Angus pretty much right on top of them now.

They were seriously going to stand there and gossip about me now? This just crossed every line I had, lines I didn't even know existed until now.

"From what I've heard, she was pretty upset but pretended she didn't care. Then he was all *I don't care either* but he definitely does. I've seen them," Lars added.

Cutty started nodding his head. "So what do you think is going to happen?"

Throwing my file down, I got to my feet. I couldn't do a round of speculation, too. I marched over, forced myself in between the four of them and put my hands on my hips. "What has or has not happened between us is not for your discussion."

Cutty looked down at me. Actually, they all did. Fate's guys were freakishly tall, up close.

Cutty looked at me assessing and nodded. "Yep, They slept together."

"I didn't say that." I knew I shouldn't raise my voice, but it happened anyway.

"You didn't say you *didn't*." Cutty turned back to

Lars. "This makes things much more difficult."

"No shit."

Cutty lifted the roll of tape in his hand. "We can't tape her to the chair, so what do you guys want to do tonight?"

"I'm not his girlfriend!"

They all looked at me and then decided to ignore me.

I poked a finger into Cutty's chest to get his full attention. "You tape me to that chair this instant!" I tried to rip the roll of tape from his hand but he wouldn't let go.

"No!" He yanked it back and held it up above my reach. "I won't do it and you can't make me."

"Let's take a vote," Lars said.

"What's the point?" the Bic said. "If she's doing Fate, what's left to do?"

"Not about her, you idiot. Where we're going out tonight," Cutty corrected.

"What about O'Toole's?" Bic said.

"O'Toole's is good with me. You two good with that?" Angus added in.

That was it? They were just going to leave? Probably to continue with the gossip over a beer. "I'm not good with that!"

"Karma, I'd like to help you out, but it's just not in the cards." Cutty threw his hands up in the air. "I'm sorry. Nothing I can do about it."

Cutty headed toward the door and the other guys followed.

I ran in front of them and tried to block the door. "No. No one is leaving here!"

"Can someone else step in here? I just can't keep doing this with her when she won't take no for an answer." Cutty stepped aside and Angus stepped forward. He put his hands on my waist, picked me up and then deposited me to the side.

"That's it?" I yelled out after them.

"Oh, yeah. Sorry. We're finished here. You need a ride or something?" Lars asked.

"I hate you all."

"Are you sure he didn't dump her cause she's crazy?" I heard Bic say as they walked out without me.

Chapter Nine

Even a cat only has nine lives.

Luck was sashaying through the lobby, her five-inch heels clicking away, when I finally spotted her.

"Wait up," I yelled, and hurried after her, wanting to catch her before she made it into the office.

Once I caught up, and she got a good look at me, the instinctive smile she naturally wore dropped into something closer to concern.

"What's wrong?"

"How much of the story did you tell people about what happened with me and Fate?"

She looked skyward, as if trying to recall all the details. "Well, you know I warned Murphy about the Cupid thing—"

"No, I mean about *how* it went down. Like the specifics of things said after the act happened." Even though I knew the truth, I was still hoping she'd tell me she held back.

"Oh, yes. I told Murphy about that too." She

smiled, like it was the most natural thing in the world.

It took a second before I could get the word to unstick from my tongue. "Why?"

"Why what?" Her face was pure confusion.

"Why would you do that? Tell him?" The words flew out of my mouth.

"Isn't that what you're supposed to do? You were upset about it, so of course I got upset for you. Well, obviously then I needed to confide my emotional hurt. You weren't in any shape to comfort me, so I talked to Murphy. That's what besties do. I've studied them." She nodded her head through this whole explanation.

I covered my eyes with my palm for a few seconds. It was hard to remember she'd never been mortal and didn't really understand the concept of a human friendship. She hadn't meant to be a complete blabbermouth.

Dropping my hand to see her confused stare, I explained, "This is the thing, besties tell each other secrets. But, they aren't supposed to repeat them to anyone."

"Yes, but Murphy is my bestie, so then it's okay to tell him," she said, quite confidently, as if she was filling me in on some inner workings of human friendship that I'd skipped over.

She seemed so proud of herself I almost felt bad about having to explain the finer details, but I had to do it. "It's okay to tell him your secrets, not mine."

She started to fiddle with the chain on her neck. "When I watch the humans, they repeat everything."

She was shifting from one foot to the other, moving out of confident territory and into flustered. I was afraid if I didn't let her off the hook, I was going to send her into a complete tizzy at any minute. "It's okay. Just no more repeating secrets."

She looked very solemn as she nodded in agreement but was staring down at the floor now. "Does this mean we aren't besties anymore?"

"No, we're still besties." How did I become the one who was feeling bad?

She kicked out a toe, making an arc pattern on the floor, still looking down. "Does this mean I can be in the manual?"

"Murphy already told you about the manual?" This confirmed it. The entire office had a huge mouth. I wasn't really trying to keep the book under wraps, but this had to be a record.

"Yes. Can I help?" She was looking at me now and smiling, clearing excited at the possibility of being included.

"Sure," I said, having known from the beginning she'd want to be included.

She leaned in closer and whispered, "It's against the rules right? I've always wanted to be a rebel."

"Hey, Karma!" Jockey, usually fairly reserved, was sprinting down the hall toward us. "You're making a manual?"

I shot Luck a look that said, *this has got to be a joke?* The whole office must know.

"Why?" Luck asked Jockey before I did. Her enthusiasm made me look a bit closer at her. Why was Luck so excited?

"Could I help?" Jockey asked.

"Well, that depends. She'll need full access." Luck

stepped forward, partially blocking me and obviously looking to be the negotiator.

"What do you have to do with this?" Jockey looked pointedly at Luck and then tried to see past her to me. Luck simply moved with him, blocking access again. If I'd been human, I might've tried to diffuse this but I'd since learned to let them do their crazy shit and stay out of it.

"I'm her second in charge." She nodded her head repeatedly. "So, full access or not?"

He eyed up Luck and then his shoulders seemed to ease a bit. "Yes. I will grant her access."

I opened my mouth to respond to Jockey, but Luck cut me off again before I could say anything. "Can we see them?"

Jockey pointed to me. "She can and only when they are ready."

Uh oh.

After an extremely loud sigh from Luck, she nodded.

"I'll come find you when it's time," Jockey said, and took off briskly in the opposite direction.

"Sorry."

Luck shrugged. "At least one of us gets to go. No one ever gets to see the Night Mares, like ever."

"Nobody?"

"Zilch! Not even Santa, and everyone's always kissing his butt to get the good stuff around the holidays." She moved a step in the direction of our office. "You coming?"

"Yeah."

As soon as we took the turn down the hallway, I

knew something was wrong. One of Mother's gardeners walked out of our office almost in tears.

"What happened?" I asked, but he just shook his head, unable to speak.

Quickening our step, we rushed in.

The office was in a complete uproar. Something was very wrong. It was so wrong in fact, that people weren't even running from Cupid, who was in the middle of the fray. Everyone was here but Fate, even some of the Tooth Fairy's dental assistants.

"What happened?" I asked as we walked over to Murphy, who was on the outskirts of the group.

His eyes dropped down and although he opened his mouth to speak, it took him several seconds to find the words. "Kitty *retired*." The stress he put on the latter word made it sound like he believed anything but.

Luck turned to me opened her mouth to speak but immediately started to sob instead. Murphy folded her in his arms.

Luck spoke on an exhaled sob and my brain had trouble processing her words. A second later it clicked and I realized she'd said, "No, she didn't."

Luck, turned away from Murphy, her breathing still heavy and erratic, but a bit of an improvement. "She wouldn't have left without saying goodbye. She wasn't even up for retirement." She dragged a hand across her cheeks. "Where are her cats?"

"They're still in her apartment, with all her things," Murphy said looking down. "We're going to go over there shortly."

As if the thought of the abandoned cats triggered another breakdown, Luck's sobs renewed their force.

Her pain was understandable. Luck had been a friend of Kitty's for centuries. She'd been a maternal figure in Luck's life; in truth, the only mother she'd really ever had, never having been human.

I sank into the nearest chair. I hadn't known Kitty for long, but there was one thing everyone was aware of, including me; she'd never abandon her cats like that.

The next thought that came into my mind was something no one else in the office would know. I wasn't even sure myself but I feared it deep in my gut.

This was Malokin. He had her, and it was because of me. The waffles from breakfast felt like an unwelcome lump in my stomach as my fingers clenched the arms of the chair.

Luck was still crying; Murphy was hanging his head so you couldn't see his face. Death was walking over and I wasn't sure how I was even going to speak to him when he got there.

I stood abruptly, even though my legs shook. "I've got a job in twenty minutes," I said, trying to scramble in my mind for details if they asked.

I didn't need a whole concocted excuse. They nodded, too consumed by their shared grief to care.

Chapter Ten

Call or fold

The card sat on the table. It was a linen blend, with his name written in black ink. I'd expected script, but it was fat, bold type. There wasn't an address or a logo, simply a number beneath the single name Malokin.

A Wal-Mart bag containing a pay-per-minute phone sat on the table next to the card. I couldn't risk using the work phone for this. I wouldn't put it past Harold to have all our lines tapped.

I knew he had her. Fate had been right; even as I'd been hoping that I could stay out of whatever this mess was, I'd feared it myself. These people—or whatever they were—had me marked as a target. If they'd gone as far as kidnapping Kitty to bring me into the fold, they weren't going to let this go easily.

I hoped just kidnapping. It was still an assumption. There was only one way to be sure. If Malokin confirmed it, there was no going back. I'd have to do something.

Or I could pretend that this had nothing to do with me. How long would that buy? A week, a month? Then what? Perhaps someone else disappeared?

And the whole time I'd be thinking of Kitty. Where she was, if anywhere. Was she gone for good, deader than anything mortal could ever be? Or did he have her still, slowly torturing her while I went about my day?

I sat there pondering my two choices, neither of them good, while a grey cat did figure eights through my legs. It was one of Kitty's cats, dropped off this afternoon. We'd all taken a cat in. I'd assumed they'd all be black, but I was clearly mistaken. Smoke, the grey cat, was on partial retirement for ineffectiveness. No one took a grey cat crossing their path seriously.

When Smoke stopped moving, I looked down and she shot me a stare. I could've sworn it was accusatory. There was something very un-cat-like about Smoke.

"I don't know if it has anything to do with me. It's just a hunch."

She let out a meow that was just short of a howl.

"Smoke, it's not that easy." I reached down and gave her a scratch behind the ears. She let out another accusatory meow, even as she positioned her head for better access. "What if I'm wrong? What if he has nothing to do with her going missing, and I'm just opening myself up to more trouble?"

The cat jumped up on the table and nailed me with a stare, then let out a flat "Meow?" Then I swear, Smoke rolled her eyes.

"It's not that simple. You're a cat. You can't understand the complications."

Smoke jumped off the table and pranced in a slow

manner to my bedroom, and then slammed the door. Great, now even the cat's pissed off. Good work.

I wished I'd asked Paddy more questions last time I'd seen him. It would help to know who I was dealing with. Maybe I should go stroll through the vegetable aisle or go get a drink.

I knew one thing for sure; if Malokin had taken Kitty, it was to get to me. It needed to end with me. I'd call and work something out. He didn't seem like an illogical sort. This could be handled with minimum exposure and limited damages.

I unpacked the phone but it took me three attempts before I was able to dial Malokin's number correctly. My nerves—which I never used to have—were making my fingers shake and hit the wrong numbers. I took a deep breath to work the fidgets out of my system, so my voice wouldn't quaver when I spoke to him, then hit dial.

"Hello?"

"It's Karma."

"I'm happy to hear from you." His voice took on a softer tone.

I bet you are. There was a gloating quality to his voice that chased my nerves away quicker than a double dose of Xanax.

"You have Kitty." It wasn't a question at all, not anymore. I'd known it for sure the second he answered.

"Yes."

I'd been expecting some denials or a run around, not a clear cut "yes;" but that's what I got. Even the people who I'd defended who were guilty had taken a while to finally spill the details, and I'd been there to help them. Things were a hell of a lot different when there was no penal code.

It was time for the scary question. "Is she okay?"

"Okay? That's debatable. Shall I say, she's as good as she was."

Even his jokes sucked. His laugh grated on my ears and flamed my anger.

"I want her released." The words came out between clenched teeth.

"Then I suggest it's time for us to meet. A proper get together, where we can discuss the situation."

It was hard enough to not punch the wall listening to him through the phone. No, he needed to have a face-to-face sit down.

I stood, crossing my one free arm across my chest. "Fine."

"Alone."

I had to think for a second on how much a response of *duh* would affect our future negotiations? Probably shouldn't. "Figured."

"I'll know if you aren't."

"*Sure* you will." This time I couldn't stop some of the sarcasm from leaking out as my eyes rolled in my head.

He rambled off an address and we agreed upon a time for tomorrow evening. As much as I'd have liked to handle this all on my own, I still wasn't sure what I was dealing with. I needed back-up. If I couldn't find Paddy by then, I'd tell Fate. I wasn't going to meet Malokin alone if it wasn't necessary.

It didn't matter anymore anyway, when I thought about it. If I wasn't going to be able to fly under the radar, I might as well join their war. Didn't look like there was much choice, because Malokin taking Kitty meant I'd essentially been drafted.

I was just about to hang up when he started talking again. "By the way, they did throw Suit in a ditch."

The pencil I'd used to scribble down the meeting details snapped in my fingers. "I don't know what you're talking about."

"Come now, I know your memory isn't that bad. Lars didn't want to answer, but I feel you deserve to know. They did bury him out back. Of course, I dug him up and gave him a proper burial."

"I'll see you tomorrow." I clicked the phone shut.

There'd been only two people in the room when I'd said that: Lars and Fate. I was certain he didn't get that information from them. As I looked around the condo, every nook and cranny took on a different light. Had that bastard tapped my condo?

•••

"Meow?" Smoke sat on the kitchen counter, staring at me as I waved a strange wand over every wall, fixture and trim.

"Don't look at me like that." I'd already gone through the living room area. The guy at the store said this would reveal any bugs. The more I searched, the worse I felt. There had to be a bug, because if there wasn't...

Not Fate, but what about Lars? Perhaps, but I didn't think so. I knew a liar when I met one. I swiped the handle past the dome light in the hallway. Beep, goddamn you!

Paddy, where the hell are you? I couldn't even say it out loud anymore, for fear Malokin would hear somehow. I walked out onto my balcony and leaned over to make sure I was alone out here.

"Universe person? You out there somewhere? Could use a little help. A note? Something?" I leaned on the railing and then looked up again. "Look, this is the thing, I know I muddled up some of your plans before, and maybe I was a bit pushy about getting what I wanted. I'm trying to say, I know I wasn't that cooperative in the past, but I'm trying to be now. Problem is, I don't know what to do."

Scanning the horizon, I waited for something. I slid down and sat on the wooden deck and just watched the waves break. After more than an hour, with no notes sailing down to steer me in the right direction, I walked back inside and closed the door.

My work phone sat on the counter and I punched Fate's number in but hit delete. I did this three more times as I paced the living room before I threw the phone on the couch.

I'd meet Malokin alone. He wanted me. As long as he did, he wouldn't kill Kitty or me. I'd go, find out what he wanted and figure out a way to give it to him. And if I couldn't, I'd figure out a way to kill him.

Time to go shopping for an arsenal, because as of right now, I was a highly under-stocked agency of one.

Chapter 11

Table for Two

Malokin had offered to send a car to my condo but I'd declined the gesture. Instead, I climbed into my ancient Honda Civic and did my ritual rub of the dashboard, before turning the key. The engine whined to life after making a couple of choking noises.

"Sorry about this." I patted the dash again. "I guess neither of us planned on sticking around this long." I switched on the FM radio and found a classic rock station before I pulled out of my lot. "Now, tonight might be a bit rough, so try and conserve your energy. We might be making a run for it later on this evening. I'm going to need you at your best." I tried to have faith in my old Honda, but if she had to be my getaway car, I was dead before I even got there.

My plan was to go, scope Malokin out and gather intelligence. Best case scenario, I discovered Kitty's location for a future rescue mission and got the hell out of there. Worst case, I might be changing

91

employers...again. Hopefully this would be a temporary position and not another thousand-year commitment.

It took me about two hours to get to Charleston, since using the doors wasn't an option. I wasn't ready to disclose where I was going, even to beings who rarely spoke and had acquired a fondness for me. More likely it was the polish I supplied them with, but I'd prefer to think it was me. Hey, we all wanted to be liked.

Driving usually had a calming effect on me but not this time. Even as I drove into one of the most stunning areas of South Carolina, I couldn't relax enough to enjoy the beauty.

Malokin's address was a magnificent old waterfront mansion, with columns framing the entrance. It looked as if it had been there since before the Revolutionary War. The guy did seem to have impeccable taste. Sticking out like a donkey in a herd of stallions, I parked in front of the house and walked up the stairs toward the grand entrance.

A servant dressed in black answered the door. He spoke before I uttered a word.

"Follow me." He turned and started up the grand spiraling staircase before I replied, leaving me to shut the door and follow. I trailed him through several rooms until I wondered if this whole tour was simply about demonstrating Malokin had money.

I felt like tapping the butler on the shoulder and saying, *Yeah, I get it, he's got some cash. Isn't there a direct route?* Finally, we made our way through a sitting room and out onto a second floor veranda, which overlooked the back gardens.

Malokin was sitting at a table in the shade of the

blue roof, two glasses of wine sat on the table, a bottle between them.

He stood as I approached.

"Join me, please." He smiled and pulled out the chair for me. "I'm glad you called."

"There are always two sides. I'm open to hearing yours." The bullshit I spewed was so thick it was amazing he didn't laugh in my face as I said it. He didn't look naïve. I needed to thread in some discontent or I'd have no shot of him buying it. "The Kitty situation will need to be resolved, of course, before we can move forward."

He walked around to his chair, dressed in another expensive black suit. I rubbed my hands along the jeans I wore and smoothed down the loose blouse. It's not like I could've worn a skirt. I had knives holstered at my ankles and a gun tucked against my ribs.

"I believe in going into a negotiation with an open heart and mind," he said as he sat down across from me.

His open-heart comment hit a note in me. Had I made sure the safety was on the gun I'd bought off the Jinxes? Hoped so, because I couldn't check it now. I leaned to the left, trying to leave a little room between my skin and the gun handle, just in case.

"I'd like to hear why you seem to have such an interest in recruiting me?" That might have been the first truly honest thing I'd said in a month. Why me? Couldn't they find someone else to drag into their mess? First Suit and now him? Don't you people ever chase willing girls?

"I'm sure you've noticed that this world isn't

running very well."

"That depends on your perspective, to a certain degree, doesn't it? Perhaps it's not going the way you prefer, but maybe it is for others?" I weighed the risk of being poisoned and decided to take a sip of wine. I'd strolled into his lair. If he wanted me gone, he didn't need to poison me.

"Have you noticed how unbalanced things seem?" His voice dared me to deny the obvious.

I'd been thinking the very same thing myself, just the other day, as I'd done a job in Montreal.

"No, not at all." I denied it anyway. Hopefully he'd assume I was stupid and therefore worthless to him.

"I can see you aren't as open minded as you'd like to have me believe, but that's okay. I have confidence you'll come around." He lifted the bottle and topped off my glass. "I think it's time for new management. I want you to join me."

"You think you could do a better job?" Of course he did. His type always thought that. To be fair, though, this place did look quite a bit better than what we had going on over at the office.

"Definitely."

"But why me? Why do you want me so badly you have to drag Kitty into this?"

He reclined back in his seat and crossed his legs. He looked like a southern gentleman, but I was sure he was anything but.

"Cigarette?" he asked, opening up a jeweled case that sat by the wine.

"No, thank you."

He lit up and then blew out a stream of smoke

94

before he began to talk. "I need people who have control. Did you know you had more control over your existence than any other human I've ever encountered in all the years I've been around?" He stared at me while he spoke, watching for a reaction.

And I was having a strong one. The idea that he'd been in my life—on some level—for longer than I knew, revolted me, but I tried to hide my disgust. "You clearly know me very well. Who exactly are you?"

"For now, let's just say I'm someone that thinks it's time for a change." He smiled and said nothing more on the subject.

I leaned back and took a sip of red wine. He could smile, because as of right now, he had all the control. In fact, he had everything I didn't; control, money, and information. I was the epitome of the underdog in this situation.

I smiled now. That was okay with me. I liked being the underdog. Victory's never as sweet as when you're coming from behind.

"What is it you want to do?"

"The short answer is, take complete control." He took another drag of his cigarette and the light glittered in his eyes, making me wonder if I was sitting with the devil himself. I knew some things didn't dwell in our dimensions, but perhaps they came by for visits?

"The first part would be the hardest. We'd have to do some restructuring of management."

Getting rid of Harold? Yikes, that was one thing I might be interested in. Why did this guy have to scream "evil dude?" Why couldn't there be a sane person suggesting restructuring?

It didn't matter. If Malokin was serious, he wasn't going to get very far targeting Harold. He was simply the paper pusher. Maybe this guy didn't know too much. That was a good sign.

"Of course, Harold doesn't pull the strings. His departure would be simply to upset the apple cart and shake a few loose." More wine, another puff and he continued. "But you have a unique in with someone who does. Paddy."

My leg stopped in mid swing. "Paddy is just an old man. Why would you be interested in him?"

"I didn't initially recognize him, but I'd never gotten that close to one of them before." He looked at me, smoke swirling around his head like he really was straight from hell. "Strange how familiar the two of you were, though."

"One of who?" I scoffed. "I'm telling you, Paddy's just some old guy I met at the grocery store." I started swinging my leg again.

"He's upper management."

"You're mistaken." *I think you're dead on.*

"I could be, but I'm not. It's like spotting a unicorn when you've never seen one before. It could be a horse, except for the massive glowing horn on its head."

And what had been Paddy's horn that had given him away? The curiosity building in me wasn't enough to ask and confirm. I agreed. I wouldn't be responsible for slipping and giving him something he could use against Paddy. Although I had no real knowledge, it didn't mean something I said wouldn't be of use to him. It was time for another subject switch. "Where's Kitty?"

"You know I can't tell you that, right now." There was no emotion when he spoke; he simply stated the obvious.

"Is she alive?" I had more emotion than I wanted, but I tried to swallow it back.

"Perhaps," he said, purposefully leaving me hanging.

It was hard not to grab one of my knives and go for his neck. "She'll need to be released for me to continue on in good faith."

"If you sign on, I won't have any further need of her or any of your other co-workers."

"And what about Kitty?"

"We'll come to a mutual agreement about her as we proceed." He stood and I followed suit. "I know that's the only reason you're here, but it doesn't matter. I have every confidence you'll find your place with us."

"What is it exactly you want me to do?" I asked as I watched him open the door to the interior.

"Don't worry, I'll be in touch." He held it open for me, signaling the end of the meeting. All I could think as I passed him was if he was standing just a few feet closer to the railing, I'd be tempted to end this now and figure out where Kitty was afterward.

Chapter 12

A Dark Ride

It was dark day at the office. Even the employees who came in weren't speaking much. After Kitty's disappearance, everyone was off balance, wondering what would happen next. I was right with them, wishing someone would fill me in as well.

Jockey strode over and stopped by my side. "You ready?"

"Ready?" I looked up at him, having no clue what he was talking about.

"To see the Night Mares."

"Yeah," I said, and grabbed my bag. I'd forgotten about our agreement, with Kitty's disappearance on my mind and now Malokin breathing down my neck.

"You have to come now. They're expecting you." Jockey turned on the heel of his riding boots and headed off.

I followed him down the hallway to a door I'd never noticed before. Strange, I'd thought I'd seen them all. This was going to lead to the stables? I'd walked around the building before and I'd never once seen a horse. I couldn't deny I was beyond curious, especially with this being such an elusive experience. Why so secretive?

It opened onto another hallway that stretched out fifty feet in front of us, this one much more dimly lit. An aged and rustic door stood ominously at the very end.

I followed him in. When the door behind us slammed closed, the lights dimmed even further. The walls and ceiling seemed to fade into the abyss. I reached out my fingers to the side but didn't feel anything.

A cool gust blew the hair off my shoulders and it didn't feel like it came from an AC vent. The screams started then, children, adults, male and female. The entire spectrum of the human race seemed to be letting their voices be heard. I walked a little quicker, following right behind Jockey while trying not to step on his heels.

"You sure this is okay with them?" I asked Jockey.

"Yes." Jockey paused before the door with his hand on the large iron handle. "I'll go first, to let them know you're here. Open this door in five minutes." He leaned in slightly and stared directly into my eyes. "Once you are in, I tell you to leave, immediately run for the door."

He turned back to the door and I grabbed his arm before he could go in. "Why? What would happen?"

His face scrunched up. "Just don't stay." He opened and closed the door so quickly I didn't even get a peek inside.

The wind kicked up again and the screams got a bit louder. It might have been the slowest five minutes in my life before I pushed open that door.

Even though there should've been bright midday sun, the sky was sparkling with stars. A field, instead of the paved parking lot outside of the building, seemed to go on for miles and miles. Grass, moist from a recent rainfall, sparkled with the reflection of the moon. Trees lined the entire perimeter. But the most beautiful vision were the horses, all black and sleek. A more perfect creature couldn't possibly exist.

Jockey made a clucking noise with his tongue and the largest of the horses turned her head and trotted over. Its sleek muscles rippled in the moonlight as they worked beneath the glossy mane. Jockey tilted his head as the horse stopped beside him and nuzzled his neck.

"So beautiful." She was massive at close range, larger than most of the horses I'd seen in my life by about a foot. I was in awe.

"Her name is Terror," Jockey said, his hand running down her neck. "She's the queen of the herd."

"May I touch her?"

"If she'll let you. She doesn't take to strangers well."

I took a hesitant step forward and reached out my hand. Terror approached me with confidence then ducked her muzzle beneath my palm. When she came closer, for a moment I feared she was going to trample me, but then she brushed gently against my side.

"She wants you to ride her." Jockey looked at me. "This is an honor."

All thoughts of bailing out politely went to hell with that statement. Why not? How often did you get a chance to ride a Night Mare? A lap or two around here wasn't going to take very long, considering the size of these beasts.

He didn't ask if I wanted to do it, just cupped his hands in front of me. I took his offer. Guess it was giddy up time.

Terror didn't have a saddle or reins so I leaned close and tangled my hands in her mane. The moment I was settled in, we were off, and within a few seconds we were flying full speed ahead, right at the tree line. I ducked low, hoping not to get clobbered by branches, but they disappeared into nothing, along with the field. The grass beneath us was gone as well.

We were galloping at full speed through nothing but blackness for a handful of seconds, and then our path was lined with images on either side. As soon as I got a glimpse of one, they changed. We whipped past them and more sprang up in a distance with no end in sight.

It was one of the most terrifying and invigorating things I'd ever experienced. Suddenly, Terror slowed to a trot and we moved into one of the scenes playing out around us.

It was Malokin, with an image of a female who looked too similar to me to be anyone but. She, or I, was standing in the center of an empty room as Malokin circled around her. From his fingers sprung a web. Slowly, he kept circling the girl, thickening the sticky covering that she struggled to get loose from. I could see her hands pressing outward as her mouth opened in a cry, but she'd lost her voice. Turn after turn, the web got thicker and denser and she struggled less and less.

"Are we in Malokin's dreams? What does this mean? I don't understand." The horse neighed in response and then we were sprinting forth again, until we were in the field once more.

Jockey grabbed my waist as I slid down Terror's side. She nuzzled my arm before taking off into the field, leaving me standing there, shaky and breathing heavily.

"It's quite a trip, isn't it?" Jockey asked, mistaking my demeanor for excitement and not the fear that it was.

"They're just dreams, right?" I crossed my arms and rubbed my palms over them.

"Yes. Everyone's. Anyone's. Where did she take you? Did you get to see a good one?"

"Just a random dream." I'd never seen Jockey so animated, and I wished I could partake in his enthusiasm, instead of wanting to run for the door.

"They can go anywhere in the dream world. Any mind that's sleeping."

"Thank you, but I really need to go," I said, my voice flat, no matter how I wanted to fake it. I took a couple of steps toward the door, wanting nothing more than to get the hell out of there.

"What about the manual?" he called after me when I finally succumbed to the urge.

"Of course. I'll give you an outline of what I need this week," I replied without stopping.

Chapter 13

On the Job Training

We met at the end of the pier in Surfside. He was already there, standing amidst a brewing storm. Thunder clapped in the near distance and lightning flashed behind him, silhouetting his body.

He was facing away from me, hands resting on the railing. His head was angled slightly to the side, just enough to catch a glimpse of me in his peripheral vision. He knew I was approaching.

I took every step towards him as if I were approaching the gates of hell. Perhaps I was. I'd still keep going, even if it were the devil himself I marched toward. If Kitty was in hell, she was simply my seat warmer. I wouldn't let her burn for me.

I stopped by his side, just close enough to hide my aversion but hardly warm and cozy. I leaned on the railing, and bent over it slightly to watch the waves churning. The ocean smashed against the pier's support, trying to take it down, annoyed at a foreign presence where there shouldn't be one. I understood the ocean's anger at the intrusion. It was how I felt about Malokin walking around in my universe.

He leaned forward as well and rested his forearms on the railing, as I was. Every action he took was intentional. It was a common tactic, to mimic someone's actions to put them at ease. He wanted me to feel that we were alike.

We weren't. I didn't care what had happened in my past life. I'd made mistakes, and had regrets, but I'd never be like him.

"I'm assuming that you're ready to start work?"

"Kitty's situation needs to be resolved." The fact that I'd walked away from our meeting with no answers had grated on me since the second I left. What bothered me even more was that I still couldn't do a damn thing about it.

"Of course." He turned and offered me his arm. It was a little too cozy, but I went along with the gesture. I swallowed back my aversion and placed my hand in the crook of his elbow.

"I know we aren't starting off with ideal conditions, but this will work out for both of us." He spoke with so much confidence it worried me. He'd been around a lot longer than I. Did he know something I didn't? Was he aware of something about me that gave him surety?

No, I couldn't think like that. I made my choices, no one else. And as soon as I started rationalizing away from that, the quicker I would be like him. Whatever he believed, I'd prove him wrong.

"And if it doesn't work out? What then?"

"Let's not make this meeting unpleasant for no

reason. You're with me now; let's think positively about the future." He patted my hand that rested on his arm. I'd let him. And then I'd use that same hand he touched with familiarity to break his neck as soon as I got Kitty out of this mess.

We walked toward the Jaguar, parked at the entrance to the pier. It was something I'd expect him to drive. He held the passenger door open for me, keeping to his gentlemanly demeanor, regardless of what lay beneath.

"No driver?" I asked as he got behind the steering wheel.

"I wanted to give us some privacy."

Or to kill me with absolutely no witnesses. "Where are we going?"

"We need to make a stop before Kitty."

"Where?" Maybe he really did want to kill me? If that was the case, he was going to get a run for his money. I wasn't going down easy.

"I wanted a little demonstration of you stopping something that was meant to happen." He looked over at me. "I've never seen you in action. You don't mind, do you?"

I found his statement odd, but nodded. "Sure."

I resisted the urge to fidget or show any nerves. When I'd done this before and killed the man in the forest, I hadn't realized the full picture. I'd seen someone about to get hurt and acted on instinct to protect them. It hadn't been a planned intervention to mess with the larger scheme of things.

This was exactly the type of thing that could kill me—as in gone forever, no passing go. You lost and you didn't get a lousy reincarnation to soften the blow. You got nothing but erased, as if you never existed at all. I knew it well now and was certain he did, too.

But I still turned and asked him, "What did you have in mind?" I asked because—right now—I didn't have any other option.

"You'll see."

It was exactly those types of answers that had my hand itching to grab one of the knives holstered at my ankles.

Chapter 14

A Storm is Brewing

He parked at a marina, not far away from the pier we'd just left. I followed him to the beginning of a large dock, lined with decent sized boats and the occasional yacht. It was empty for the most part, due to the rough weather caused by the hurricane riding up the coast.

The ones that moved their boats were smart. I knew about the storm Mother was sending our way. She'd been carrying on about it, back at the office, for more than a week, raving to anyone who would listen that it was some of her best work to date. The fact that we weren't in hurricane season didn't seem to take the wind out of her sails, or anyone else's.

Without a word, Malokin indicated a boat all the way at the end, which was holding up under the waves better than the smaller vessels. It had to be a sixty-five footer, a beautiful craft, with multiple decks made of gleaming teak.

Light from the inside cabin filtered through the

shades and I could see shadowed movements within.

"There are two men on that boat tonight who are arguing." He looked at me intently and I dreaded what words would come from his lips next. "One will shoot the other in the next thirty minutes."

Oh God, what did he want me to do? Make sure they both died? So much for going undercover to spring Kitty. I was going to have to bail on the first job he gave me. What had I really expected, though? I'd be handing out fliers for the election of a new President of the Universe?

My hand tensed in preparation for a possible fight. If we left here without him getting my cooperation, Kitty might be dead by midnight. I wasn't sure if I could take him. There was a power that simmered underneath his exterior, just waiting to explode, and I felt it. Either way, someone's blood would be staining the dock beneath our feet.

If I did manage to kill him, would I be able to find Kitty? Or would I be condemning her to death anyway?

I shifted my stance, getting ready to go for a knife. I should've brought the gun. Why didn't I? I knew why. I was afraid I was going to shoot myself with it. But somehow, the knives they just felt natural in my hands.

"I want you to stop them."

My entire body relaxed with those words. I didn't have to kill anyone. A scream of relief wanted to burst from my chest, but I held it in. Saving someone, now *that* I could handle. I felt a kernel of doubt about my abilities but nothing compared to the overwhelming anxiety of a minute ago.

But what if I couldn't? It didn't matter; I'd figure it

out. I'd saved people fated to die before.

I took a step forward and he followed. "I'll come just close enough to see you in action."

So much for the southern gentleman act. I hoped he carried a handkerchief. Drooling over blood wasn't a good look.

Shaking my arms out, I cleared my mind and pushed Malokin's presence from it. I focused all my attention on the boat, on the job at hand. If I didn't get it done, three people could lose their lives tonight.

With Kitty on my mind, I headed toward the yacht. The screaming was audible before I even climbed onto the deck. I wasn't working with the Universe on this but against it, as evidenced as soon as one of the ladder rungs broke beneath my foot. My hand firm on the side rail, I plowed ahead.

Also, there would be no cloaking of my presence. This was going to be all me, and I had no idea how I was going to do this.

No need to get worked up. Baby steps. Who knows, my appearance alone might calm the situation. The shooter wasn't likely to want witnesses.

Two men, both in their late twenties, with very similar features, stood in the main room right off the deck, arguing with each other.

"Hello?" I approached the large room they were in, separated by glass doors.

They paid me absolutely no mind at all, just continued to scream at each other. I didn't care what their argument was over, but it was hard not to pick up on the particulars as I stood there.

It seemed one of them had been caught embezzling

109

the funds of their jointly owned company. Of course, the accused denied this vehemently and screamed how the accuser had been slacking in his obligations. He'd deserved more. It didn't matter to me one bit. The only goal I had tonight was that nobody died because of it. Looking at the two of them and their cracking skin, it wouldn't have been a big loss.

"Hello?" I repeated, quite a bit louder, and accompanied it with some pounding on the door.

I needed to handle this and in an impressive manner. Not because I cared what Malokin thought of me from an ego point of view, but because the more adept I appeared, hopefully the more leverage I'd have. Standing at a locked door and screaming didn't look very impressive.

Not sure what else to do, I thudded on the door even harder, as if I really meant it this time. I had the first time as well, but this was an *open up or I'll break your door down* kind of pound, or at least my best impression of one.

Finally, they turned to me. The larger of the two opened the glass door and then they yelled in unison, "Who the hell are you?"

I put on my best lady in distress appearance. It was a bit of a stretch after the pounding on the door and my black cat-burglar outfit. "I have a boat docked a few spaces away and—"

"Get the fuck out of here!" The guy who opened the door screamed so loudly I could see spittle flying in the air. This is how you treat a woman in need? Animal. It almost made me sorry I'd have to save one of them tonight.

"But…" I fluttered my lids, trying to work up a good cry.

I didn't have time to force tears before they each grabbed an arm. I was then manhandled off the deck and over the railing. My fingers grabbed for the ladder just as they released me, not caring if I fell or not.

I had to save one of these jerks? It might have been better if I was supposed to kill them both.

They loomed over the railing, ensuring my departure. My feet hit the dock and I proceeded to take a couple of steps away while their eyes were still on me.

Malokin was watching from the end of the dock but I paid him no heed. If he had a complaint over how it was going, he could take off his nice suit jacket and get his hands dirty. Otherwise, in my opinion, he could shut up.

The sound of the boat door slamming closed spun me on my heels. I doggedly headed back toward them, trying to think of a new approach and getting angrier as I went. What if I'd really been stuck? What kind of men were they? Either way, one of them was getting some saving tonight, whether he wanted it or not.

I slinked up the side of the boat, ignoring the breaking ladder as I went. This time, I stayed out of sight and simply watched the fight escalate. The argument took a turn for the worse with a shove, and the smaller guy fell into the table behind him. The larger one, already having the upper hand, turned his back and pulled out a gun. Well, that wasn't very nice.

Plan or not, I was out of time. Running across the distance, I yanked the handle but the door didn't budge.

111

This was going to have to happen the hard way. Backing up several feet, I launched myself through the door. Glass shattered everywhere and scraped along my skin in various places. That wasn't the tough part. It felt like I'd hit a cinder block wall right beyond it. In truth, what I was hitting was the Universe's resistance to what I had in mind. I didn't remember it feeling quite this bad last time. When I'd saved that woman in the woods so long ago, I'd experienced pushback but not of this caliber.

My legs felt like they were being tugged at the ankles and I'd been laid out on an ancient torture device, like the rack. There was even more pressure against my torso, to the point I lost my breath.

I forced my way through it until it gave and was shot through the room like a torpedo. I took the guy down just as the gun went off.

The bullet skimmed across my back, just as I landed on top of the intended victim. There was a trail of burning pain, but I could breathe normally. No puncture wounds, just a graze. It was manageable damage, as long as the guy didn't shoot again.

"Who the hell are you?" the voice across the room asked in a mixture of shock and agitation. I looked up to see him staring at me, the gun pointed in my direction.

I stood, slowly moving off the guy beneath me. I raised my hands in the air, in an effort to mentally disarm my current foe.

"Who are you?" he repeated, screaming; his intended victim was looking at me, as well.

"I'm no one. Just a random stranger who saw what

was happening." My voice was as calm and level as I could make it.

He eyed me up and down. The hand holding the gun was shaking as it pointed at my chest.

"How did you do that? Dive through the window like that and tackle him so quickly? How? I didn't even see it happen. It was a blur. What are you?" The last sentence was screamed. He used his gun to point to the shattered glass all over the floor.

"What I did doesn't matter. You can't kill him." I motioned to his intended victim, still lying on the ground at my feet, where I'd left him. The guy looked more scared of me than his possible murderer. Good; hopefully he wouldn't do anything stupid.

"Says who?" His voice betrayed his fear of me. I just wasn't sure if he was the fight or flight type.

"I do." *The scary person.*

"What if I just kill you, too?"

He was quickly falling into the fight category. Time to dig deep and do something really badass, or we'd both be dead soon. If I went for one of my knives, and it got out of control, he might end up dead by my hand. Adding more weapons to the situation might not be a good idea.

The gun was waving in front of me and I knew I could reach it with a kick, but could I pull that off? I remembered back to the night I'd leapt onto that guy's back and snapped his neck. Maybe I could.

Everything physical was easier now. I could run up several flights of stairs, taking three at a time, with the same level of difficulty as a leisurely walk down the street had once been. I shifted my weight and went for it. My foot shot up and knocked the gun from his hand.

Wow, I'm definitely badass. That could've been in a Bruce Lee flick. This is why transfers needed a manual. Someone should tell us about this sort of thing.

I grabbed the gun from the ground before either of them could get to it first. Stepping back, I kept them both in view. "This is how it's going to go." I waved the gun towards the guy on the ground, "Get up. You're coming with me." I pointed to the other one. "You. Stay here. On your belly."

Neither of them put up an argument against the crazy lady with a gun and perhaps a black belt. They just nodded their heads.

"You, up, now!" The intended victim got to his feet as his would be killer dropped to the ground.

I took a few steps backward, with the guy following me out towards the door. I walked backward, keeping them both in view, as we made our way across the deck. The whole time, I imaged how badly I'd ruin my new persona if I fell on my ass.

Once we got to the ladder, I waved for him to go first. "Climb down and get the hell out of here." I'd just saved the guy from being shot. This was exactly what he wanted, so there wasn't an argument. He took off over the boat and ran down the dock.

I climbed down a bit more slowly, trying to keep the gun ready. Who knew if the lunatic in the boat had another one stashed somewhere? Crazy people often had a multitude of weapons at their disposal. If you dipped your toes into the crazy pool, you needed to be prepared for a swinging machete to come your way.

The wooden dock felt solid beneath my feet as I

stepped off the boat and saw Malokin waiting. His hands were in his pockets and the look on his face was a cross between satisfaction and surprise. I wasn't sure which emotion was stronger.

His eyes shot to my neck. I'd thought I'd caught a couple of scratches there, but nothing compared to the damage he couldn't see on my back. It was making my shirt stick to me, but it wasn't lethal; just enough to be annoying. I walked slowly and deliberately in his direction. The last thing I'd want him to think was that my back was hurting. A position of strength was crucial in bargaining. His smile became more generous as I neared him.

I lifted my chin slightly. "I want to see Kitty."

"Certainly." He turned and I followed him back to the car. "That was impressive."

That? Yes, I'd moved quicker than a human could, and had more agility, but it wasn't something any one of us probably couldn't have pulled off. If he couldn't figure that out, I wasn't going to inform him, especially since we were heading where I wanted. Instead, I said a simple, "Thank you."

We'd just gotten to the car when the downpour started. He held the car door open for me, ever the gallant and I grabbed the rain jacket I'd brought with me. I'd had a feeling there might be rain in the forecast and now I could use it to shield the damage on my back from his eyes.

"She's close by," he said as he got in the driver's side. He pulled out and let the engine loose. It felt pretty fast, but maybe I was just used to going at my Honda's max speed of thirty.

115

It took us about ten minutes to get to our destination, neither of us speaking much during the ride. I'd been too distracted, waiting for my phone to ring the entire time. No irate Harold? I'd definitely pissed off someone with the golf ball sized hail that was coming down. I was pretty sure Malokin didn't talk because he was distracted by the dents being made in his hood.

We pulled into an indoor parking garage, leaving the suspicious storm behind, his car looking worse for wear. He proceeded to the elevator and pressed the top floor button when we got in. How many places did he have? My guess was they were countless, to make it harder for someone like myself to track him.

"Why did you want that man saved?" I asked, breaking the silence in the elevator.

"Just to see if you could." He smiled again. It was as if this whole situation were his private joke.

What was I missing here? I could feel my blood, or whatever it was that ran through this body, start to spike and boil. I wasn't used to letting guys like this walk all over me, and it chafed at something integral to who I was. "Why do you think you can run things so much better?" I asked, my temper slipping out.

"Just a feeling," he said with a shrug, completely unperturbed by my question. He stood there, next to me, as if he already owned the world.

I gripped the railing behind me so as not to grip his throat instead. The floor buttons lit up one after the other as I wondered how many floors it would take to kill him. Could I do it the space of time it took to travel three floors? It was tight, but my anger might give me the burst of speed needed. Too bad I couldn't find out.

We didn't stop until we reached the top floor. There was only a small private hallway and a single door on this level, which was already ajar. It opened up to a large suite, where five men already waited. Three were sitting on the tufted leather couches, the other two stood by the windows. Of course he'd have thugs. He was Big Bad, after all. He'd need to have the prerequisite brawn surrounding him just to keep up appearances.

I walked in confidently but was anything but. If I did manage to walk out of here tonight, what condition would I be in? Would I be walking out or crawling? I could take the beating, but I wasn't so sure how I'd hold up to a gang rape.

Malokin waved his hand and all but one man left the room. He was the smallest of them and didn't look like much. His dark navy suit had a soft sheen that slid across his narrow shoulders as he walked toward us. The blue of his suit made his hair an even blander shade of brown.

When I'd met Malokin, I hadn't immediately been sure of who he was or how to take him. This guy I hated instantly. It might have been the way he strutted across the room toward me. His eyes openly assessed every detail of my face and form, giving some aspects way more attention than others.

I'd worked for and defended some pretty sleazy people. I didn't use the word hate easily.

Malokin patted the man's back as he stopped by his side. "Karma, I'd like you to meet Luke."

"Hello." I held out my hand in greeting even

though I didn't want to touch him. Not only did he take it, he brought my knuckles to his lips. A smile was beyond my capabilities. Luke was lucky I didn't yank my hand back.

"Luke is my right hand man. He oversees many of my interests. You and he will be getting well acquainted." Then he looked at Luke, "Luke, if you wouldn't mind giving us a moment?"

There was a slight narrowing of the eyes that told me Luke would mind. It was less than a second's slip before the pleasant expression was back in place. So, Luke didn't like playing second fiddle. Still, he nodded his head and exited gracefully into the room where the other men had gone.

"I want Kitty, now." My patience for a meet and greet or Malokin's fake niceties was over. I'd put some skin in the game, now it was his turn.

"Come with me."

He turned and walked in the opposite direction of where the other men had gone. We stepped into an interior office, decorated with wall-to-wall polished wood. Any space that didn't have wooden bookcases, had intricately carved paneling. He stepped behind a desk that had a monitor sitting upon it and pulled out the chair.

"Have a seat." Everything felt like it was going to be a trap, and between that and my still bleeding back, it was wearing me down. I felt an inner shakiness, born from operating on an empty tank with nothing but adrenaline fueling the engine.

I perched on the edge of the seat to not stain his chair with my blood. It wasn't out of politeness; I didn't want him to see how badly I was bleeding.

He leaned forward, over where I sat, to reach a button on the monitor, distracting me from my injuries again. He swerved the mouse around and clicked an icon. The monitor flickered onto an image of Kitty, lying on a twin bed in a cement-block room. There was nothing but grey to be seen. She could've been next-door or halfway across the world.

I switched my gaze to him.

"I want her released."

"You know I can't do that. You'd walk."

I'd known, and yet I'd hoped in spite of it. Kitty was his leverage and I had none.

"You expect me to take this as proof she's alive? This could be days old. She might already be dead. I'm new to this game and nowhere near as old as you probably are, but that doesn't make me stupid."

He pulled a phone out of his pocket and dialed. "Bring our guest a glass of water."

Two minutes later, a man walked in, wearing jeans and a t-shirt and placed a glass of water on her table. He wasn't one of the men who was in the room when I'd arrived. Kitty looked up as he walked into her cell but didn't move other than that.

I shrugged. "Doesn't prove anything. Have him bring her a glass of iced tea, with a piece of lime."

"Lime?"

"Yes. Lime. You want to prove she's alive?" I leaned forward. "You want something from me? You'll do it. Because unless you prove beyond all doubt that she is, we're done."

He stared at me for a moment, and whatever he

119

saw there, he believed. It was easy to convince people of something when it was the truth.

He lifted his phone to his ear again and repeated my request. "It'll be a few minutes. They don't *have* lime."

"I'm not in a rush." I folded my hands behind my head and leaned back, blood be damned.

Eight minutes later, the same jean-clad man walked into the room with an iced tea, a lime slice perched on the side of the glass.

Kitty's head popped up, then her whole body seemed to perk up. She looked at the glass and then around the rest of the room.

That's right Kitty, I'm coming for you.

Chapter 15

Locked Up Tight

Last night, after meeting Malokin, I'd gone to bed with a storm shaking the condo's very walls. I'd told myself it was just Mother's hurricane. It wasn't the Universe. When I'd killed the man who was supposed to have lived, the storm had only lasted about forty minutes. This one went on for hours.

The sun was finally shining when I drove to the office that morning. Considering how bad the weather had been, the damage seemed minimal. A few ripped awnings here and there, and some debris and dead branches that had finally lost their grip, but nothing earth shattering.

I parked in the lot and strolled into the building, coffee in one hand and manual in the other. Last night, I'd decided no matter what else I did, I needed to remain calm and take this day-by-day.

I'd locate Kitty and everything would be fine. She wasn't in the Shangri La, but she looked sound.

121

Everything would work out. For now, I needed to go into the office and act as if nothing was amiss.

I opened the door and found the place in an uproar and a small kernel of fear started to unfurl within me. *Don't get crazy. This probably has nothing to do with you.*

Taking a few steps in, I overheard one of the Jinxes say, "How could he have *not* died?"

And there went my pancakes. I managed to keep them down but it was a fight. Maybe I should start skipping breakfast altogether.

Everyone at the office had already been on edge before. After Kitty disappeared suddenly, without a single goodbye, no one was feeling very secure of late. I'd seen a list of the *retirees* in the last few years. It was staggering in its numbers. They had a reason to feel like they were hanging over a precipice. Problem was, they couldn't see how deep the fall was. Neither could I, for that matter, but we all felt the chill blowing up from the chasm below.

Still, I hadn't expected this amount of upheaval because I had saved a single life. Again, this was when a manual might come in handy.

They were all gathered around Harold, even employees who preferred their own office space, like the Tooth Fairy and his assistants.

Fate was here too, but he wasn't hovering around anyone for details. He was perched on the side of my desk, eyes only for me as I walked farther into the room.

His stare was condemning, but he couldn't possibly know I'd had anything to do with it. Still, he looked like he not only knew but was royally pissed about it, too.

Ignoring his presence the best anyone could with Fate, I neared the cluster of people questioning Harold. I watched as the slender redhead raised his hands to quiet them down.

"There was a change in plans. Everything was approved." His words would've been much more believable if he hadn't had a hitch in his voice.

Crow raised his hand like he was still in grammar school. "But the bird I sent out—"

"I have nothing else to say about it at this point. As I explained, it was just a last minute change." Harold turned abruptly, walked into his office and slammed the door shut. The sound echoed through the room, followed by the lock clicking into place as everyone was still staring at the spot he'd just occupied.

Scanning the group, Murphy seemed the most likely source for reliable information. He was also standing the farthest away from Fate. With a tug to his arm, I motioned for him to follow me to the outer limits of the room, away from prying ears and a few more feet from the condemning stare.

"What's going on?"

"Someone who was supposed to die last night didn't." The extent of the calamity he believed this to be was there in the urgent pitch of his voice, but I didn't understand why.

"So what? Things change all the time," I said.

"These things don't. It was a Lock."

"You're right, I don't get it. What's a Lock?" I crossed my arms, getting slightly defensive. "And don't give me that look."

"What look?"

"The '*oh God, the transfer doesn't understand again*' look." I tried to mimic the way I was sure they said it to each other.

"I don't do that." His face scowled but then shifted into something closer to doubt. "Do I?"

"Yes."

His eyes shot over toward Harold's door and his voice dropped another octave as he asked, "As bad as Harold?"

I shrugged and relented on that score. "Not as bad as him but worse than Death."

"That's not fair." Murphy took a step back, as if he'd just been put into the ring with Muhammad Ali. "You can't use Death as an example. Do you know he waited over a month once to collect a stubborn soul? Do you know what it's like to compete with that kind of patience?"

I sighed. "I understand. Death is a saint." Wait, that didn't sound right. "Maybe not a saint, I don't know. Forget about this." I waved my hands trying drop the subject. "Just tell me about these Locks."

Murphy went to perch on the corner of the desk near him before he remembered it was Kitty's. He stopped himself and leaned the other way. "Most things have flexible futures and many possible outcomes. These narrow as the time of events near, but every now and then, there are certain courses that have been set in motion for years and years. They are referred to as Locks. They've been predestined, you know about them way in advance and they never change. You'll get your orders for a Lock sometimes decades in advance."

"But things change constantly? If nothing else is fixed around these events, how can that be?" I should probably bang my head against the wall for asking. Looking for logic here was akin to asking to speak to the sanest inhabitant of the asylum.

"It doesn't matter. That one thing will not change." His eyes shot to Harold's closed door. "Or hasn't, until now. One of the most common Locks is when someone is going to die. Not every death is a Lock, just certain people who are slated to move on at very precise times. No matter what these people do, when they wake up that day, they're getting called up. Locks can be getting a job or having a child. There's all different events, but if it's a Lock, it's written in stone."

"And this person's death was a Lock?" Then why didn't he fall off the boat and break his neck on the dock or something? What exactly did I do last night?

"Yes. He was supposed to die and he didn't." Murphy's eyes were back on me, but I could see them dart to Harold's door every so often.

I crossed my arms again and then undid them immediately, dropping them into what I thought looked like a relaxed position. "Well, maybe the Universe changed its mind, like Harold said? And what's the big deal? Things will just settle in a different direction."

Murphy gave me a '*the transfer isn't getting it again*' look, but I let this one slide. It was better than the reality of what I was really doing, which was clinging to denial.

"It's sent ripples through everything. I had a job last night that got canceled, minutes before I got there. A Lock event is something woven into the fabric of the

Universe and time. It's like taking all the water out of the ocean. It can't be done. I've been here centuries and not once has this happened."

The air felt like it was thinning. No matter how deeply I tried to breathe, I couldn't get enough. I stared at the door, plotting a direct pathway to it, without having to talk to anyone. I grabbed my purse and slung it over my shoulder.

"Where are you going? Don't you want to stick around and see if we get any more information?" Murphy looked at me, surprised by my imminent departure.

"I forgot I've got to get Smoke some cat food. Call me if you hear anything."

He nodded and then went to gather at Harold's closed door, where everyone else was still standing.

I needed to get out of the office into the empty hall. Having a panic attack in the middle of everyone might wave a couple of red flags. And since when had I started getting panic attacks? That was easy. Since I'd started hiding things.

I needed to relax and be my normal logical self. It wasn't that big of a deal. So I'd messed up a Lock. So what? Murphy was always melodramatic and overreacted to situations. I just needed to hold it together until I got out of here.

Two more feet to go and a set of fingers wrapped around my arm. I didn't need to look to know who it was.

"What?" I snapped, my nerves getting the best of me.

He dropped his hand, daring me to walk away from

him. But he didn't say anything—just stared—and it was a thousand times worse. There was something about the way he looked at me. There was an intensity when his eyes met mine; everything else fell away and all I saw was him. Sometimes it was unsettling but not altogether bad. Other times—like now—it made me want to hide.

When my hands started to fidget, I shoved them in my pockets. Let him stare. It didn't matter.

Then I blurted out, "Are you going to speak?"

He did an obvious scan of the room. It was like he was erecting a visual barricade that told everyone else to keep their distance. We were already separated by a good ten feet in every direction, and after that look, I didn't expect anyone would be coming closer.

I looked around now, too. Yeah, they'd gotten his message and had their own interpretation. "Stop doing that. It looks like we're having a lover's tiff."

"Where were you last night?" he asked, not caring a bit how it looked.

"I don't answer to you."

His hand reached out and grabbed my shoulder, but something changed in the way he was looking at me, his eyes softening slightly. "Tell me what's going on."

If he'd come at me with more bossiness or anger, I might have shut down. But he didn't. I wasn't sure if it was concern or friendship he was offering, but something in me wanted to respond to it and tell him everything. I needed help, and this was exactly who he was after. He could handle this.

Maybe I'd missed the bug in my condo. Or maybe Lars was playing both sides. But I could trust Fate. It was just something I felt. He'd keep this quiet until we figured out a plan.

I've always been independent but never stupid. There was no denying I could use some help. Being an agency of one wasn't a lot of fun.

I bit my lower lip as I contemplated the outcome of either choice. Then I nodded. "Come outside with me." He didn't even know anything yet, but just the prospect of unloading on someone else loosened the vise on my chest. The tension in my muscles unknotted slightly. I didn't have to do this alone.

His eyes softened and he nodded back. He walked toward the door and the moment I started after him, my phone vibrated, alerting me to a new text message. The caller ID told me it was Malokin.

I looked back up as Fate turned to see why I was lagging behind. I didn't want to pull out my spare phone in the middle of the office, but my purse was large enough for me to see the text message that just buzzed its arrival.

I wouldn't do that if you care for Kitty.

I let go of the phone like it was poisonous. How had he known? Was the office bugged too? Was there someone here watching me? My eyes scanned the room frantically. No, it wasn't anyone here. The only person who had been in both places was Fate and I'd seen every move he'd made in the last two minutes.

The vise around my chest was back and it was even tighter than before. I didn't know how he was getting his information but until I did, I couldn't let anyone in.

The feeling was altogether horrible.

Fate's eyes were on me. *Don't fidget or act upset. Keep your composure. Remain calm.* No, that wasn't an option, especially not around him. My best option was *pretending* I was calm.

I walked toward Fate but stopped him with a hand to his arm when he thought I was ready. It was better to tell him here, than alone outside.

"You know, right now isn't a good time, actually. I think maybe tomorrow would be better." I rattled on another few sentences about bad timing, not even aware of what I was saying anymore, just spewing out whatever line I thought would stall him.

His deep-set eyes sunk even deeper with the furrow that formed on his brow. My excuses picked up their tempo until his stare, so condemning, robbed me of my voice altogether.

"What was that?" His eyes went right to my purse.

"What do you mean?" I pulled the strap up firmer on my shoulder and tucked my purse snugly under my arm as I answered.

"What did you just look at in there?" His fingers went to grab it, but I turned so that he couldn't.

"Nothing."

"Show it to me." His hands were firm on the straps now, and I started to wonder if we were going to end up in a brawl over possession of my purse.

"What I do is my business." I yanked my purse out of his hands and took a step back.

He wasn't going to concede. This was going to get ugly, and it was going to happen in the middle of the office, with everyone watching. Alone might have been the better choice. I could feel the sweat forming on my brow.

"Please, not here. Not now."

There was the slightest softening around his mouth, but I didn't know if it was going to be enough to make him let it go.

"Fate!"

We both turned to see one of Mother's gardeners coming down the hall.

"Mother's having a tizzy," he said, winded as he stopped next to us, oblivious to the tension.

Fate looked at the gardener. "Not now."

The guy visibly swallowed and then blurted out quickly, "But she says she's going to take out the entire continent of South America."

He was staring at me; I was staring back, and the gardener just stood there, staring at both of us.

I could hear him taking deep breaths. It was clear what he wanted to do, but he wouldn't. He'd go with the gardener because, well, it was the entirety of South America we were talking about. No rational person would let a whole continent go down just to see the contents of a purse.

I was right, wasn't I? I wanted to scream, *leave, go save the continent, already.*

Just when I thought he might let South America go down, he walked away.

Chapter 16

Wasted Mornings

"Like I told her, I can't do it."

Death was standing there in his khakis and sweater vest, a regular Mr. Rogers. Fate stood next to him in head-to-toe black. Logic would dictate that it should've been Death in all black, but I'd given up on such foolish concepts as logic.

They were standing in the hallway off the lobby and hadn't noticed my arrival yet. A polite person would've notified them of their presence. I found a nice spot behind the fake potted plant. Common courtesy was another thing I'd given up in my adaptation to my new surroundings. My death had really brought out the best in me.

"There's no way?" Fate asked, clearly talking about me. The thing I couldn't get my head around is when he'd decided he was in charge of everything in my life.

In the beginning, it made sense. Harold had assigned him the position because I'd been even more clueless than I was now. But why was he still at it? I couldn't turn around without finding him two steps behind me. After yesterday, I'd had to write off showing up here again. If I hadn't wanted to try and search Kitty's desk for some clues, I wouldn't be anywhere near the place.

"I wish I could help," Death continued, looking honestly sad.

The throwaway phone in my pocket buzzed against my hip. Fate's head popped up and I shot around the corner and hightailed it out of the door. I should've confronted him on his meddling, but it wouldn't change anything. No, avoidance was still the best option with him.

I didn't check my phone until I was in my Honda, a block away. The area code was all zeros, obviously someone with Malokin. Where were they calling from? End of the World, U.S.? It was better than three sixes, although that might have been a more accurate fit.

I hit call and perched the phone on my shoulder as I drove, trying to put more distance between Fate and me.

"Hello?"

"It's Luke." His voice was nasal, and unnaturally high for a man. "Time to go to work." He rattled off the name of a restaurant I knew and told me to be there at seven forty-five that evening. Didn't ask me if I could make it, or if I needed the address. He just hung up.

The cell phone bounced on the seat next to me where I threw it. "What a dick." Kitty was the only thing that kept me from telling him so.

But Luke was right about something. It was time to

132

get to work. Sooner I found Kitty; the sooner I could kick his ass.

It took me about twenty minutes to get to the hotel Malokin had taken me to the other night. I fished through my trunk, grabbed a baseball cap, sunglasses and a paperback, and snuck in through the side gate.

The place had a beautiful oceanfront pool, with lounge chairs pointed right at the lobby. I kicked up my feet, tugged down my hat and opened the book. It didn't matter if Kitty wasn't here. Eventually, I'd tail someone back to her location.

"Miss?" I looked up to see a young woman in a hotel uniform, approximately fifteen minutes later.

"Yes?" I was expecting her to question my right to be there. Instead, she handed me a note with a smile and left.

I hope you're enjoying the sun this morning. Unfortunately, I won't be able to join you.

In the future, please refrain from these types of actions. They could lead to some unfortunate consequences. I'll know, just as I know every single move you make.

No one had followed me from the office. I was positive of that. He wasn't tracing my phones, because I'd left them both at the condo. How was this happening? He knew what was said in my home, but that could've been from a planted listening device I hadn't found. Then he knew I was going to go speak to Fate. Now this?

I leaned back on the lounger, my hat falling off as I

pushed my hands through my hair. It didn't make sense, and all I could think of was the web I'd seen in Malokin's dream, tightening around me and stealing my voice.

Chapter 17

Undesirables

The parking lot at the restaurant was full, except for a small spot next to the dumpster the Honda barely squeezed into. If that wasn't an omen of the job to come, I didn't know what was.

I locked the door for no particular reason other than habit, from my human years, when I'd had a nicer car. The gravel crunched under my feet and played havoc with the heels of my shoes. I was running out of available tactics. If a snug black dress and high heels gained some leverage, I wasn't above using my newly improved looks.

My heel got caught in a particularly troublesome patch of gravel as the smell of smoke hit my nostrils. Turning back toward the rest of the driveway, I didn't need to look far, or wonder too hard, to find the source.

The beautiful Maserati I'd admired on my way in had flames shooting through the cracks of the hood. The explanation stood not more than five feet away, with their blond heads bent over, laughing. Their skateboards were tucked under their arms and they were passing around a bottle wrapped in a paper bag.

What were the odds they'd be here right now, before my meeting? Was this some sort of set up? I was starting to wonder if I was the one who was jinxed.

I turned quickly, hoping they wouldn't notice me and almost walked into Luke. I stopped just short of a collision and took a step back.

"Karma." His eyes darted behind me, probably looking at the car fire that was quickly attracting a swarm of attention. People from inside the restaurant had begun piling out to see what the hubbub was about. The burly owner, identified by the girlish squeal at the sight, was in the lead.

I hoped the whole place swamped the parking lot, as the more people who poured out of the restaurant, the better. I didn't need the Jinxes to see me here with Luke.

"Let's—" I was right about to suggest we move to a different locale when I was interrupted.

"Hey, who's the loser?"

If I hadn't recognized Bobby's voice, I would've known it was him anyway. There were few beings in existence who were that naturally abrasive.

The look on Luke's face was nothing new either. The Jinxes didn't have a large fan base. It was an expression I'd come to expect when I was around them.

"Give me a minute?"

Luke nodded and I ushered the Jinxes several feet away and over to the side, hoping the uproar around us masked our discussion. The parking lot was becoming chaotic with fire engines screaming in the distance.

"So? Who's the jackass?" Buddy said, Billy nodding so vigorously in agreement his baseball cap came loose.

"You steppin' out on Fate?" Bobby said as he took in my display of rarely seen cleavage. He was the most vocal, and the defacto ringleader of the three terrors.

"I'm not with Fate." I shifted some of my hair in front of my breasts.

"I can't believe you're doing that to our boy." Now their little heads were all shaking.

"This isn't a date! And I'm not dating Fate, either. I'm dating no one." Three little scornful, jaded faces looked at me. They would've been a tough jury. "Look, I need you to keep your mouths shut about this." I snuck a quick look back over where Luke was waiting, his arms crossed and his lips pursed. Not a good way to start off.

"What's it worth to you?" Bobby asked.

More than you can know, right now. "What do you want?"

They took a few steps away from me and whispered amongst themselves. When I saw the nodding, I knew they'd decided. Bobby took the lead again. "Gallon of scotch, brand of our choice, every week for a year."

I'd expected chocolate or rides to amusement park, maybe accompaniment to an R rated movie. "I can't buy you scotch. You're kids!"

"Collectively, we're over a thousand years old. Who you calling kid?" Buddy added.

They had such little angelic faces it was hard to

137

remember their true age. "Fine."

"First delivery within the next couple of days," Bobby added, and looked like he was jotting it into his phone calendar.

"Fine! Now go. And remember, one word of this to anyone and you're cut off." I pointed an arm away from the restaurant, not caring where they went, just desperately wanting them gone.

Buddy, the quietest of the three looked at me quite somberly. "Don't worry. This isn't our first extortion. We're consummate professionals. Once we're paid, you won't hear anything from our lips."

They left then, carrying their boards under their arms, while high fiving each other on their negotiations. As soon as they hit solid pavement, they hopped on their skateboards, grabbed a passing truck's bumper and hitched a ride

Luke stood waiting in his expensive suit, platinum watch and shiny shoes. The Jinxes were right; still a loser.

"Sorry about that," I said, as I imagined delivering a kick to his face.

"Here." He shoved an envelope into my hand. "These are the details of your next assignment."

He turned to walk into the restaurant and I went to follow him.

He stopped walking. "What are you doing?"

"Coming with you. I thought we were going to discuss them?" I said holding up the envelope.

"Are you illiterate?"

"No," I replied, not understanding where he was going with this yet.

"Then I have dinner plans." He turned and walked away.

What a *dick*.

Chapter 18

Take a Hint

The brown envelope rested on the dashboard. I'd been staring at it for a good ten minutes while I sat in the parking lot.

It was ridiculous. It's not like it would magically disappear if I didn't look. I ripped the seal open and pulled out the beautiful ivory sheet inside.

At eleven pm tomorrow evening, the blonde girl must die.

There was a local address included.

I was right. I wish I hadn't looked. I couldn't do it. I wanted to save Kitty but not at the expense of some other innocent woman. They'd need to understand that even with my back against the wall, there were limits. I dug out my second phone and dialed the number I had for Malokin. No answer. I dialed Luke next, and again, no answer. I was positive they weren't answering on purpose. They didn't want to hear it. I punched the dashboard a second later.

I got out of the Honda and looked upward. "Paddy! Where the hell are you?" I screamed not caring who heard. I spun around in the parking lot, keeping my eyes upward and raising my hands as well. "Anybody?"

It took another hour of me sitting in my condo for it to sink in that Paddy wasn't going to show up this time. If I called Fate, Kitty would be dead anyway. I'd already been warned once of that so he wasn't an option and Harold had never been. This was all me.

I needed to figure out some way to get to Kitty. That was proving near impossible and had zero percent odds of happening before this assignment tomorrow night. Since I couldn't even make a step without them knowing, my options were very limited. I'd have to figure out a way not to kill the un-named blonde but still perform the task given to me.

I am a smart woman. I can handle this. They might know every move I made, but they couldn't read my mind. I could figure a way out of this.

If I killed her, I'd have fulfilled my obligation. Nobody said she had to *stay* dead, though. It was risky but possible.

I reached under the kitchen counter for the butcher block with the scribbled face on it, grabbed the new pair of knives I'd bought this afternoon and started throwing them.

I didn't stop until I had one in each eye.

***

Today could go very badly. It wasn't a great plan to begin with. No matter how long I'd thought it over, I hadn't come up with a better idea.

Fate's car wasn't in the office's parking lot. Strike one.

I grabbed my purse, which I'd placed on the dashboard when I got in the car, along with the instructions and information underneath. Malokin and Luke were both men, they'd have no idea how unusual it was to place your purse on the dash.

I shut the car, the paper in plain view now and headed into the office.

A long-sleeved shirt hid the address and time I'd scribbled in pen on my skin. I had all the red flags lined up. Now I just needed the opportunity to wave them.

I pulled out my manual and flipped to my page to distract myself as I waited.

Karma

The page was still blank. It should've been the easiest one to write but every time I started, the words that came out made me cringe.

Karma - in charge of equalizing the balance of people's actions.

I tore it out, crinkled it and shot it into the garbage.

Karma - a complete fuck up, who can't even save herself, let alone fix anyone else.

Nope, that wasn't good.

Karma.
Duties: equalize people's actions and sometimes
throw the Universe into even worse shape, just because
you don't know what else to do.

That was fairly accurate, but I couldn't leave it in. Another paper ball hit the trash as I shut the notebook, giving up on being productive to simply wait it out.

I watched people come in and out all afternoon but still no Fate. When the clock struck four, I was starting to believe he wasn't coming in today. What if I needed a stand in?

Crow stood next to the water cooler with a bird perched on his shoulder. He'd be useless. Even if he did notice the address and time scribbled on my skin, he'd never figure out it was a clue. Plus, he didn't go out into the field.

Bernie was flitting around. He was always looking down, and unless I could promise him a yard full of clovers, he was another waste of time.

Luck was perched on the corner of her desk. She'd been quiet since Kitty disappeared. Murphy was pretty sure she'd only slept with one new guy in the last couple of days. Definitely in a depression, and too unreliable.

If I managed to get Murphy, the girl might end up worse off than dead. Saving wasn't his forte. His natural inclination was to compound a problem. I didn't want him anywhere near me tonight.

Jockey strolled in through the door. Nah, not him

either. The Jinxes skated in a few minutes after. Bobby tilted an imaginary bottle to his lip and threw me a wink. Billy and Buddy high fived. *Definitely* not them.

Finally, just when I'd about given up hope, Fate arrived.

His eyes scanned the room and moved right over me. Then he walked over to Harold's office. Today, of all days, he was giving me peace? This had to be some kind of karmic joke. Except I *was* Karma and I wasn't laughing.

I fiddled with the book in front of me until I saw Fate stepping out of Harold's office again.

Time to make a nuisance of myself. I wasn't sure what actions of mine tipped off Malokin and his people, but they couldn't read my mind. If I did this just right, I could pull it off.

Fate walked in a straight line, heading for the door, and I did the same. His eyes narrowed as I edged in front of him, entering the hall first. The second I reached the hallway in front of him, I slowed down to a snail's pace.

His eyes narrowed. "What are you up to?"

"Nothing." I squatted down to tie my sneakers, the ones I'd worn on purpose and just for this occasion. He'd have to step over me to get out of the hallway.

"You're acting stranger than usual."

Red flags shot off in my brain. I couldn't have his words tipping them off. Those bastards heard everything.

"Because I had to tie my shoe?" I stood, raising my arm to tighten my ponytail which flashed the time and address.

144

"What is that?" His eyes shot to the ink scrawled on my forearm, and I lowered it quickly but not too quick. Hopefully, he'd seen enough and would remember.

"Just a note to myself. Mind your own business." I put as much nastiness into the reply as I could squeeze in. I had to. If they knew what I was about, it could be a disaster.

I strode off down the hallway with him staring at my back. He'd be there.

Chapter 19

Domestic Bliss

The blinds were up at the Cape Cod house located at the address on the instructions. It was a nice home on a quiet street. There was a reserve along their backyard, and I hid easily among the trees as I peered inside the large windows.

A couple in their early thirties sat on the couch, watching Lord of the Rings in their den. The guy's karma wasn't horrible, but he was a bit dull around the eyes. The girl, also my supposed target, was glowing. It made it all the worse.

It's not like I was going to kill her; not for good, anyway. But the risk would've been easier to handle if she'd been all dark and dingy. What if I didn't manage to get this worked out, would she end up dead by someone else's hand later?

I couldn't worry about it tonight. In approximately twenty minutes, something was going to happen. No clue *what* but something. That would be my opening to push things in the direction Malokin wanted. Hopefully, Fate would show up and undo whatever horrible thing I was about to set into motion.

The clock on the wall ticked along the slowest fifteen minutes of my life as I waited. I knew Fate would come, but where was he? What if he'd read the address wrong? What if he hadn't read it at all and I'd misinterpreted the entire hallway scene?

Three minutes left on the clock when she reached for the remote and paused the movie. The light turned on in the kitchen as I saw the man open the back door. I ducked further into the shadows.

He shut the back door and walked around to the trashcans for garbage night. She was making popcorn in the kitchen. She was the one in trouble, so I had to keep my eyes on her, but the sound of the loud wheels of the can grinding against the pavement drew my attention back to him.

He pulled them to the corner and turned around. I looked back at the woman standing in the kitchen. She was choking.

He was just about to go inside, and I knew what was supposed to happen. I was supposed to stop him.

She couldn't breathe. If I stopped him—or even simply delayed him—she'd die. If he went in, he'd save her.

The man's hand was on the door and Fate still hadn't arrived.

Kitty's face in my mind urged me forward and I took a step toward him but froze. I couldn't do this. Not for anyone. Not if I wanted to be able to live with myself. This was a decision that would define who I was, and I didn't like the definition attached to the action.

The man walked into the house and I took a step closer. Not to stop him, but to help if he failed to save her.

"Why are you here?" Fate stepped forward to stand beside me. I hadn't heard him approach, not even with my improved hearing. How long had he been there watching?

"Nothing. Was just in the neighborhood," I said, for the benefit of whoever might be listening.

When Fate didn't say anything, I looked at him. I was letting him in on what was happening and he knew. It wasn't a lot. There wasn't some great opening up of details and information, but it was acknowledged, and I guess it was enough for him. For now, anyway.

We stood next to each other as we watched the man in the kitchen giving her the Heimlich. Once, twice, then she was breathing. Their panic slowly turned into relief and then the type of elated laughter that's born from escaping a close call.

As I watched their shared joy of surviving, I couldn't stop feeling the dread of Kitty's possible death that might accompany it. I hated that their happiness was causing me such dread.

I started to walk away, and Fate's hand reached out, grabbing my wrist and stopping me. My eyes immediately shot to where we made contact, as if that were the only part of my body I was aware of anymore. Why did I react so strongly to his simplest touch?

"You touch me a lot," I said it before I thought

better of it. He immediately dropped his hand from me, as if trying to prove he didn't have to touch me at all.

"No, I don't."

But he did. He touched me every time I saw him.

"Should I expect more of these meetings?" Fate asked, changing the subject.

"I have no idea what you're talking about." I threw my hands up in the air, silently gesturing his guess was as good as mine as I did walk away this time.

There wasn't a doubt that as soon as I got in my car, my phone in the glove compartment would be ringing. Time to give the devil his pound of flesh, if he hadn't already taken it himself.

Chapter 20

Born to Fight

We stood in a different hotel suite, this one a block away from the first. It was equally elegant and the top floor again. Constantly changing things up had distinct advantages for him and made it impossible for me to find them.

"How did Fate know that you'd be there?" Malokin asked from where he stood, facing out the window. He watched my every move in the reflection.

"I can't imagine."

"But I think you can." He turned back to me and walked over, propping a hip on a table, leaning just like Fate did. I rejected the thought immediately. He was nothing like Fate.

"We could have a beautiful relationship. Don't make this ugly." He picked up a random pen, letting it drop and bounce off the wooden surface.

"I'm telling you, I have no idea how he ended up there." What did liars always say? Deny until you die? I might be taking that advice quite literally, today.

His eyes shot to where I had my arms crossed in front of my chest. "Did you wash all the ink off your arm yet?" He took a step forward and yanked my arm away from my body. I let him, without putting up a struggle, while I stared at his neck. He was so close. Could I take him on? Reach over and break it, ridding the world of this monstrosity. Risky or not, I'd try, if it weren't for Kitty.

"I see you did." He dropped my arm and I wanted to run in the bathroom and scrub where he'd touched me.

"I do things like this all the time. I've got a horrible memory." I twirled a lock of my hair around my finger, as if implying, *what's a ditzy girl to do?*

His lips pursed into a thin line. "You *gave* him your location."

"Prove it." My hands started shaking in anger, and the words came out before I thought about it. I wasn't a meek person, ever. Certain pretenses were a real stretch.

"I guess it's going to be the hard way, then." He walked away from me toward the door to exit the suite.

He was leaving, and I had no idea what was happening to Kitty. If I asked, it gave him more control, but he had it anyway. I had to know. "What about Kitty?"

I heard him stop somewhere behind me. "We'll call this your first infraction and leave her out of the repercussions for now."

"Because the second she's gone, so am I."

"Don't press the issue. You don't know what I'm

151

capable of." He was inches away from my back now and I forced myself to remain calm.

"Are we done?" I didn't bother turning around. I already knew it wouldn't be this easy.

"I am. You're not."

I didn't breathe right until I heard his steps retreat away from me.

He walked out and several new sets of feet walked in. The door closed. Instead of turning to see them, I kept staring straight ahead. It was an arrogant move—maybe even stupid—but I just didn't care at the moment. I wouldn't huddle in fear and I wouldn't go down easy.

Three of Malokin's thugs came and stood before me. They were all much taller than I and easily twice my weight. This wasn't going to be pretty.

But they were human. I could tell by the dull skin and rank odor. That gave me an edge.

"Malokin said no marks on her face," one guy with light brown hair said to his two companions.

"We allowed to rape her?" the other one asked.

I kept my face stone still, but inside I was in pure panic mode. *Please, don't let this happen.*

"No."

"Never get to touch the pretty ones." The way he looked at me let me know exactly what he wanted to touch, too.

The relief of that being taken off the table made me cockier than I should've been.

"You guys are a bit overdressed for a beat down, aren't you?" And those ties might come in handy for me. Kitty or not, I knew myself. There wasn't a chance

152

in hell I could do this without instinct kicking in and fighting back. Everyone has a fight or flight instinct in them, but the day I was created, they must have been handing out a double dose of the fight part.

My body went loose and limber without me even thinking about it. It was strange actually. In my mortal form, I would've had no idea what to do. Now, it was somehow instinctual. I'd heard that once someone's mortal skin had been shed, what they truly were released without any constraints. Apparently, deep down, I'd always been a fighter.

I eyed up my opponents, waiting to see who'd be the first to step up. The largest of the three made a move, separating himself from the others and coming just close enough for me to nail him with a roundhouse kick to the side of his head. No one had instructed *me* about leaving their faces unmarked.

The other two didn't look so smug now that their friend was holding his head, unsteady on his feet. I wasn't unrealistic. The odds were still stacked against me, but I'd give them some souvenirs before it was over.

"Get her!" The one I'd struck said to the other two, though he wasn't anxious to come at me again himself.

The guy I'd already hit was still keeping his distance, but the other two spread out slightly, preparing to come at me from different sides and limit my maneuvering room. They were big but slow. It was invigorating to know if it had been a fair fight, I would've taken one of them down with ease. As a mortal woman, more often than not, you're at a physical disadvantage in a fight with a man. Not

153

anymore, though; not in my case.

They inched a bit closer in conjunction. I needed to make a move soon, before they pinned me down. I wouldn't be able to strike without being within reach of the other if I gave up another foot.

I made a quick move to the right and dropped down low. I leaned against my left hand while kicking out with my right leg. Thug two hit the ground. I quickly jumped to my feet again, like I'd been making that move since before I'd learned to crawl.

"Your turn," I said in a singsong voice as I turned to thug number three, the only one unscathed so far. There was a chance I might walk out of this place in one piece, after all.

The other two were taking steps away from me as I eyed up my next victim. Hopping back and forth from foot to foot, I slowly inched my way closer to him. Adrenaline pulsed through me, making me feel more alive than I'd ever felt in life. I wasn't sure if I was getting off on the physical exertion or just being able to kick these guys' butts. But something felt really good.

Thug three would be expecting a kick to the head or a shot to the legs. The midsection wasn't as good a target if he had a lot of muscle. It was advantageous that this guy looked the softest.

I moved in quickly, relying on the stronger strength of my legs to deliver the blow but didn't realize my mistake until it was too late. Leg already extended and in a forward motion, I couldn't do much when the target's eyes shifted right above my shoulder, alerting me to the danger too late.

I tried to abort the kick and drop to the ground,

planning on rolling to the side but the lamp hit my skull before I could.

My head was reeling but I still tried to get up, pushing on my hands beneath me. Unfortunately, this just made it easier for one of them to kick me in the stomach. The force of it pushed me upward and flipped me over.

I was quickly losing all ability to defend myself, when I heard one of them warn the other to stay away from my face.

"They won't see the bruise through her hair." The kick to my skull finished me off.

***

A scratchy cat tongue licked my eyelid, bringing me back in to reality. The tile under my face was cool and sticky with blood. It was also tan, just like the front hallway of my condo. How nice. They drove me home. I'd have to remember to thank them, next time I saw them, right after I kicked in all their teeth.

"I hope you had a better night than I did," I said to the cat, sitting on her haunches appraising me.

Her "meow" led me to believe it had been so-so.

My right wrist folded under the pressure of my weight as I tried to use it for leverage. Good thing I had a spare. My body creaked in strange places as I pushed to my feet and limped into the kitchen.

Everything seemed to still be functioning, if not quite to the same caliber it had. I grabbed a bottle of water from the fridge to wash away the taste of blood in my mouth and looked down.

Smoke had fed herself, as demonstrated by the two bowls of cat food in the kitchen. In truth, she was more like having a roommate than a pet, especially when she was hogging the bathroom.

Smoke, content I was alive, went over and settled onto the couch to watch her soap operas. I wasn't sure how much she actually understood, but I had a feeling it was quite a bit. Sometimes I'd hear a tirade of meows being shouted at the screen when they did something she didn't care for.

Stripping down, I made my way to the shower while the bathroom was still free. I avoided the mirror as I stepped under the hot water.

There had been a price for yesterday, but the scoreboard had a one under the home team. Or were they the home team? I really hoped not. It felt better to think of them as the visitors.

The water started cooling before I would've gotten out and forced me into reality again. I made a large pot of coffee to recharge my battery. I was a little worse for wear today, but caffeine and a hot shower could get me pretty far. We'd see who won in the end.

"I'll see you later," I yelled to Smoke on my way out the door. The cat raised a paw as I left.

Chapter 21

Anything but Coal

"I need you in my office." Harold was standing next to my desk five minutes after I'd gotten there.

"Sure." The red headed bane of my office existence—if we didn't include Fate on his bad days— had some sick sense of exactly when I wanted to speak to him the least.

His pace was brisker than normal as he walked back. I strolled while he waited. He shut the door behind me, a little firmer than I deemed necessary; it didn't do my headache any favors.

I took the extra chair and reclined as much as I could, but it was a fairly cheap model with limited movement.

"I've heard about the manual."

I debated whether I should just tell him now that I didn't care or should I wait and leave him in some suspense?

"I'm guessing you don't like it?" That was definitely stating the obvious.

"It's against the rules." His face was becoming tinged with pink.

"How was I to be aware of that? If I'd had a manual, I would've known." Speaking to him as if he were five wasn't my smartest move, but something about Harold brought out my most immature self.

"You can't write all this stuff down!" He was quickly turning from pink to red.

My eyes made an obvious scan of the room. Stacks of papers were everywhere I looked. It was a ridiculous argument and I said so silently.

He stared back at me, refusing to take my hint, so I stood and grabbed a stack of *written down papers* and waved them in front of his face.

"You're really going to make me spell this out?" I dropped the pile in front of him.

"A manual hasn't been approved." He was completely unbending.

I tilted my head back and stared at the ceiling. "Can you help me out a bit? I'm really not in the mood for this today, and I could use some support here. I'm not sure if you're on vacation or what these days but come on, already. A girl's got her limits." I shook my hands at the ceiling.

Harold stood and pointed at me with his bony little finger. "Stop trying to go over my head to upper management!"

I managed not to laugh at him, but I couldn't stop the smirk. A person only has so much control. If he knew what I was dealing with lately, he'd understand it was next to impossible to worry about him.

He leaned over his desk, placing his palms flat on its surface. "Don't think I don't see you."

"Well, I certainly hope so, with those glasses." I made a circular motion with my finger towards his face. "I'm not sure there are thicker lenses available, so it's a good thing they're working out for you."

"That's right, make your jokes." His fist slammed the desk. "But I know there's something wrong. I knew it when you first came on. I knew it when you walked in here one day, somehow different." He leaned as far over the desk as he could. "And I know it now."

"Well, I did get my hair cut and caught some rays last week. Could it be the tan?" I squinted like I was pondering the changes in my appearance.

"You don't want to make an enemy of me." His voice was soft and low, and the threat in it threw me over the edge. I was being threatened from every side these days, and I wasn't going to let one more go unanswered.

I stood and inched closer to him, helping him out, since he seemed to be looking for the close proximity. "Now, let me tell you something. When I came here, I was looking for help and guidance. What did I get from you? You dumped me in a parking lot and shoved me off on Fate. Still, I went to you again, asking for help. What did you say? 'Go figure it out on your own.'"

I straightened and walked over to his door, hand on the knob and paused. "So, you should understand if I'm figuring it out on my own, now. If you don't like the way I'm handling things, you should figure it out on *your* own. You know why?" I let go of the door handle

159

and walked back over to his desk and stabbed my finger down. "Because I. Don't. Care."

By the time I was done, he was leaning away from me. I turned and walked out, leaving his door wide open as I did. Every head in the office swung to look at me when Harold slammed it shut a minute later.

Bernie, not far from me, nodded his head toward the office. "What's his problem?"

"He was looking for some together time and I said I felt like playing alone. He's feeling a bit rejected."

Bernie accepted this information with another nod, as if it were completely logical and normal. There were some perks to working in a place where everyone was crazy. Since I'd been here, not once had I heard anyone say, 'No way, you've got to be kidding.'

I grabbed my notepad out of my desk drawer and headed over to my table. Technically, it was the office's table, but I'd staked out my claim well enough that no one sat there.

"He's back! The big guy's in the house!" The Jinxes did know how to make an entrance. After they lapped the place on their boards, making sure they disrupted every possible person they could, they skidded to a stop by me.

"Really? Santa's back? I thought he wasn't coming until next week?" I immediately told myself to shut up. Too many questions all bunched together like that and I'd sound as nervous as I was.

"Got an early flight. Said he was starting to burn," Bobby said. He leaned in close then, "Where's our shit?"

I'd hoped they wouldn't ask, but I'd been prepared

anyway. The corner liquor store was on my way to work and a gallon of scotch, wrapped in the prerequisite brown paper bag, sat in my car. "In my trunk. My keys are in—"

"Don't need the keys." Bobby signaled to Buddy and Billy. "Our target has been located in the rust bucket."

They called my car the rust bucket? Well that was just rude.

I watched them take off on their skateboards and hoped they could hold their liquor.

They cruised through the excited crowd. Crow was doing a little hop, Murphy was clapping and everyone was heading toward the door. Santa was here.

I'd wanted to meet Santa but not anymore. What if he knew I was on the naughty list? What's worse than not meeting Santa? Meeting him and being told you were getting a lump of coal.

Luck, as happy as the rest of them, came running over to me. "Come on!" she said, and grabbed my arm, trying to pull me toward the door and everyone else.

This was the most animated I'd seen her since Kitty disappeared.

"I don't know. He's got so many people going to see him. I don't want to inundate him when he's just getting back. We should let him get settled in." I leaned back, resisting her urging.

She dropped her hand and stood back, assessing me. "Why are you acting so weird?"

"What do you mean?" I shrugged.

"What's wrong with you?"

"Nothing." She didn't know what was wrong, but

161

she knew there was something. For someone most people would write off as a flaky trollop, she had laser point instincts.

Oh no, she wasn't getting more secrets out of me today. I plastered a smile on my face. "You're right. I really do want to meet him. Let's go."

She relaxed and smiled as I stood and started to walk next to her.

I really hoped there wasn't a physical list pinned in the office somewhere. Forget getting caught, everyone would know I was naughty!

It wasn't like I wanted to be doing any of this or was trying to hurt anyone. Wasn't saving Kitty a good reason? Hell, I only made sure people didn't get hurt. If I was on that naughty list, I'd be giving Santa a piece of my mind.

Okay, time to get a grip. I was rationalizing and making excuses to Santa and I didn't even know if I had been caught, yet. When had I changed from nerves of steel into bones of Jello? Death really had messed with me. I'd become rude, sarcastic and blood thirsty. Now I could add paranoid to the list. In the three minutes it took to get to Santa's floor, I'd talked myself into—and back out of—innocence four times.

By time we reached Santa's door, everyone in the building was there. Mother and her gardeners, the Tooth Fairy and his assistants, Death, Bernie—basically, everyone in the building—and all I could think of was the amount of possible witnesses to my shame. I was going to have to add self-absorbed to that list of changes since death.

The door opened to a sour faced elf. "You're all

here. What a shock," he said, in perfect deadpan delivery. Put a glass of booze in his tiny fingers, and a cigarette hanging out of his mouth, he'd be ready for stand up in some little dive in New York.

"What's with the cranky elf?" I whispered to Luck as we walked into a very unimpressive office, not much different than our own.

"It was his turn to work off season. They always get really prickly when they work straight through." She waved her hand as if it were no big deal.

"Can't he take some time off?"

"Yes, but none of them ever want to miss the prime season." She was whispering now, since the elf we were gossiping about was giving us the eye, like he knew.

"Single file, you know the drill," cranky elf said.

So, I'd be going in alone? It was something, at least. Luck rattled on as we made our way up the line. My *uh huhs* seemed to satisfy her enough, but it was a good thing she didn't need more. I had no idea what she was even saying to me by time we made it to the front of the line.

"Make it sometime today!" the elf said as the door loomed in front of me, no bodies buffering the way any longer.

Luck gave me a shove from behind and my feet took over after that. The door looked similar to Harold's, so when I swung it open, I was expecting a small square office of the bland variety.

Instead, I walked into the North Pole. The place was enormous, and I realized that just like with the stables, I wasn't in the office building anymore. Elves

163

were running here and there in a bustle of activity. Conveyor belts ran up and down in a maze of angled paths through the three-story room.

A freezing gust of air blew in from the right and some elves started shouting to seal it up, whatever that meant. I turned to see two large red doors, just starting to close on snowy fields that stretched as far as my vision could see. Reindeer, being tended by other elves, were walking into the large area.

"This way!" A small female elf grabbed my hand and started to tug me along after her, toward another entrance off to the side. A plaque above the rounded door read "Santa's Office."

"Go in," she said, and motioned with her small hands for me to enter.

The whole place smelled like a bakery, but his office had the distinct smell of chocolate chip cookies baking. Santa himself was sitting behind his desk when I walked in.

"Hello," he greeted me. He looked exactly as one would expect; long white beard, and a thick head of white hair. His cheeks were rosy and he truly did look jolly when he smiled at me. "You're the new Karma."

"Yes." I smiled back, all the while waiting for the scolding.

"Would you care for a cookie?" He motioned to the heaped plate on the corner of the desk.

"No, thanks." I didn't want to get thrown out mid bite. He was Santa. He knew everything. Any second, he'd tell me to get the hell out of his office, throwing coal at me as I ran.

He stood up from his chair and walked around to

the fireplace that blazed in the corner, lending the space a warm light.

"Would you like to sit?" He motioned to the two well-stuffed chairs in front of it.

"I don't want to take up too much of your time. I can see you're busy." I made a step backward toward the door.

"I've got time for you."

Guess I was going to have to see this thing out until the coal started flying. I watched as he sat. He was still smiling. I took the seat across from him. Maybe he didn't know?

"I know why you're nervous."

Well, there went that.

"Karma, sometimes there are grey areas in life. Things that don't fit neatly into wrong or right."

"Okay?" At some point soon, my phone was going to start ringing like crazy.

He leaned forward and took one of my hands. "I trust you to make the right decisions."

"And what would those be?"

"That's not for me to tell you. Those are your choices. Your inner compass will point you in the right direction." He nodded his head as he said this, as if he was imparting some great wisdom.

My jaw dropped as I contemplated grabbing him by the beard and screaming, *I'm glad you're sure, because I'm lost right now and would someone care to fill me in on what the hell I should be doing?*

Fairly certain that wasn't the right approach, I tried to think of a better way to discuss the situation.

I never got the chance. Elves swarmed in,

interrupting our discussion with a work order problem. He left, telling me an elf would show me out.

I'd missed my chance to ask him what happened if my inner compass was spinning around like a bad ride on the teacups. The only thing it was telling me was to go puke my guts up, and hang on for a lousy ride, because the operator was drunk.

Chapter 22

Point your arrows somewhere else.

My steps immediately slowed once I spotted Fate leaning beside my condo door. I could still leave as he hadn't...

Nope, he had seen me.

Whatever he was here for, it was probably something I wasn't going to like. I wasn't in the mood but that wouldn't faze him.

My keys jingled as I yanked them out of my purse and slid one into the lock. He followed me in.

He didn't say anything. No hello, or how are things. He toyed with the manual I was working with and then moved on, taking in the rest of the place. He was looking for clues, and I was letting him. Unfortunately for both of us, he wouldn't find anything, and I was too scared to leave him any more unless I got desperate again.

I kicked off my shoes and walked into the kitchen, noticing the container on the counter. At least he'd brought iced tea with him. Good thing, because I was out.

He followed me into the kitchen as I took a glass out of the cabinet and offered him one. I sort of had to, since he had brought it. He nodded.

He took his tea and chugged most of it down in one gulp. He nodded toward me. I'd never had such a tense glass of iced tea in my life.

"What's with the outfit?"

I smoothed the dress down, tugging on the hem. "It's Luck's. Santa's elf led me out through their kitchen and there was a mishap with the flour."

"It looks good on you." His eyes slowly moved up my legs.

I drank the iced tea in my glass so as not to have to respond.

He needed to stop staring at me like he was ready to eat me. What the hell was wrong with him, today? He was too smart to get caught by Cupid, but he was acting awfully interested. The worst part about that was the more interested he looked, the more my body seemed to respond. Forget *him*, what the hell was wrong with *me*?

My breathing became more erratic. I tugged my hair loose of its ponytail and pulled it over my shoulders, trying to hide just how excited certain parts of my body were becoming. It backfired because he took it as a different type of sign and closed the gap between us.

One hand reached and threaded through my hair as I tilted my face upward. I felt his other palm land on my hip but it didn't stay there long. Slowly, it slid down and then wrapped around until it cupped my ass and pulled me upward into contact with his hips, where I could feel just how much he wanted me.

His eyes never left my face, surely seeing how every point of contact affected me. There was something so intensely sensual as he watched, waiting for me to acknowledge the need between us.

He looked at me as if I were the only thing that existed. It was frightening in its intensity, and yet I couldn't move away.

I was sinking and quick.

"What are we doing?" My voice was breathy with anticipation of what was to come, even as I feared the ramifications. Hadn't I just convinced myself how bad it was to do this with him? And yet here I was, first sexual overture in weeks and I was putty.

His mouth quirked up as if to say, *don't pretend you aren't with me every step.*

The smirk was gone again and his hand in my hair tightened, tugging me closer to him.

If I let this go any further, I'd never be able to stop it. His mouth was a mere inch from mine when I acknowledged to myself that not only did I want this, I needed it.

I was drowning and this felt like a lifeline. It didn't matter if it was an emotional Band-Aid, simply masking the injury. This was the only thing in my existence right now that didn't cause pain. At least not yet, anyway. Tomorrow, or next week, would be a different issue.

My lips parted and it was all the welcome he needed. His mouth covered mine and then it became a

169

frenzied battle for dominance as both of us tried to take what we needed from the other.

I quickly became the aggressor as I pressed him back against the fridge, pulling his head down to mine. He reached down, grabbing a thigh in each hand and hoisted my legs around his hips.

Our lips never broke contact as he started walking into the other room. When he would've pulled away, I held his head to me, fearing any break would let reality sneak back in. He somehow sensed my desperation and instead of pulling back, he deepened the kiss.

We only made it a few steps into the other room before we were on the floor. He pulled my breast above the low neckline as I reached down and unbuttoned his pants. My hands reached lower and urged him into me.

I threw my head back on a moan as he entered me. His mouth moved to the peak of one breast as his teeth nipped and then licked the hardened nub. My legs wrapped around his hips, urging him deeper within me.

Nothing mattered right now. All I cared about was how my body felt alive wherever he touched me. My hand gripped his head as his mouth bit my lobe. I wanted to climb inside of him, and if I couldn't do that, I wanted him pressed inside of me as deep as he could.

Waves of pleasure started to wash over me and I felt him thrust. Arched over me, his weight partially on his forearms, his hands gripped my head as his eyes— almost wild, now—stared into my own, and then his mouth covered mine. There was something different this time, though. I felt it in his stare and I felt it in the almost claiming of my mouth.

The pressure of his lips increased and when I

would've turned my head he held me there. His hips picked up their pace. It went from too much to not enough. The last little bit of hesitance, which had been buried within me, died, and I found myself clinging to him as I cried out.

He collapsed next to me on the floor of the living room, both of us still dressed. The reality I'd avoided was coming back quickly now, as the air cooled my skin. What the hell had we just done?

"What happened to your leg?" he asked.

They weren't exactly the post-coital words most women long for. I looked down and saw the bruise. It looked like the shape of a boot, and I quickly tugged my dress down.

"I was moving the TV and dropped it." I sat up, self-conscious now, and adjusted the top of the dress, the air becoming chilly.

He sat up as well, leaning on his one arm and eyeing me suspiciously. "Take off your dress." His voice wasn't husky; it was determined and it scared me, not because of what he'd do but what he'd see.

His eyes squinted and his gaze dropped to my torso before rising.

"No." I got to my feet, looking to put some physical distance between us, just in case he wasn't willing to let the subject drop. "I don't strip on command."

"Either take the dress off or I'll do it for you." He got to his feet as well. Somehow he seemed larger now that he was possibly going to try and rip my clothes off.

"We're done. I think it's time you left." *Don't let him unnerve you. Stay in control.* If I showed panic, he'd smell it. If he saw the bruises...I couldn't even think about that. I knew what they looked like. What I looked like.

We stared at each other, only a few feet between us, as I waited to see how far he'd push the issue. My eyes darted around, trying to figure out a plan if he did.

Then something changed in his expression. "Why wasn't that iced tea in the fridge?"

"What?" I looked at the half empty bottle sitting on the counter. "If you wanted it in the fridge, why didn't you put it there when you brought it?"

He adjusted his clothing while he was mumbling curses under his breath, ripped the iced tea off the counter and left the condo, slamming the door as he went.

I didn't care. I was too stunned about what had just happened. How many times had I told myself I wasn't going to do that ever again, and a couple of steamy looks from him and I'm all in?

I fell on the couch with a loud sigh and covered my brow with my arm. A feather gently landed on my nose as I lay there. Opening my eyes, I held it up, thinking it had broken loose from one of my down pillows and made the journey from the bedroom to the living room via Smoke.

It wasn't that small though, and it had the strangest iridescent quality to it. Where had I seen this shimmer before? It was right at the edge of my brain but didn't want to break loose.

And then the memory slammed into me.

Cupid! I'd seen feathers like this flying all over his office. He'd been here. That hadn't been Fate's iced tea.

The ramifications ran through my head. He'd caught on way before me and hadn't been happy about it. He must have realized something was wrong, because he couldn't understand why he was so attracted to me. It's not like he'd come on to me once since that night, months ago. Every detail that came to mind just compounded my embarrassment.

This was why you didn't drink things when the tamper seal was broken. I jumped to my feet and dug my work phone out of my purse. Scrolling down my contact list, I knew he was here somewhere.

I scrolled down and hit send.

"What did you do?" I said, the second he answered.

"That was fairly quick, no?" Cupid said. "I feel as though you two are seriously wasting my gifts with these slam bams."

"Why did you do that?"

"I'm going to tell you the same thing I just told him, darling. It's my job." Cupid's voice, in comparison to mine, was the epitome of calm. "And I'm exceptionally good at it."

"I didn't want to have sex with him!" Perhaps I shouldn't have even admitted it happened, but my embarrassment was quickly morphing into other emotions.

"Oh please, sure you did. I didn't get to this pay scale because I sucked at seeing the signs."

"I really wish you hadn't. I thought..." My words trailed off, not wanting to say the rest.

"That he wanted you, too? He does, you idiot."

He called to someone in the room to go fetch him a latte as his words sank in. Fate had wanted to have sex with me without Cupid's interventions?

I needed to keep this in perspective. Even if he did, it was a far cry from "I love you," and "I can't live without you." Still, it was better than having him ask me what time my flight out was.

It couldn't matter either way, right now, as the other phone started vibrating in my purse. Not with the current status of my life. "I gotta go."

"Toodles."

It was Luke.

"Yes?"

"If you're finished over there, it's time for work."

My hand clenched on the phone. I'd already wondered if they'd know. Would it have been too much for him to have kept his mouth shut and given me the illusion of privacy? I wrapped an arm around myself, as I replayed what they might have seen.

"I'm assuming you're ready now?"

"Just tell me what you want."

Chapter 23

Leave a message at the beep.

The last two days had been hell. Even if Fate had been looking for me, he never would've found me. I'd had two jobs for Malokin and a legitimate one for the office.

Just when I'd thought I'd have a break, I received another call from Luke. I'd been lucky though. They'd all been "save" jobs.

I was starting to wonder if Malokin threw me softball jobs to keep me off balance. As if he dragged me to the very line where I was about to snap and then eased me back.

It was a type of mental warfare I could imagine Malokin playing with me. Keep me off balance until I didn't know which direction was up anymore. And I was sure it was Malokin. Luke was too stupid to play these games. He was more of a "hit them hard and obvious" type.

In the wee hours of this morning, I'd had to save a

junkie, who was holding up a convenience store, from getting shot. He'd been one of the worst humans I'd seen in a while, and it made me wonder what Malokin was up to. Why was I saving these people? Now, I also had the additional knowledge that any of these saves might be a Lock and cause further turmoil at the office.

It was one of the things that drove me to come to the office today. I needed to know what I was dealing with, and see if I'd caused another uproar. But instead of going in, I sat in the parking lot, my fingers running across the leather-bound manual.

Harold had told me to stop working on it, but I couldn't. When everything else seemed chaotic, this gave me some sort of control. I'd flip through the pages and make notes. Even when my life had no semblance of order, inside this cover, everything was how it was supposed to be. Somehow, working on this had become my mental salvation.

Sanity; I'd looked up the definition of it the other day. According to Webster's Dictionary, it was the ability to think and behave in a normal and rational manner. Such a thing didn't exist in the realm we operated within. At best, the office was in short supply.

I placed the book on the seat and reached for the glove compartment. The door was holding on by one hinge when I opened it and the Advil bottle fell with a hollow sound. Popping the lid, there was single pill stuck to the side. At least it was an extra strength. A couple of bangs against my palm set the pill free and I swallowed it dry.

A quick check in the mirror showed the makeup job over the side of my face wasn't the best. Nothing a quick rearrangement of my hair part couldn't fix. I'd just have to remember not to push it behind my ears, as I liked to do, and try and stay on everyone's left side. That store clerk had certainly had one mean right hook.

My old Honda's door creaked and I gave her a pat on the hood after I shut it. "I feel you, old girl, all too well. It feels like we're both hitting the end of the line."

Step by step, I walked toward the building, trying to concentrate on not limping. I'd hurt the already sore knee during a different job last night, when I'd jumped a fence as the police pursued me. They'd been under the misconception I'd just knocked off a jewelry store. In truth, I'd just helped the burglar escape.

I walked into the office suite, and I noticed the receptionist watching me from behind a copy of Stars Magazine. Her narrowed eyes followed my steps. They were starting to catch on that something was off with me. It was in their eyes, when they thought I wasn't looking.

"Are you walking funny?" she said, just as I'd made it to the interior door.

"Nope. Not at all," I said, hoping she'd take the hint and drop the subject. Maybe I shouldn't have risked coming in today, but I had to know if any of my last jobs were a Lock. I wasn't going to make it too much longer, at this rate. I needed to figure out what Malokin was up to, because if I didn't...

Try as I might, I couldn't see a way out of this mess. Kitty could be anywhere. I was no closer to finding her than the day she disappeared.

And Paddy. Where was he? His absence made how much I'd relied upon him being there to catch me brutally obvious. I was jumping without a net, these days.

The receptionist dropped the magazine onto the desk, dropping the subterfuge of not watching me with it. "Yeah, you are."

"It's these shoes. They aren't that comfortable." I was wearing sneakers.

She forced her mouth into a smile, but it didn't wipe the doubt from her eyes. I smiled back and hoped I did a better job of faking it than her.

I pulled open the interior office door to the back, never noticing the full weight of it until now. My knee felt like it was going to tell my shin it wanted to go its own way. I focused on walking as normally as I could, while maintaining a face that showed anything but pain. Even annoyance would do.

I took a quick inventory of its occupants. Luck wasn't in, which was a good thing. She read me better than most and almost as well as Fate.

"Hey, guys," I greeted, as I made my way past Crow who was talking to Jockey. I waved to Bernie as he watered a potted four-leaf clover on his desk and went to sit over at my table by the window.

Gripping the chair, it helped support my weight as I sat down. I whipped a book out of my purse and pretended everything was good in my world. As if I wasn't fighting the force of the Universe on a daily basis and barely escaping.

The arrival of Buddy, Bobby and Billy, the Jinxes, was heralded by the skidding sound of skateboards. They knocked into the table I was sitting at, pushing its leg into a collision course with my knee. I grimaced before I could stop myself and then forced my teeth to unclench.

"Chickie, you don't look so good," Bobby said, and Billy and Buddy didn't hesitate to back up his opinion.

"I'm fine. And a gentleman should never criticize a woman's appearance," I replied, hoping to shut down this line of questioning.

It had the opposite effect on the three of them. They looked at each other and made mocking faces before breaking into a fit of laughter. Yeah, I wasn't operating on all cylinders today.

"Chickie, that's the funniest shit we've heard in a decade!"

The Jinxes were laughing so hard I didn't notice when Fate walked in. I was clued in to his arrival as soon as I saw the Jinxes start to lean on the table, wall, windowsill or whatever else they could place their little hands on.

He was heading in our direction. I could feel the way his eyes bored into my skin as he neared. Every inch of my body seemed to become more alive, as if it had some sort of intrinsic awareness of him on a cellular level, or whatever it was that my body was now comprised of. Or maybe it was a heightened sensitivity after our last romp.

"Hey, what's up?" Buddy addressed him, leaning on the table with his ankles crossed, trying to play it cool.

Fate looked over, as if he hadn't noticed them until they spoke. He nodded, and then turned his full attention back to me.

"Need to talk." His tone meant business, but I wasn't sure which business it was. Did he want to talk about our *moment* the other day, to put it nicely, or was this about the job he'd shown up at a few nights prior? I could still see that woman choking in my mind.

Either way, it meant getting up. That would, in turn, lead to him noticing my limp. Fate saw everything; I'd never be able to hide it from him if I couldn't even make it past the receptionist.

"Right this second?" I motioned to the boys, as if I didn't want to leave their company. I knew it was a stretch.

"Now." He didn't scream the word; he didn't have to. And yet somehow the whole office heard him say it anyway. Maybe it was because they had an ear in our direction every time we were together. Fate and I were the hottest piece of gossip currently circulating through the building.

The Jinxes looked at Fate, then me, then each other, and quickly decided the other side of the room looked more appealing. Couldn't blame them. He wasn't happy, and a pissed off Fate was a scary Fate. Not that I was particularly worried. Fate wasn't threatening Kitty's life, or kicking me in the gut, so he wasn't listed as a top threat in my book. No one got that honor these days until they'd nailed me in the head with a metal-reinforced boot toe.

I remained in my chair and looked out the window. His presence hovering over me was palpable. He wasn't going to leave. I couldn't hide the limp and after that last knock to my knee, I wasn't completely sure I could even stand, yet.

Waiting him out wasn't going to work. "Why don't you sit?" I motioned to the empty seat next to me.

"No. Not here." He grabbed my chair and pulled it out for me, banging my knee against the table leg again. An instant burst of pain exploded, causing me to catch my breath. I was impressed I hadn't screamed or made a noise, but my cover was completely blown.

His brow furrowed and his eyes squinted accusingly. The vein pulsed in his neck and his body seemed stiffer than it had been even a minute ago. That was impressive. If he got any tenser, he might turn to stone.

"Do you need me to carry you?" The words were said softly but with a definite edge. He looked so angry I wasn't sure if he was mad or trying to help.

"No." The last thing I wanted was to be carried out of there.

I turned in my seat and tried to get a read on him. An idiot would've known he was pissed but beyond that I got nothing. Why was he the only person in my life I had so much trouble reading?

He started to lean down and I realized that I was out of time.

"Don't you dare," I said, trying to delay whatever action he was preparing to take. Looked like my stall quota had been all used up. If I'd had any delusions of him cutting me any slack because of what had happened between us, I was quickly realizing how wrong I'd been. He seemed even worse.

He moved closer and grabbed me under one arm. But not hard, and I realized he *was* actually trying to be helpful with his previous offer when he tried to assist

181

me in getting up.

"Stop," I hissed under my breath, not caring what his intentions were, at this point, everyone was staring at us, and he was drawing attention to the fact I was wounded.

He gave me space as I pretended everything was fine. I stood, waiting to see if my knee would hold my weight. His jaw was clenched and he wasn't leaning while he waited. When Fate didn't lean, it was bad. The less horizontal he was, the worse it was. A happy Fate was at full tilt.

I went to grab my things, but he did it for me. He threw me a look that said "don't you dare argue." I shrugged it off, like it wasn't a big deal, and made my way outside, now with an obvious limp, him maintaining less than a foot distance behind me.

Once we got into the hallway, he pushed open the door to the stairwell that was right near our office entrance. Stairs? I was wrong about him again. He *was* trying to aggravate me.

I wasn't going to argue or say I couldn't, so I limped through the door he held open. The second it closed he shoved me against the wall.

"What are you doing?" His stare sent a chill through me, the flecks of green looking almost gold and ablaze. Last time I'd looked at his eyes, I would've sworn they were darker. I tried not to shrink away, not that I could. He had a hand on each shoulder, pinning me to the wall.

"What the hell is your problem?" My voice was a few notches above normal but not quite a scream.

He moved in even further, until my breasts were

pressed against the front of his shirt. "When did you hurt your knee?"

"I was running and tripped on a rock." It was so lame I was embarrassed at my lack of creativity.

"You don't run." I could feel his breath fan my cheek as he spoke.

I rolled my eyes. "That must've been why I hurt it. It was right after I saw you last. Too bad you ran out of there so quick. You might have been able to warn me." My cheeks grew hot at what I'd just revealed but hadn't meant to. I hadn't even admitted it to myself how bad it had felt when he'd just up and left.

I got it, though. It was Cupid again, or at most a base sexual desire. At least it had been for him. In all honesty, I didn't know what it was for me.

He his head bent down slightly and he lowered his voice. "I didn't mean to run out like that. I just had to—"

"Call Cupid? Yes. I know." I didn't need any fake excuses. I had enough lies in my life without adding his to the heap. It was what it was. He wouldn't have done it without Cupid, and I probably would've. He didn't need to know that part, though.

"Then you know it was the iced tea." He sounded slightly relieved, and it hurt me more than the throbbing knee or the bruised ribs.

It hadn't been a question, but I answered it anyway. "Yes. It wasn't a big deal. Let's not make it into one." I tried to shrug his hands off my shoulders. "If that's all you wanted, I need to get going."

He didn't budge. "Where?"

For someone who was so relieved to be let off the

hook, I couldn't shake his grip loose. If anything, his hands on my shoulders were even tighter. I wasn't in the mood to put up with him. I'd given him an easy out; he needed to take it.

"I thought we just established that the other day wasn't a big deal, so why don't you back off?" I'd had trouble maintaining eye contact before from embarrassment, but that was quickly fading as my anger rose. My back was against the wall—literally and figuratively—and I was ready to fight my way out.

"We have other matters to discuss."

Now the real panic started. This went beyond embarrassment. We were heading into lethal territory.

I stared at him, silently asking what had happened to the unspoken truce I thought we'd had. The night at the house, I thought he'd realized. Then at the condo, again, he seemed to know not to ask, even as I let him survey my home. And yet here he was, pushing the issue.

As if in response, he raised his hand and brushed the hair back from the bruise I'd covered with makeup. It was such a gentle gesture that if I didn't get away from him soon, I'd melt right in place. I forced myself to remember how he'd basically rejected me twice, now. I couldn't let myself fall apart because of something so small.

"If you don't get your hands off me, I'm going to kick the shit out of you." I stared into his eyes; I had my own anger. I was doing the best I could by myself, and I didn't need additional shit from him. I didn't need someone messing my head up worse than it already was or walking in and out of my life whenever they felt like it.

"Try."

It was a low blow, but I brought my knee up. The rage I felt was swallowing me up whole. Given any excuse, it flowed out of me. Having him stalk me and now manhandle me made it explode like a volcano a thousand years past its due date.

He blocked it with his knee and took a step between mine. His hands shifted down to my arms, pinning them to my sides. In that moment, I would've torn him apart if I could've.

"I can help you." I was wrong. He wasn't angry. He was frustrated. I saw the concern there, and it drained everything I had.

I stared at him, wishing I could speak. My body sagged against the wall. *I wish you could help. I don't want to do this alone, but you can't.* But I couldn't say any of that to him. More than anything, I wanted to collapse into his arms and tell him everything.

He stood in front of me, not budging, our eyes locked in a nonverbal standoff. As we stood there, something started to change. The tension shifted from something combative into a different type of beast. My chest rose and fell a bit quicker as I wet my lips.

He seemed to get closer and closer, until his forearms were resting on the wall behind me, and his body pressed against mine.

"Karma..."

I wouldn't find out what Fate was going to say, because a buzzing sound came from the purse I'd dropped by my feet. It was the throwaway phone. The work phone wasn't muted. I'm not sure why vibrate is considered silent when it's so goddamn loud, sometimes. The thing sounded like it was filling the whole stairwell with noise.

We both stared down at it intensely but for different reasons. My body went rigid again, blood was pounding in my ears as my heart thudded. I had to answer that call. Luke wasn't the type to wait, and if he had to, either Kitty or I would pay for it later.

It stopped vibrating.

"That wasn't your work phone." Fate's attention had returned to me completely.

"Yes, it was." How could he possibly know?

"No, it wasn't. I know the rate of vibration on your work phone."

Who—even someone supernatural—knew the sound of a different rate of vibration? It was insane but completely believable if you considered this was Fate.

"So what? You've got a second phone."

"Exactly," he said.

How had that point gone so wrong? I was getting rusty. The stress of the situation was dulling my brain. I used to operate better under high-pressure conditions, like a well-tuned car opening up on the highway. Now I puttered and died, hoping to limp along the shoulder.

Maybe it was the Kitty element. Holding an innocent life in your hands was a whole different type of pressure compared to trying to beat a drug charge for a junkie.

The phone started vibrating again, and my breathing got rougher. If I didn't answer it this time, there'd be hell to pay.

His eyes moved from my purse to nail me with a

condemning stare. "Are you going to talk to me, or should I just answer it and introduce myself?"

"I'm done playing around with you. Let. Me. Go." I licked my lips. With every burst of vibration, I felt more and more desperate.

"Who's playing?" His hands slid down again, his grip just beneath my shoulders.

I tried to lift my arms from my side again but couldn't.

Then his hands were gone.

He took the tiniest step back. "Answer it."

"No." I moved to grab my purse but he got to it first and pulled the phone out, while I fought to get it from him.

"Hello?" he said, his eyes on me the entire time. He took the phone from his ear. They must not have spoken, because Fate lowered it without another word.

He dropped the phone into my purse and handed it to me. I grasped it and turned my back to him, digging into my purse. But the phone wasn't in there. He had taken it with him. I turned back quickly, but he'd already left the stairwell, the door shut behind him, my phone in his possession.

I yanked at the door but it didn't open. Slamming a fist repeatedly, I screamed for someone to let me out but was ignored. My fist was sore when it finally opened a few minutes later.

The Jinxes stood in a line in front of me. They threw their hands into the air. "Hey, don't bust our chops! He told us to do it." Bobby, front and center, thumbed the air in the direction of the lobby.

I was furious at them but the only thing I could

come up with was, "Don't look for your scotch next week."

I sprinted out of the building, ignoring how my knee burned in pain and their yells about how unfair that was. By time I got outside, Fate was gone, along with his car. He'd left and taken my phone with him. And I didn't know Luke's number by heart, I only recognized it from the three zeros in the area code. Why hadn't I written it down? Sloppy. How could I be so careless?

The Honda sat ten feet away and I rushed to it. In my haste, my fingers fumbled and dropped the keys. My knuckles scraped on the pavement in my rush to retrieve them.

"Are you alright?"

I let out a small yelp, startled by the voice. It was Fred, the accountant and single human occupant. "What?"

"Are you okay?" The words *you don't look it* didn't come from his mouth, but his expression was screaming them.

"I'm fine. Just in a rush. I forgot about an appointment." I smiled half-heartedly.

"Okay." He nodded politely and moved away slowly, as if he doubted it was the right direction.

The door creaked open as I got in and I drove straight to Wal-Mart, while I tried to remember Luke's full number. The last two digits were stubbornly evading my memory, but I'd try every combination until I got him.

By time I got to Wal-Mart, my knee refused to bend, but it also didn't want to completely straighten

188

out. It was clearly rebelling against the sprint. I grabbed a cart to lean my weight on and headed off toward the electronics section.

It didn't matter what phone it was, I just needed it quickly. Dodging children and adults, I grabbed the first pay-as-you-go phone I saw and handed it to the teen behind the register, shoving bills at him before he had a chance to ask.

"No bag." I grabbed the phone back and started trying to tear into that horrible hard plastic. It would have been easier to break out of handcuffs than to get this hard clear stuff off the phone. The young man behind the register took pity on me and handed me a pair of scissors.

"Thanks."

I nearly jumped out of my skin when it rang the second it was torn free. The area code to Nowhere, USA, displayed on the ID. I'd forgotten; as soon as I knew the new number, so did they.

I answered it while returning the scissors. I hobbled as quickly as I could to the front of the store, afraid I'd lose the signal.

It was time to do damage control, because Luke was going to be pissed. Losing connection now could be disastrous. "Hello?"

He rattled off an address. "Be there at eight o'clock."

"Sure." He didn't say anything about Fate answering the phone. Maybe it wouldn't be too bad. Perhaps he wasn't that mad.

"And don't *ever* let that happen again."

No, he wasn't mad, he was furious, and either Kitty

or I would be paying for it later. I just hoped I could afford the price.

Chapter 24

My own private horror show.

The address was a one-story cinder block building located at the end of a dirt road, in the middle of no man's land, South Carolina. There was no one around to hear the screams but the birds.

Luke was smiling when I walked in. If I hadn't known it was going to be bad, I would've known now. Luke wasn't happy unless he was inflicting pain.

I kept a close guard on my expression, but that wouldn't always be the way. One day, I'd be the one smiling as I ripped his head from his neck. It wouldn't be a quick death, though. There was a debt that could only be repaid in pain.

That thought was one of the things that got me through this: Kitty, and imagining the pain I'd inflict. Today might have belonged to him, but tomorrow was wide open. It lurked just around the corner, and the opportunities were endless. Every morning I woke might be the day I'd get my revenge.

He tilted his head toward a back area, his smile never faltering. I didn't want to follow but did anyway. No matter what was to come, in my mind there was no choice. Kitty was worth a beating, or worse.

I'd discovered I could handle the pain. A blow here and there wasn't as bad as it looked. It was the day-to-day loss of control, and the eyes I knew were always on me, that kept me from sleeping. It was Kitty, imprisoned under the control of a sadist like him, that woke me in the middle of the night. When I did step into that room though, I'd thought whatever was going to happen would happen to me.

The far wall was lined with black curtains. Luke pressed a button on the wall and they drew back automatically, to reveal a window to another area. Kitty sat tied to the chair, blindfolded. This wasn't where they normally kept her. I was positive of that.

A man entered to her left. He stopped behind her and loomed. He was so large; he made her appear the size of a child in comparison. I might still be paying part of the bill today, but it was clear I wouldn't be the only one picking up the tab for my earlier misstep.

There's a huge difference between taking a beating and watching someone I cared about take it for me. I could handle the pain but not this.

"No. This isn't the agreement." I moved in front of Luke, my back to the window. "I work for Malokin and she remains safe. That's what I was told. *That* was the agreement."

Luke shrugged. "Unfortunately, you haven't been working that well. I thought you needed a little inspiration." He motioned to my hand, which was already digging out my phone. "You can call Malokin. I assure you, he knows." He rocked back on his heels, waiting for me.

I slipped my phone back into my pocket. I knew he was right; I didn't even doubt it.

"This isn't fair. Whatever you plan on doing, do it to me." There was desperation in my voice, but I didn't care. This is what he wanted. Control. He had it.

He was still smiling, and that's how I knew the answer was no without him having to speak. He knew what this was doing to me, and he reveled in it.

"Let's see, we had the issue of him answering the phone." He held up a single finger to the man.

I ran to the door that connected the two rooms, but there was no surprise it was locked. Even if I could break it down, I knew there were men behind the other door across the room. I could smell their rotting skin. I'd never get Kitty out. They'd kill her before I did.

"Stop. I'll do whatever you need." If I had to beg and grovel for her, I would.

"Too late. Come." He pointed to the space next to him, like I was a dog he was bringing to heel. "You'll need to witness this, so that I know you are fully aware of the ramifications of your actions. We don't want to have to do this every day, now. I've got a busy schedule."

"I'm not watching." That's what this was about. Inflicting pain upon me. If I didn't watch, he wouldn't care what happened with Kitty, and maybe I'd just catch the beating I now so desperately wanted.

"You'd deprive her of food and water on top of what's coming? Would you condemn her to sit, tied to that chair, in her own filth?" He didn't blink or budge from his spot. He meant every word. He'd do it. "I will leave her there, until she dies like that. Of course, I'll move her to a new location you'll have no hope of finding, but you'll have this lovely last image to remember."

My spine stiffened. "No, you won't. Then you'll have nothing to keep me in line." This was not going to happen, I wouldn't let it. Somehow, I had to stop this.

"If she dies, we'll just get another one of your friends. That Murphy guy looked like an easy mark." He looked up at the ceiling, as if he was pondering some great thought. "Or maybe Lady Luck? I bet she'd be a lot of fun to break. I know the guys would enjoy trying." He smiled, as if he were picturing it in his mind.

I tried to keep my breathing calm and not attack him right where he stood.

"You think we can't? We took her easy enough. We can take others. We know everything." He gave up his physical position and walked over to me, and then let his fingers trail along my shoulder and down my arm. "Or maybe we should bring in Fate? How would that make you feel? Would that bother you? You act like you don't care that much, but I think differently."

He slowly walked back to his spot in front of the glass. The soles of his dress shoes hit heavy and rang in my ears like a death toll. He pointed to the spot next to him.

My first step toward him was the hardest. The short walk to stand by his side represented something I couldn't wrap my brain around. There wasn't a name for it; not yet, anyway. But it was dark, unnatural and made me feel like I'd walked a mile in a swamp and didn't think I'd ever feel clean again.

One final step and I was standing beside him. I kept my eyes on the large man as he reached down to where Kitty's hand was tied to the chair. He made jerking motion with her right hand. When he let go, her thumb was jutting at an unnatural angle.

She hunched over as much as the ropes tied around her chest would allow. Although her eyes were covered, I knew she was crying, because of the sobs coming from the speaker by the door. She might not be able to hear us, but I could hear everything.

"Who are you? Why are you doing this to me?" she cried desperately.

My chin notched up even as my stomach clenched. "Are you finished?"

Luke didn't answer right away, just looked at the watch on his right hand. "No. That would've been it if he'd only answered the phone, but this little issue we had today cost me an hour."

He held up another finger to the man inside the room.

All reason disappeared and I snapped. My hands went around Luke's neck before another thought had a chance to take over.

Sometimes in life, you reach the limit of your tolerance, whether it's physical pain, or worse, mental. At that moment, you snap. You revert to the most animalistic instincts that still dwell in your core, the basest part of you that always lingers deep inside. It lies dormant, waiting for opportunities just like these.

Logic ceases to matter. You become a creature without higher thinking. You attack because it's all you have left.

We were falling to the ground and I had the best of him until a Taser gun hit me from behind. I'd known they were waiting in the shadows, from the moment I'd walked in the room. But the beast inside me—the one that had grown a little more every day since this ordeal had started—didn't care. It had urged me forward, no matter the price.

My body stiffened and I couldn't control my limbs as I fell. When it finally stopped, two sets of hands gripped both of my arms and his goons hauled me to my feet.

Luke, still prone on the ground where I'd knocked him, wasn't smiling anymore. If I'd had half a second longer, I would've killed him. As it was, the damage was already apparent. Blood marked his nose where I'd gotten a good blow in, and there was a gouge where I'd almost taken out his eye. Once I had him on the ground, a few moments more and I would've been able to overpower him and snap his neck.

"Put her front and center," he said as he regained his feet and picked up his cell phone, which must have slid during our tussle.

Since my legs weren't working well, I was dragged to the middle of the glass and supported in place.

Luke dialed a number and said three words that crushed me worse than two goons ever could. "Break them all." He slipped his phone into his pants pocket and crossed to where I was now, with one of his men on either side. I found little satisfaction in him keeping some distance.

"Now, let's watch what *you've* done to your friend."

By the third break, Kitty was crying in agony. The tears burned at my eyes but I wouldn't let them fall. I moved my stare to a spot over her head but a hand yanked my hair and forced my gaze to her again. So instead, I forced my eyes to go out of focus.

At the beginning, each break was punctuated by a scream. I counted down, knowing there'd be an end and clinging to it in my mind. After the fourth, there was only a soft mewl marking the breaks. I told myself that it wasn't Kitty in there. It was a stranger who meant nothing to me.

My spine stiffened as my eyes burned. If I wanted to get through this, I couldn't feel. I had to be like them, cold and empty, a machine.

The noises finally stopped and the room went black, turning the window before me into a makeshift mirror. All the horror I felt turned toward the image reflected before me. My hair was tousled and my clothes were wrinkled and stained. It took most of the energy I had these days just to continue on. The girl in the mirror was weak.

Where was the strong attorney, the woman who could handle anything? Nothing had scared her. She'd never backed down from anyone, ever. She was her father's daughter, a Marine with steel in his bones. Or she had been.

Luke walked forward to stand in front of me, but I held my ground, no matter how pathetic I felt. The disgust for the woman in front of me held this new person I'd become in her spot. I would not let them break me.

"Next time, it'll be worse." He stared at me and I could see him searching for something, a softness. He could look all night. It wouldn't matter. It wasn't there anymore. Any emotion that wouldn't get me through this, or help Kitty, would be squashed as soon as it appeared.

He stood still in front of me, neither of us moving or saying a word. He stared into my eyes, a small smirk lifting the corner of his mouth.

He took a couple of steps around me, but I remained staring straight ahead. "Shame, really. I thought you'd offer me a much better run for my money. You'd started out with such promise. Who knew how easy it would be to break you with the right tools." His hand trailed over my back. "I didn't even know our kind could lose weight. You look so bad lately, you aren't even worth the effort of rape." His fingers grazed across my hip. "But you never know. Maybe if I get bored enough."

He was wrong. He wasn't breaking me; he was honing me. His words didn't matter anymore. His threat of rape didn't faze me. Even if he did do it, it wouldn't change anything. He couldn't take something from me I'd already shed myself. If that meant giving up all I had been, so be it. I'd deal with what I was becoming after I got Kitty out of this. Or maybe I wouldn't. Maybe I was better off like this, an animal like them.

I didn't budge; just let him grope me as he pleased. Luke seemed to become more agitated the more I didn't react. "I've got plans. Drop her off somewhere," he said to the two men at my sides.

The Taser gun hit me again and I lost consciousness.

Chapter 25

Almost Miracle Grow

When I woke, I was lying in a muddy field in the middle of the reserve. My purse lay next to me in a puddle. I guess they'd forgotten my address, this time.

I coldly surveyed the damage. My knee would require a lot of wrapping before it would be able to take any weight at all. From the feeling of my midsection, Luke or his goons had given me a couple parting kicks to the ribs.

It took some effort to push myself up out of the mud. A hard glove under my elbow startled me, and I jumped back to see the guards there. One of them was holding out a polishing rag for me to wipe the mud from my eyes.

"Thank you," I said, as I took the offering.

"Bad," the guard said, looking at me as his word reverberated through me.

"Looks worse than it is." And not as bad as Kitty was doing right now. "I didn't call you guys. How did you know I was here?"

"Paddy."

Paddy; the only person I felt might be able to handle this situation, and I couldn't find him. He clearly knew what was happening, though. For someone that had been so interested in the beginning, he'd shown his true colors quickly.

"Where is he?" There was an edge to my voice I couldn't hide.

They shook their heads and then dropped them, as if sad they couldn't help.

Fuck Paddy. I didn't need him. I was handling it myself.

I struggled to get to my feet to move forward, allowing myself to lean on the guard who walked beside me.

***

After staying at a hotel in my effort to avoid Fate, I swung by the building I'd met Luke at yesterday as soon as I could get out of bed. It was abandoned.

The window that had framed Kitty being tortured was smashed. The chair she'd sat in was there, the ropes still hanging from it. They knew I'd come back and were sending me a message. They wouldn't use it again. I looked through the place from top to bottom anyway, all the while knowing I wouldn't find her.

Mid-step into the other room, the phone vibrated in my pocket, area code from nowhere calling. I hesitated for a split second before I answered it, as my distaste warred with my duty to Kitty.

"What?"

"Why so angry?" Luke mocked.

I closed my eyes for a second and calmed myself before I asked, "What do you want?"

"There's a job to be done, as soon as you finish chasing your tail."

"Text me the details." I hit end on the phone before he replied and left the building.

***

Another "save" job; a new person to keep alive for Malokin's grand plan, which I was still unable to fathom. I could live with those on my conscience. Keeping someone alive could be undone. Killing them was final and a line I'd avoided crossing so far.

If I knew why he needed them alive, maybe I'd change my mind, but one job at a time was my motto. Still, I dreaded the day when I'd understand his purpose.

I was hidden behind some bushes when they walked into the clearing. Two guys pointing a gun directed some other guy they called "Tom" on where to go. As far as karma, it was a close call on who was the worst of them. They were all dull and had cracks running along their skin.

"Move it," one of the guys with the guns said.

"Please," Tom pleaded. "Don't do this to me. I didn't do what he said."

Tom kept talking, but I didn't bother listening. It would be easier to save him if I didn't know what he was being accused of. Didn't look like the henchmen were listening, either.

They were five feet past where I was crouched when I jumped out. I nailed the guy closest to me with the hilt of my knife to the back of his head. He landed flat on his stomach, alerting the other two to my presence at the same time.

The second henchman spun, his gun aimed at me, now. Their hostage froze, not knowing what to do. Seriously, did I have to do everything for this guy? I kicked the gun out of the guy's hand and yelled to his hostage, "Run!" since he didn't seem to have the instinct to do it himself.

Tom took off into the woods and I was left with the last conscious henchman. "I don't know who you are, but you're going to pay for that."

"If I were you, I'd leave now." This was one of those times I wished I looked like a linebacker. Even in my all black "don't mess with me" clothes, no one took me at my word. Seriously, how could he miss my "I mean business" ponytail?

He circled me and I followed, keeping him in sight. "You dumb bitch, you don't know who you're dealing with."

"You need to leave this alone." I watched his face get angrier as I spoke. "I'm really not looking for a fight. I don't want to have to kill you." I held my hands up. See?

It didn't matter what I said. He came at me. I ducked his swing and took out his legs in the process. I turned back and saw him already getting to his feet. His friend started to moan, alerting me he was awake now, too. That would complicate things. It was harder to keep two of them off me without doing any mortal damage.

This went on for a while. One would swing and I'd take him out and then the other would come at me. I could've done it all night, until there was a gun pointed at my head. Somebody had been a bad henchman and found it while I'd been busy trying to not kill his friend.

"You don't understand, I'm trying to let you guys go. Don't do this." I kept shaking my head, hoping they'd eventually catch on that I'd been going easy on them and leave.

"Who do you work for?" The one holding the gun asked.

"Name's Malokin." I found a perverse humor in telling them. *Good luck doing anything with that information.*

One guy's face scrunched in concentration. "You know that name?" he asked his friend. When the guy shook his head, he turned back to me. "Who the hell is that? And why's he getting into our business?"

"I have no idea. I'm just the hired hand, but I think it's time to call it a day."

They decided not to, and the next thing a bullet that I barely managed to dodge was whizzing past my ear. Then it really got ugly. They had a friend. There was a punch in my kidneys and then a kick to my shoulder.

It became crystal clear once I felt the stab in my side that it was going to come down to them or me. If I didn't start playing for keeps, I wouldn't be walking out of this forest; I'd be buried in it, fertilizing the trees.

Chapter 26

What a fate.

My elbows dug into the soil as I dragged myself on my stomach into same brush I'd jumped out of. It wasn't far enough away to do me much good, but it was all I could manage at the moment until I recouped some strength.

By time it was over, it had become a blood bath. I'd only narrowly escaped with my life. So much for not killing anyone. I'd taken out three humans who shouldn't have died, even if they might have deserved it.

It hadn't been easy, either. I wasn't in top form, these days; I'd only made it out by sheer force of will.

Closing my eyes, I tried to pinpoint the pain. Towards the end of the fight, the blows were coming from every direction, but I'd stopped noticing them. I'd gone from conscious choices and maneuvers to pure instinct, blocking out everything—including pain—that I didn't immediately contribute to my survival.

Even my memory of the fight seemed hazy now, as if I had stepped outside of myself in those moments. Now, I was definitely back in my body, and it was telling me a pretty gruesome story of what had happened.

I was covered in blood, and more than a healthy amount of it was mine. Everything hurt, but I had to prioritize. Staunching the bleeding before it stole my consciousness needed to come first.

It was a new moon, making the evening even darker. That wasn't normally a problem anymore, except for the black spots floating around my vision. I shook my head, trying to clear it, and ran my hands along my body. I'd sprung a bad leak somewhere, and I didn't want to wait for the puddle to form before I found it.

My lungs didn't want to work either, and there was a sharp pain near my ribs. I tried to think back to a first aid class I'd taken. ABC: airway, breathing, circulation. My airway was clear, but my breathing was getting rough. That trumped finding the leak.

I ran a hand over the spot and found the source of the breathing and the bleeding. I had a stab wound and perhaps a collapsed lung? I put my palm over it. Needed to maintain the integrity of the chest cavity, or I wouldn't be able to breathe at all, soon.

Oh no, this wasn't going to be the end. There was no way I was going to let myself die in the woods while Malokin and Luke walked off. With determination, I groped around in the dirt and twigs, feeling for my phone. If I could call for a door, the guards would get me help. It didn't matter if they dropped me in the middle of the office, a bloody mess. I came up with nothing but branches.

No, I hadn't gone through all this crap to end up bleeding out in the dirt. I tried to push myself up. My car was a mile away. I could get there. I'd lie here for a few minutes and then I'd drag my body there, inch-by-inch, if that's what it took.

I heard a branch snap in the distance and then a rustle of leaves. Someone was approaching and quickly. Had someone been waiting for the guys' return? If they came looking, they'd see the bodies and then find me. I hadn't had the energy to hide them but left them in the middle of the clearing for all to see.

I tried to pull my legs in closer but that meant being able to use the muscles in my abdomen. It didn't appear to be an option.

Dragging my body onto my stomach with my good arm, I made it a couple more inches into the brush and stopped. It was too noisy. I was better off lying still and hoping the dark shielded me.

A hand flipped me over. Before I could let out a scream—or attempt to, depending on how much air I could get into my lungs—I saw Fate looming over me.

"What happened?" His voice was cold, clinical. His hand lay over mine, where I was trying to keep the air from entering my chest cavity. "Never mind. Don't talk. Just keep your hand there. Nod if you can do that?"

I nodded. Something about him being here, right now when I needed him, made me want to break down, but I didn't. Even still, the relief was staggering.

"How did you know I was here?"

"Paddy." His eyes met mine. "Stop talking."

"I'm not in good shape," I said, as it weren't obvious.

"I thought I told you to stop talking. And you're not going to die. I won't let you." There was no softness in his tone. It was more of an order, and it tripped a switch in my brain. Why did I feel like I remembered this? It was right there, a memory just out of reach. "You've said that before. When?"

"You really don't listen well. Stop talking."

I didn't have the energy or breath in my lungs to argue.

One arm lifted my shoulders while his other went beneath my knees. I bit my cheek to stop myself from crying out.

"I know it hurts. Just hang in there." His voice was soft against my ear.

He took off at a run with me in his arms. It hurt, but I didn't say anything. I could see a set of doors looming in the distance and knew it wouldn't be long.

He paused just before he went through, to speak to the guards. "Nothing. Not a word, or you'll wish all you had were dings in your armor."

It stunned me. I could get my head around him keeping me alive, but why was he protecting me, when he knew I was probably working with the very people he was seeking? It was a fleeting thought before we were moving and the pain drove it out.

"Will protect her." Their voices rang out deeply, sending vibrations through me. It was the longest thing I'd ever heard them say.

We were through the doors and climbing the steps

to his house the next minute.

"My condo." Those two words were all the protest I was capable of at the moment. It shouldn't have mattered, but I felt vulnerable already, and coming here seemed to magnify that feeling.

He ignored me as he walked into his house and into his bedroom. He laid me on his bed and started making calls. I lay there and wondered if I did survive this, was the cat so far out of the bag that I'd be the walking dead anyway? How far over the line could I go before someone would step in and say "enough?"

Paddy had sent Fate to get me. He knew what was happening, but how much? Would he try and kill me now? But why help me first?

No amount of pain could distract me from how bad this looked. Fate had seen the dead men. That was definite. He'd had to step over them when he carried me from the scene. Neither of them had been slated for death. If they had, the Universe would've been a little more helpful. As Fate, he'd know this. He knew when most people were going to die. The only salve to my conscience on that was they'd all been evil men, with sallow, ugly auras, but it was a blatant rationalization.

I turned to locate Fate and see how bad the condemnation in his eyes would be. He'd already disappeared out of the room. When he came back, he had scissors, plastic wrap, tape and gauze in his hand.

He placed the items on the bed next to me but wouldn't look at my face. He started to cut my shirt open and panic ripped through me. If he couldn't look at me now, what would happen when he really saw?

"No." I grabbed his hand with my free one.

"Stop," he said, pushing my hand away and finally looking at me. "I've got to bandage it."

His face was closed off, not even the smallest sign of what he might be thinking.

He started cutting again. There would be no pretending after this. Not that he'd believed my lies before but having the proof written all over my flesh, which was about to tell its very ugly secrets, was worse.

I closed my eyes and waited as I heard the scissors work their way through what was left of my shirt. When the sides were laid open, and he said nothing, I thought it was safe. Maybe I didn't look as bad as I thought. It wasn't like I was looking at myself every day in the mirror. I'd taken to getting dressed and then assessing the exposed flesh for evidence. Maybe I didn't look too bad?

I opened my eyes and looked down. Even from a limited vantage point, my entire torso was a mish mash of bruises in all different shades. There were healing cuts, with fresh scabs crisscrossing in some places, and newly formed scars in other spots.

Fate said nothing. The proof was clearly before him but still not a word or a look. If I'd been working in unison with the Universe, I never would've been injured like this. My past deeds screamed out their guilt in a rainbow of injuries.

He kept working, wrapping the wound that was affecting my breathing and disinfecting other areas. The only sign he was angry was his refusal to make eye contact with me again.

"You need to tend these wounds better. You aren't immortal." His voice had an edge in it that raised my own ire.

This was the condemnation I'd expected, finally leaking out. Who was he to cast judgment?

"You're hardly innocent yourself. If you find this so objectionable, then you don't need to help me." I tried to push off the bed, but he pressed my shoulders back down.

He hovered over me, where I was pinned to the bed. "I'm mad because you're in over your head and currently too stupid to realize it. How long do you think you can keep this up?" He stared at me, waiting.

As long as Kitty was alive, I couldn't answer that question. "Why don't you ask Paddy what's going on?" I wasn't sure if it was anger or desperation that spurred me to say it. It was probably a combination, as they were both overwhelming me lately. I never should've said a word though, not with all the ears listening.

Something shifted in his expression and he backed up. Perhaps he had asked Paddy already. What did he know? The worst thing about it was I couldn't ask. If he told me, they'd know as well.

"Whoah, someone's been busy." Cutty was standing in the doorway. His eyes immediately took in my mostly exposed torso. He whistled low. "You aren't looking so hot," he continued. "Someone in this room hasn't been playing by the rules. I say we all get one guess who that might be." He cleared his throat loudly and jerked his head repeatedly toward me.

Who knew Cutty could have a sense of humor? I guessed he was one of those people who became funnier as the situation worsened. It was a relief, since the tension in the room had been reaching an unbearable level.

Fate stood and backed away from the bed. "I've got the worst wound bandaged, but she needs some stitching. You're better at it." He pointed to the supplies he'd placed close by.

Cutty came and took a seat next to me on the bed and pulled out a flask. "Here, take a good swig." Cutty pushed the container toward me. "Although I'd say the stitches are going to be the least of your pains. Probably won't even notice, looking at the rest of you."

"No, I'll get you something better." Fate grabbed the flask and disappeared for a minute while Cutty was figuring out which cut to tackle first.

"Here, it's Maker's Mark," Fate said, when he came back holding out a glass.

I took it and gulped liberally as Cutty started to sew up one of the gashes on my side.

"You're a tougher chick than I gave you credit for," Cutty said, obviously impressed I wasn't crying like a total baby.

I wanted to, though.

"Too tough," Fate added. "Stay with her. I'll be back."

The second Fate walked out of the bedroom, Cutty leaned in closer and asked in a soft voice, "What the hell is going on? You're a wreck and he looks like he's about to kill someone."

"Nothing."

"You're really going to lie here and say nothing?" He raised a hand and made a sweeping gesture over my dilapidated form.

"Can you at least tell me why he's so pissed off?"

His head bent over my torso as he resumed stitching. "Least you can do, I think, considering I didn't duct tape you to the chair and now I'm stitching you up better than a Build-a-Bear."

"I have no idea why he's mad." And in truth, I didn't. It wasn't like he played by the rules, so to be angry with me for not playing by them as well was simply hypocritical. Hell, he didn't even believe in rules, by his own admission. Why he felt like he was in charge of what I was doing was beyond my reasoning, as well.

There was a crash in the other room, and both of our heads swung around. After the next crashing sound, Cutty's eyes met mine. "Seriously, what the hell did you do?"

"Maybe you should go in there and make sure he's okay?" *And buy me some time to sneak out of here.* I was held together by tape, string and plastic wrap, but it was enough. The longer I stayed here, the worse it would be. I needed to keep my distance from them. Everything that happened in front of me, Malokin would know. Every word that might be said could endanger someone else. No one realized the threat I posed to them.

"Fuck no. You did this. You check on him," Cutty said, but there was no anger in his words.

Another crash. What the hell was he doing in there?

"What if he's hurt?" I had to get Cutty out of here so I could leave as well.

"The only one that'll get hurt is me, if I get in his way." Cutty met my eyes, humor fading into something

213

more serious. "Really, what's going on between you two? Fate doesn't get like this."

"Nothing. He just gave me a ride."

He tied off another knot and placed the needle beside the bed. His eyes went to the door, back to me, and then he shook his head. "Not good. I was worried about this."

"What?" I was curious and defensive all at once. I could feel the blame for something heading my way.

He looked at me. "You know, for a bright girl, you can be *awfully* stupid."

"I don't understand." What was Cutty seeing that I didn't?

"I hope whatever this is between you two doesn't fuck with the rest of us." Cutty stood up and started walking out.

"That isn't because of me, and it's not my problem." I almost added that his friend was a control freak and just didn't like being out of the loop. If I did, I'd have to explain what loop he was out of, and I certainly didn't want to go there.

He threw his hands up into the air. "I can't talk to you if you're going to be this much of an idiot."

"Huh?" He just kept walking out. I pushed up off the bed to try and follow him. My head immediately started to swim and not from blood loss. Someone had taken perfectly good Maker's Mark and spiked it on me.

Chapter 27

On my own.

The morning light was shining in my eyes, as I lay on Fate's bed, alone. Looking next to me, I could tell I'd had company at some point. The spot beside me was wrinkled, like someone had slept on top of the covers.

I ran a hand over the wound on my ribs, which was freshly wrapped. I gave my lungs a try and got a fulfilling sensation deep in my chest. Well, deep might have been stretching it, but I could breathe, so who was I to complain?

The t-shirt I was wearing came almost to my knees and smelled of Fate. He'd already seen me naked, so it shouldn't have been a big thing. And yet, it was. It didn't help that my legs were a mishmash of bruises and cuts.

It shouldn't matter. It couldn't.

I shoved it from my mind with the force of a Mac truck barreling down a highway. I didn't have room for softness or worrying about what Fate thought.

The only sound in the house was the AC churning out cool air and the distant pounding of waves coming from the beach. Empty. Good.

I needed to get out of here before Fate got back and the questions commenced. Swinging my good leg over the side of the bed first, I dragged the bad one after it and limped over to his dresser.

His top right drawer held a nice supply of sweat pants. I grabbed the first pair I saw and rolled them up to accommodate my shorter stature.

Still silent, almost too much so. Why wasn't the phone ringing? Close proximity to Fate usually warranted a couple warning rings, at the very least.

I moaned. That might be because my phone was buried in a mud pile somewhere. Wal-Mart was going to get their money's worth out of me in throwaway phone purchases, and I was going to need a raise from someone. Two different employers and I was still poor. Something was very wrong with this picture.

Realizing I had nothing else with me, my hands felt bare. All of my possessions had been left scattered in the forest last night. I was going to have to go digging around the condo complex for my stashed keys, not to mention I was going to have to limp to get there.

Peeking around the corner, the house appeared empty but a complete mess. Piles of glass sat under stains on the wall. A hutch lay on its face, shades torn from the windows. I tiptoed past the mess and was almost to the door when I heard him come up behind me. Not so empty, I guess.

My body froze but I didn't turn around. The front door was only a few feet away, taunting me with the small distance. A couple of steps more and I would've been gone.

I should've known better. Fate never made things that easy. Everything about him was complicated. Even if it started simple, it didn't stay that way.

"Where are you going?"

"I'm sorry, did you miscalculate how much you spiked my drink?" I said, sugary sweet as I turned to face him.

"Actually, I did. If I could've trusted you to rest for a while, it wouldn't have been necessary," he countered, clearly not feeling the least bit shamed by his actions.

"I've got a job." I started walking forward, but I knew that wouldn't be the end of it. I opened the door and he slammed it shut, leaving his hand firmly against it as he stood by my side. He was so close his chest pressed against my shoulder.

"Who are you working for today? You're not going anywhere until we talk."

I wanted to scream in frustration. *I can't talk!* I kept my eyes forward and stared at where his hand was splayed against the rich dark wood. It might as well have been iron bars, under my current physical condition. He needn't try so hard to keep me in.

My fake composure slipped on like someone else threw on a raincoat. Bracing myself for the suspicion I'd find in his eyes, I turned to face him. "Sure. What's up?"

It was worse than I'd expected. He wasn't just suspicious, there was worry in his eyes, and it threatened to chip away at the wall I'd erected around myself.

"You're a mess. There's barely an inch of unmarked skin on you." He sounded almost violent when he said it, but there was something raw there too.

It made me think of the other day, in my condo, and my breathing sped up and my palms grew damp. When he was like this, my body responded to him without any consent from me.

Every line of him, the tilt of his head, the way his eyes stared at me; he was alive like no one I'd ever encountered. There's no way that his life force could have ever squeezed itself into a mortal husk.

"What would you have been?" I slipped, not able to contain my curiosity. Instead of being mesmerized by him, I needed to get out of there. But the question was out now, and I couldn't stop myself from hoping he'd finally tell me.

"You share and maybe I'll do the same." He looked me up and down.

Why *would* he tell me? I'd told him nothing and had no right to ask for anything in return. The wall between us that had slipped for a minute was right back up.

"I fell down the stairs at the condo. I'm horribly clumsy." That had to be the lamest line I'd ever uttered. I needed to stop watching Lifetime movies. Still, it didn't matter what I told him. He'd know it was a lie, and I didn't have the strength to pretend I was being honest.

I couldn't tell him the truth, and there was nothing else to be said.

"You're in over your head. Can't you see that?" He

slammed his hand against the door.

I knew he was frustrated. Whatever his motivation was, he did want to help, and that made it so much worse. How many times would I be able to swallow back the words? I looked at him and got angry he even made me feel this way. Weak.

"How do you know what I can handle?" My voice cracked as I said it, angry at his assumption and worried he might be right.

His hand suddenly grabbed the edge of my t-shirt and yanked it upward violently, displaying my bruised and damaged skin underneath.

I didn't mean to flinch, but I couldn't stop the reflex. It wasn't that I was afraid of him. We might have our differences, but he was probably the one person in my life right now that I would stake everything on not hurting me.

But natural instinct, born mostly out of the beatings I'd taken recently, made me. Get the shit kicked out of you enough and you'd flinch at the Mother Mary making the sign of the cross if her finger waved a bit too close.

I tried to play it off like it wasn't a big deal. I yanked the shirt out of his hand and pushed it down quickly.

"Yeah, you've *really* got this under control." His hands dropped to his sides, but he didn't move away. The look in his eyes made me uneasy. "Why did you flinch? You really think I'd touch you like that?" he asked, roughly gesturing to where he'd just revealed my injuries.

"No." I rubbed my hand against the back of my

neck, and I was the one who couldn't look at him now. "It was just…"

"Can't you see you're a wreck?"

Nervous laughter bubbled up, compounded by embarrassment. Of course I saw. I wasn't blind; I was stuck. He was the one that couldn't see. I'd been thrown in the deep end without knowing how to swim, but I was doggy paddling my ass off. I'd get out of this, even if I did it on my own.

"I'm leaving now." Sensing a calm moment, I moved to open the door.

"Why should I let you?"

"Because unless you intend on keeping me here and guarding me night and day, you have no other choice. I am not your responsibility or your concern." Each word closed the door a little more snugly, and made me more and more trapped, but this was the way it had to be.

Even still, as I took the last few steps out the door, my feet dragged and I felt like I'd stumble under the weight.

I was committed to seeing this thing through alone but not because I wanted to. Deep down, I felt weak because I wanted him to stop me, but asking him to was akin to killing Kitty by my own hand.

Chapter 28

Not so alone after all.

"Large iced coffee, please." The cashier handed me the change from my twenty and I exited the shop and walked across the street.

The benches were fairly comfortable at the Murrell's Inlet Marsh Walk. I angled my leg out along the length of one. It was aching but not as badly as it had been two nights ago when I'd ended up at Fate's. I'd wrapped it tightly in anticipation of the job I'd be assigned tonight.

A gentle breeze blew the reeds across the wetlands. A pelican, perched on a wooden stump, gave me a condemning eye. There weren't any pelicans employed by the agency that I knew of, so it was hopefully only my imagination that it was judging me.

The time on my phone indicated Luke would be here any minute, unless he'd decided to mess with me and be late on purpose. I wouldn't put it past him. Every move he made seemed to have some sadistic undertone.

The pelican took off from its perch and flew across the marsh but turned sharply to fly inward. He dipped over one of the bars that lined the outdoor area and right over where Fate sat on a stool, a drink in his hand.

He raised his glass to me. I just stared back. Why would I ever have imagined he'd just let me go along my own way? Had I learned nothing about him? A selfish part of me was elated for a moment. I couldn't do anything with him in tow, which meant I couldn't do the job tonight.

The relief didn't last long. If I knew they wouldn't torture or kill Kitty, maybe I could use the excuse that had so neatly fell in my lap, but that wasn't the person I wanted to be. Every day had become a battle to overcome what I desired to do, for what I needed to do.

Decision made; even if I did secretly want him there, he was a problem nonetheless. I couldn't meet Luke, or anyone else, until I got rid of Fate. My brain finally kicked into gear and I dug through my purse for the spare phone.

"We have to postpone our meeting for a little bit," I said the second Luke answered.

"Why?"

He didn't know Fate was here? They knew everything and usually immediately. Maybe he was too far away from me, or more likely, Luke did know and choose not to say.

Fate's stare met mine again as he watched me talk on the phone. He tilted his glass back and waved over the waiter, not once losing sight of me.

"I got a call from Harold. I have to go in to the

office," I blurted out quickly.

"Tell him you can't." His voice was like a hammer, slamming away at my nerves.

"I think he's having me followed. I don't think we should take the chance." He still said nothing about Fate. Why wouldn't he know? They always knew. Was I going to pay for this later?

"You said you were careful."

There was a dangerous edge to his voice and I felt a tremor go through me. Who was this person I was becoming, that trembled at some low life's accusation?

"That's what I'm being now."

Fate got off his stool.

"Fine. Tonight."

He hung up, leaving me to wonder what would be in store for me later. There'd be something.

I threw the phone back in my purse as Fate walked toward me in a determined yet calm manner, fresh drink in his hand. He sat down on the bench next to me like it was the most normal thing in the world for him to be stalking me.

"You're following me." It wasn't a question. I was simply putting it out on the table.

He shook his head. "Coincidence. This is my favorite place."

So now I was going to be the questioner and he was going to lie? Guess I deserved that.

"Good food?"

"Great drinks." He held up his glass.

"Are you going to be staying a while?" I found myself enjoying this game more than I should have.

"Not sure. What do you think you'll be doing?" He

leaned back and smiled at me, daring me to do something about it.

I tugged my purse higher on my shoulder and crossed my arms. "Getting chilly out. I think I'm going to leave."

"You know, I think I'm going to leave as well." He placed his glass on a nearby table and waited to see what direction I'd walk.

My car was parked across the street, but I couldn't leave with him following me.

The shops across the street called to me like a beacon. I crossed, with him following behind me. Stopping in the center, I searched for the perfect place for his downfall.

He didn't say anything, just smiled as if this didn't bother him at all. His torture started with the sound of tinkling bells on the door and the perfume of melting wax. Let's see how well he stood up to the candle shop. If that didn't break him, it would be the Christmas store, next. He had no idea who he was up against. He'd be begging to leave me in a few hours.

Four hours later and I'd gone to every touristy shop there was. I stayed in each one until the shop owners eyed me suspiciously. I was about to cry mercy as I watched him. How the hell could he look so interested in a collie shaped key chain?

And more surprisingly, I hadn't received a phone call. What had started out as a joke was quickly wearing down my nerves to nothing. They had to know Fate was with me, by now. Why weren't they bombarding me with implied threats and other such nefarious outcomes? Did they think Kitty's torture had finally put me under their control?

Had they succeeded? It was a repugnant idea, but there wasn't any chance I'd tell Fate anything after the last time I'd seen her. It hadn't even occurred to me. It was the first time since this began that I was seriously considering the possibility that they were controlling my thoughts. But I was making the just choices, wasn't I? What decent person would risk their friend's life?

When Fate put the Collie down and picked up a German shepherd, I'd already lost a sizeable amount of my control.

"I'm leaving, and without you." Hands on hips, I dared him to say otherwise. "I thought we'd reached an agreement the other morning?"

He turned and surveyed me, still holding the shepherd and not anywhere near as agitated as I was. "I don't remember that." He turned back to the key chains. "What about the golden retriever?"

"I told you I was fine on my own and you accepted it." I took a step toward him and then back again, not sure what to do at this point.

He put down the golden retriever keychain and gave me every ounce of his attention. I wasn't the only one who seemed finished with the games. "I think you misunderstood what conclusion I came to. I've come to the point where I've accepted you aren't going to be logical or make sane decisions. So, now it's going to be like this."

"Like this?" I was tense before I even heard his reply.

"Yes. Me, you, all day, every day."

All the lightness was gone from his voice. He

meant it. My eyes darted toward the door and back to him.

He was getting to me and I couldn't handle pressure from another source. It was starting to cloud my judgment. No, he was bluffing. He couldn't stay with me all the time, not with our positions.

"And what about when you have a job?" I asked and I couldn't help but infuse the question with a little bit of an, *aha, I've got you now* attitude.

"I'll take you with me." He shrugged.

"And when I refuse? What are you going to do then?"

He smiled but it wasn't warm; it was chilling. "I wouldn't do that."

He'd knocked me out twice, since I'd known him, and attempted it another time. He wouldn't hurt me, but he had no qualms about playing dirty.

Shit. He had me and he knew it.

I walked over to the restroom with Fate following me. He came within a foot of the door before I stopped.

"Even in here?"

He stepped around me, surveyed the bathroom, and I guess not spotting any windows, deemed it safe enough.

Shaking my head, I went inside and dug out my phone.

"I need a favor," I said in a hushed voice. "And you little jerks owe me after locking me in that stairwell. You ever want to see another bottle of scotch from me again, you'll do this." I gave the Jinxes the details and hung up.

Fate was leaning against the wall outside the

restroom when I walked out.

"So, where to now?" he asked, as he followed me out of the last shop in the small outdoor mall. "I think there might be a stand over there, way back in the corner, we might have missed."

I looked around the mall area and stopped in front of a couple windows I'd already looked at before. The Jinxes moved quickly. They'd only need five minutes, they'd said.

After ten had passed, I turned to Fate. "I've got some things to do at the office."

"I'll drive you."

"I'm not leaving my car here. You can't think I'm going to outrun your Porsche?" I didn't give him a chance to argue as I walked toward the parking lot. His car sat not ten feet away, and I wondered how I hadn't noticed that when I'd parked here earlier. "Follow me if you want, but I'm taking my car."

I got into my Honda and turned the key in the ignition, letting the engine wheeze to life just for effect. It must have been enough, because he walked away and headed to his own car.

Not bothering to wait, I pulled out of the lot. Looking in the mirror, his car was still parked. His Porsche looked to have stalled.

Chapter 29

One Big Happy Family

My palms were sweating as I knocked on the suite door. After the canceled meeting with Luke, I'd figured we'd be meeting at an obscure location that had the benefit of no witnesses and no one to hear the screams. I couldn't imagine why I was at another hotel suite, meeting with both Luke and Malokin.

I pushed my hair out of my face and shoved my shaking hands into my jeans pockets while I waited. The energy transferred to my feet and I had to consciously force myself not to pace.

What would they do to me? It would be easier on my nerves if I could go down fighting. It was the prospect of submitting to them, for Kitty's sake, that pushed me over the edge. But I had the short stack, so I either went along or did something desperate. Desperation wasn't a good place to operate from.

Luke opened the door and greeted me with the usual dose of underlying sadism in his eyes I'd become accustomed to. Without any words exchanged, he told me he'd like to nail me right where I stood. With him, sexual overtures never had anything to do with sex and everything to do with power.

He smiled, knowing I was rattled. He turned his back on me and walked into the suite, leaving me wondering just exactly what was to come. None of the possibilities seemed good, but I took a deep breath and followed him anyway.

I turned the corner and spotted Malokin. It was who I saw over his shoulder that made me freeze. Fate was sitting on the couch across from him.

What was he doing here? Was he the spy? Was that how Malokin knew everything? It felt like the floor was spinning, even though I was standing still. My first instinct was to lunge across the room and rip his heart out of his chest, but I couldn't. As far as Malokin knew, coerced or not, I was cooperating.

Malokin stood and greeted me; Fate just stood.

It was a struggle to make my legs move, but I managed. No, he couldn't be the traitor, could he? I'd *slept* with him.

"Karma, I think you already know Fate?" Malokin turned to him, a smile on his face. My lips formed one as well, even as I was planning to kill him if it were true.

Malokin was obviously pleased at having Fate here. Luke was smiling, but his looked more forced than even mine was. I could understand that. Fate could upstage anyone, and Luke wasn't happy being second in command. Third must have seemed dismal.

"Please, have a seat, Karma." Malokin waved me

over to the couches to join the party. Luke followed behind me and was practically breathing down my neck as I went to sit on the loveseat. Before I could, Fate stood and wrapped an arm around my waist, to steer me toward the couch he'd been sitting on.

Luke, making a move to follow me, was cut off as Fate stepped between us. They stood so close it looked like the tips of their toes touched.

"Find another seat," Fate said, packing each word with such potent violence it even gave me a chill, and I wasn't the target.

Maybe I should've cared, but at that moment, I didn't like either of them. If they wanted to fight it out over who would have the opportunity to be rejected, I didn't see the point in getting involved. One less "no" to say.

"Who the hell do you think you are?" Luke asked. He was used to being—well, if not top dog—the favorite sidekick, who always got his way. I had a strong suspicion the only reason he even had the nerve to get in Fate's space was because Malokin was nearby.

Something strange happened then. A tingle of energy shot across my skin. The pretense of who, or what, Fate was slipped just a hair, or more accurately, was lowered on purpose.

"Do you really want to find out?" he asked Luke, who was starting to cower and back up. In spite of myself, or my doubts about Fate at the moment, I couldn't help but enjoy watching Luke being knocked down a peg or two.

"Luke, I need to see you in the other room." Malokin said. It was clear he was simply trying to diffuse the situation, and it worked; Luke now had an excuse to run from the room.

The door shutting echoed through the living room of the suite. Left alone with Fate, my anger boiled over. "Really nice to see you here." My voice was bitter, counteracting my words. "So, how long have you known Malokin?" *How long have you been a traitor?*

"Not long at all. I couldn't keep waiting for you to invite me, so I made some calls myself."

With numbers he got off of my stolen phone. At least that made sense. My instincts, no matter how jumbled, had resisted the belief he'd been in cahoots with Malokin this whole time.

We sat staring at each other from opposite sides of the same couch, weighing reactions and subtleties, neither of us willing to reveal anything in words.

His arm was slung along the back, his fingers raised slightly in my direction. "How long have you been working a double shift? My guess is since the Lock?"

"Pretty much." I folded a leg underneath the other as I choose my next words. "In what capacity will you be helping out?"

"There's one area in particular that I think needs to be fixed." The way his stare was focused on me left no question as to what—or who—that area was.

The sound of glass breaking drew both of our attention to the closed bedroom door.

"You promised her to me!" Luke's scream was so loud it was heard clearly through the door. Nothing about what he said surprised me, though. I'd expected something like that had been arranged. I was too exhausted to care anymore. If it wasn't happening today, it wasn't a problem I worried about.

Still, I'd rather Fate hadn't heard it. The whole situation was degrading. The fact that I sat there, and didn't charge into the room and tell them both to go screw themselves, added to my humiliation.

I didn't want to turn my head back toward where Fate was, but his movements caught my eye. He walked over toward the closed door, where Malokin was with Luke, and went in without so much as a single rap.

He was back out in less than a minute and standing before me.

"Get up. We're going." His voice was deep and strained, and drew my eyes.

"I can't." I looked at the door, then back to him as I shook my head.

"Get. Up."

Why didn't he understand I couldn't leave? He looked like he was about to explode in front of me, but I knew what could happen if I did. Luke's threats were never far from my mind. First it would be Kitty, then someone else—maybe Luck. I inched back on the seat, shaking my head. "I can't leave."

I watched as Fate's chest rose and fell several times before he spoke. "I told Malokin we're leaving. He knows. We have to do a job for him."

His voice was calmer now, but I still felt uneasy. "He knows?" I asked, looking at the door to the room Malokin was in.

"You just saw me go in there. It's okay." He stood there, hand outstretched to me. His voice was low and reassuring, so different than it had been a minute ago.

I placed my hand in his warm one, his fingers wrapping around it.

***

Fate was barely a foot behind me as we entered the parking lot. When I slowed my step, he urged me forward with a hand on my back. The moment of ease I'd felt upstairs in the suite was quickly disappearing.

If this were a problem, my phone would be ringing. Malokin was okay with whatever job we were going to do. Was Fate really going to go to this job with me? I hoped it was another "save." I wasn't going to kill anyone. Would he? My head was spinning with all the possibilities, when he grabbed my arm and diverted me toward his car and opened the door for me.

"I'm driving. Get in." I didn't have the energy or the will to fight with him or care enough. His car or mine, what difference did it make?

I slumped into the passenger seat. I had bigger issues than who drove. How was I going to maneuver this to make sure he didn't kill anyone? That was the line I wouldn't cross. I couldn't come back from that and I knew it. But how far was Fate willing to take this charade? He'd been after Malokin before he'd even known his name. What was this worth to him?

"Where are we going?" I asked, when he turned off the highway and down the road that led to his house.

"I want to pick up some more gear." It seemed like a plausible enough explanation, and I relaxed back against my seat, hoping he wasn't going to be armed to the teeth. That could cause a problem with my no killing plan.

"What's the job?" I asked, as we pulled into his garage a minute later. No, I didn't think Fate would actually take it that far. He was only involved in this for two reasons: because he couldn't seem to stop himself from getting into my business, and because he was trying to dig around and find out what exactly Malokin was, and what he was after. The weapons were probably more for our protection than for killing.

Still, when he turned to me and said, "Come in. I've got some things for you, as well," it felt eerily like a stranger offering me candy.

"Sure." Something was wrong about this, and the longer I was with him, the more I felt it.

I needed to dump him. I'd get him in the house and then sneak out alone. It was the only way. My head was spinning with plans and plots by time I walked in after him and saw him move toward a storage area.

He was watching me. Yes, something was very wrong here, and he knew I was catching on. He watched me like he was expecting me to make a break for it at any minute. Not surprising, since I was.

Why had I come with him? When he'd ducked in the room with Malokin though, it seemed like it was okay. No one had tried to stop us, either. But still, it didn't feel right. He was watching me too intently.

There was no way to outrun him. I needed to knock him out. My eyes scanned the room for possible weapons. The lamp? Too unwieldy. The bar area caught my eye. Cutty Sark. The bottle was perfect.

"Want a drink?" I asked, making my way to my weapon of choice, forcing myself not to rush.

"Sure, thanks," he said from around the corner.

I gripped its neck and pulled it off the shelf, holding it upside down like a bat. I was getting the feel of it when a hand wrapped around my wrist and I felt his front flush against my back. "Were you going to pour me a drink or hit me over the head?"

He let go of my wrist and grabbed the bottle from my grasp, placing it back on the bar.

"Just noticing how heavy a full bottle feels." I was still playing the part, even though I was pretty sure the final credits had already rolled.

"Sit."

Chapter 30

What don't you understand?

There was a single light on in the room as we sat across from each other on opposite couches. A paper-thin pretense hung between us, as we pretended that he was going along with Malokin and that I was here willingly.

The clock ticked by slowly, every minute counted if I was going to figure out a way out of this. I hadn't gone through everything just to have Fate blow it wide open and get Kitty killed. I hadn't taken more than one beating for nothing, or suffered Luke to let it fall apart at Fate's whim. Still, some contrary part of me was relieved he knew, even if it changed nothing.

We stared at each other. I didn't move, because I didn't know how to get out of there. What was more nerve wracking was why he wasn't stirring. What was he waiting for? I knew he had some plan in motion, and it wasn't a huge leap to guess I wouldn't like it.

Every second that went by wound me tighter, and I

shot him several accusatory stares. They ranged in different degrees of rage that mostly conveyed, *you think you're helping, but you're fucking things up.*

He retaliated with his own variety. His were more along the lines of *you're so stupid, what did you think would happen?* Occasionally, I caught a hint of *you were going to get yourself killed* in his look. That one didn't last very long before it reverted back to *you're so stupid* again.

Getting up, I went to his bar area, daring him with my eyes to stop me. He didn't move; he just shrugged, as if taking me down wasn't a concern. Tomorrow I might possibly find that insulting. Tonight I was just happy to get a drink without a fight.

The bar was devoid of Maker's Mark, so I poured a Cutty Sark neat. I flaunted my glass with a flourish as I walked back to the couch. *Yeah, see that? I don't need ice anymore because I'm a badass. I don't need ice and I don't need you.*

I threw back a healthy gulp, realizing how ridiculously I might be acting.

He rolled his eyes, confirming it.

The booze burned its way down to my stomach, and I felt the tension ease slightly.

"What time are we leaving to do the job?" I asked, putting him on the spot, since I knew without a doubt we weren't going.

"We'll be moving forward shortly," he said. He had the nerve to smile at me.

Those ominous words had me downing another gulp. Whatever it was we'd be doing, it wasn't going to be for Malokin or Luke.

237

Those two might be able to hear everything said, but I was pretty sure a lot of smaller movements were lost through however they got their information. I placed the glass down on his wooden table between us, purposefully avoiding using a coaster from the stack right next to it. I fisted my hands and gave Fate the double finger. The double, for when one just wasn't enough.

The jerk laughed.

Having depleted the double finger gesture, I was at a loss for an appropriate silent reply.

Then two things happened at once; Lars tapped on the glass back doors and my throwaway phone started vibrating.

We got to our feet at the same time. I didn't want him to let Lars in. I didn't have specifics, but I knew it would be bad news for me. He didn't want me to answer my call.

My purse sat to the right, on the dining room table. Lars stood waiting to the left, at an approximately equal distance. Lars or the phone?

Fate made the decision for me when he took a step toward the door. Abandoning the phone, I lunged for him. He was too much larger than me for a clean takedown if I jumped on his back. I dived straight at his knees. My arms wrapped around his legs as we both thudded hard against the hardwood floor, but I didn't let go. I wrapped my entire form around his legs, locking my ankles and wrists together.

He leaned over and I thought he was going to start prying my hands apart. He didn't. He tickled me under the arms and then above the knees.

238

I released him by no choice of my own, as my body convulsed with giggles for a few seconds, which only mad me madder. "That was an undignified way to fight," I yelled as I got to my feet. "Do not engage in tickling again!"

Fate didn't answer, he just headed toward the door again. I ran and jumped on his back this time. I got a satisfying "umph" as I landed on him, but it didn't stop him. Legs free, he walked to the door with me clinging to his back and making unsuccessful attempts to put him in a chokehold.

He unlocked the door even as I tried to wrap my arms as tightly as I could around his neck. I wasn't trying to kill him, just make him unconscious. He opened the door and stepped out of the way to let Lars enter, as if I wasn't in the middle of attacking him. It dawned on me that he might be a bit stronger than I'd given him credit for.

With Lars in the room, I jumped off his back and switched tactics, which had absolutely nothing to do with the strange looks Lars was giving me.

I quickly realized my best option was to grab my phone and get the hell out of there. It was still vibrating where it sat, in my purse. I hesitated a split second and it cost me my opportunity.

Fate had an arm wrapped around my stomach and was swinging me back toward him. "Not gonna happen."

"Let go of me." I tried to rear back with my head but only connected to his chest.

Ignoring me, he addressed Lars. "Is everyone in place?"

I swung a lose arm backward, trying to nail him with an elbow.

"Just like you asked," Lars said, as his eyes kept shifting to me. "She looks mad."

"We need a minute." I could feel Fate's voice vibrate through me.

"Sure," he said. "I'll wait out there." He hooked a finger toward the beach, looking more than happy to leave us alone.

The room quiet again, I could hear the phone vibrating, over and over. Both of Fate's arms were wrapped around mine when he spoke. "I'm going to let go of you. Don't go for the phone."

His arms dropped and I spun on him the second I could. My legs were shaking from the exertion I'd put into trying to stop him from letting Lars in. Or maybe it was from the panic I felt. And I was panicked. No composure left. All of my attempts to keep things afloat were about to come crashing down around me if I couldn't get out of here.

I didn't know what would happen to Kitty, and who might be next? Fate may be able to handle Malokin, but what about Murphy or Luck? He didn't understand; I couldn't be here.

"You don't understand everything that's going on. You need to let me go." I felt like I was talking to a crazy man in a hostage situation who hadn't yet seen the ramifications of his actions in a hostage situation.

"No." And the crazy man looked like he was digging in to his position.

He stood there and I knew he was serious. The phone didn't stop vibrating as my gaze darted back to my purse again and then to him. How many times had they called?

It didn't matter what I said now, or if they heard me; if I didn't get to Malokin, none of it would matter soon. He must have known Fate wasn't really with them by now. They also must know what Fate was planning. It was time for damage control.

Closing the gap between us, I gripped the front of Fate's shirt in my hands. "He's got Kitty. If you don't let me go, he'll kill her and then someone else after that. I have to go." I waited for the understanding to show in his face.

He stared at me where I clung to him, practically begging, then shook his head. Why was he looking at me like he was sad?

"Don't you hear me? They've got Kitty." My tone was frantic and I needed to stay calm.

"You're not leaving." His voice was soft.

"You don't know what they're doing to her. They're torturing her." What was wrong with him? He needed to understand what was at stake here, and then he'd change his mind.

"What about what they've done to you?" His palm came up and cupped my face, and there was that sadness again. "Can't you see what's happening?"

I stepped back away from him. "What? A couple of bruises that will heal," I said defensively. "They're going to *kill* her."

"They've got you twisted up like a pretzel." The anger was coming back into his voice and I was grateful for it. I could handle the anger. The sadness—verging on pity—I couldn't.

241

I started pacing the room while he kept himself strategically placed in between the phone and me. He was right. I was a wreck; I knew it. He wasn't getting it though, and I didn't care anymore about my secrets. He had to understand. I had to leave.

I stopped pacing and tried again to make him understand. "This is my fault. She's there because they want me. Because I was a shitty fucking human being, who cared more about her career than people. They thought they saw potential in me." Both of my hands were in my hair, and I felt like I was going to go completely crazy at any moment. "I deserve this, not her."

He didn't say anything. "Don't you hear me?" I shoved at his chest with both my hands, but he didn't budge. "Don't you get it? They only have her because of me. Let me go and we can still save her. You've never wanted me here anyway."

"I don't care what you think you deserve. I'm not letting you do it." He said it so calmly it only agitated me more. He wasn't listening to me.

He was unmovable and I shoved at him again as hard as I could. He wouldn't budge, and I had this irrational feeling that if I could force him from his spot, I could jar him out of his current thinking.

"Why not?"

His hands were on my shoulders then, pushing me up against the wall. "Because I can't!"

He quickly let go and walked away from me. I pushed off the wall, following him. "Yes, you can. You do everything else you want. Why can't you? That's bullshit!"

He spun on me and stopped my pursuit. "You're right. I can. I don't want to."

"Why?"

"Because I've seen your death and..." his words dropped off, and he ran his hands through his hair.

All the steam left me. It was the last thing I'd expected him to say. Some crazy part of me had almost wished he had said Harold was forcing him to do this. Or even crazier, that he cared for me.

"How do you know?"

He was leaning away from me, his palms resting on the back of the couch, his head hanging down.

"Because I saw it," he said, on a long exhale.

"You can't see our fates." He was trying to trick me and convince me to stay.

"But, I did." He pushed off the couch and walked over to the bar, pouring his own drink.

"Maybe it was just a normal dream."

He shook his head. "I've seen it more than once and not while I was sleeping." He threw back the contents of his glass and then poured another.

"You can't see my fate. You said it yourself." I didn't want to believe him, but I was starting to anyway.

"I know. But somehow I can, at least this part." He wasn't trying to convince me, and that lent his words more weight than anything.

"Maybe it was me retiring that you saw." I knew that wasn't what he meant though, and he shook his head again, confirming it.

When he looked at me, I saw in his face that he had more details. His expression warned me not to ask.

Did I want to know? When I'd been mortal, I'd debated this very question with Charlie, over a bottle of wine, one night. He'd said he would never want the details of his death. I'd said I would. Theoretical musings were a whole hell of a lot different than the reality of such knowledge. I'd thought I'd known how I would feel, given the option, but I didn't. And yet, my answer was still the same as it had been that evening.

No matter what Fate told me, it wouldn't change anything. I'd still leave there tonight, by any means I could, to save Kitty. I guess I just wanted to know if I'd never come back.

"Tell me." I walked over to his couch and sat, but then immediately got back up to pace.

"I don't have the exact details. I don't even know when." Fate stood in the center of the room, just watching me.

"But you saw me die." I stopped pacing to glower at him. "If you're going to tell me that part, then you can't start cherry picking which details to divulge."

"You were lying on the ground, in a puddle of blood." He stiffened as he spoke, anger pouring off him as the words came out.

"Are you sure it was my blood? And I could've just been knocked out or hurt badly." It was just an image. He could be wrong.

"You were dead." His words sounded as final as their meaning. There was no doubt in his mind about what he'd seen. "Your neck was sliced open."

I swallowed hard and lifted a hand to my throat. I didn't even realize I'd done it until Fate's hand was there, pulling mine away.

"I'm not going to let it happen."

"Why? You don't even like me, most of the time."

"*Liking* you has nothing to do with it." His hand dropped from mine and he walked a little distance away.

"This doesn't change anything."

I watched as his frame straightened and tensed. "No?"

"I told you. She's there because of me."

"And I told you, I'm not letting it happen."

Chapter 31

Finishing the job.

Fate and I had hit an impasse. The tension was so thick when Lars walked back in that it had become a palpable thing in the very air I was laboring to breathe.

"Did you bring everything?" Fate asked Lars, seeming more at ease than I; or maybe he was just better at hiding it.

Lars lifted his hand and I saw the bag he carried his tattoo gun in, which I'd been too busy to notice before, my attention drawn to the phone vibrating. It was a continuous chain of calls in an attempt to stop whatever was coming. That's how I knew whatever Fate had planned would be a deal breaker between Malokin and me, and mean the end of Kitty. I had to stop this.

"Is everything in place?" Fate continued.

"Exactly as you wanted."

Trying to go unnoticed, I edged further toward the door in the smallest movements, no bigger than a shifting of my feet. I didn't make it more than an inch farther before Fate's hand wrapped around my wrist.

The tiniest shred of dignity I had left was the only thing that kept me from trying to pull myself free.

"Doesn't look like she wants this though, man," Lars said, as he took a step backward, physically trying to put distance between himself and something he felt morally questionable about.

"Want what? What are you going to do?" My breathing was obviously labored now, as my adrenaline raced to keep pace with my rising panic.

"She doesn't even know?" Lars held up a hand and took another step back. "We don't force anyone. Isn't that why we broke out? Isn't that what we're all about? Making our own choices?"

"She hasn't made her own choices in weeks." Fate's grip on me didn't loosen at all, even under Lars's doubts. He was actually pulling me closer, demonstrating his commitment to the choice he'd made.

"I don't know. This feels really bad. It'll cut her off permanently." Lars was shaking his head, clearly conflicted between helping his friend and going against his morals. "When did we start forcing people? You didn't even do this final step."

I realized my last hope was standing right in front of me. I hadn't given Lars enough credit in the past. Maybe he was a better person than I'd known. "Please, Lars, don't do this," I pleaded, looking straight at him. "You know it's wrong."

I didn't know what the consequences of being cut off permanently would be, and I didn't want to know. I was already losing Kitty. Murphy might be next, and who knew who'd fall victim to Malokin after that, and all because of me.

"Lars, this has to be done." Fate wasn't asking anymore.

Lars looked off through the windows toward the beach for a minute, but then nodded.

After that, Lars wouldn't look at me again, and I knew I'd lost the fight. My dignity was officially gone as I tried to pull free of Fate's grasp but couldn't.

Fate was slowly pulling me in closer to him, as I started to completely break down. Sobs wrenched my body now, and I must have looked as unstable as he said I was.

Fate walked over to the couch, pulling me with him, as Lars grabbed his ink and gun out of the bag. Fate sat angled in the corner, pulling me down along with him. His arm wrapped around mine.

"You're killing Kitty. Right now, you are killing her. They have her and not letting me go is killing her." My breathing was becoming more erratic, and in some part of my brain I recognized I was hyperventilating, maybe even having a panic attack of some sort.

Fingers gently moved the hair out of my face and Fate's hand rubbed up and down the outside of my arm before he spoke, "*They're* killing, Kitty, no one else. But if I let you go, it'll be you in her place. Maybe not tonight, but soon."

"Why do you care?"

One arm was wrapped around my waist and the other crossed in front and wrapped over mine, pulling me slightly more snugly to him. "I just do."

"This isn't your choice to make." I was still arguing, but the fight was slowly draining from me.

"I don't have a choice. You don't see what he's

doing to you. You aren't thinking clearly anymore. You aren't making rational choices. And if I need to shoulder the weight of Kitty's death, then I will." His voice was somber as he said it, and gave me the impression he didn't actually want to do any of this. He wasn't gloating over besting me, and I felt myself finally giving up.

The constant battle I'd been fighting was being taken from me. The guilt was overwhelming, even if I did let him shoulder some of the blame. But I didn't feel better; I felt disgusted with myself.

An image of Kitty being eradicated from all existence made me shudder, as Lars kneeled down in front of us, tattoo gun in hand. Fate's one arm stayed wrapped around my torso, holding me snug to his chest as he opened my jeans enough to expose the ying yang tattoo.

He could've let me go at that point. I had no fight left in me tonight. I knew a lost cause when I saw one, even when it was myself.

"This will only take a minute. I just need to add a few more strokes in this different ink to the tattoo I gave you initially. See, this started the process but…" Lars looked at me and then stopped talking. He focused on the tattoo again.

This time felt different, and there was no mistaking it. A connection I hadn't realized existed was being severed. Each stroke of the tattoo gun felt like a dull saw, running its blade across my midsection.

"This feels wrong," I said to Lars.

I couldn't see Fate's expression, but Lars's was alarming. He knew. He looked down quickly again, but he answered, "That's how it's supposed to feel. I'm finishing what we started before. This is what it feels like when you're completely severed from..." His eyes shot skyward and then quickly down again, purposely avoiding my face.

"It has to be done," Fate said. "This is how he was monitoring you."

If I wasn't so destroyed over the repercussions that would come from this, I might've actually been happy to know that at least I was getting my life back. But any joy I might have felt from being free was swallowed by the dread of everything else it entailed.

All this time, wasted; the effort, the hurt, all for nothing. Malokin would surely kill Kitty now. And what were the rest of the ramifications of such an action? What happened now?

"I'm done," Lars said, and placed his equipment on the table.

His words might have benefitted Fate, but I'd already known. The last stroke had felt like an elastic snapping back against my skin, but it didn't just smart with pain. There was a void left.

"I'm going to get out of here." Lars looked up to Fate with a nod and then started repacking his things. He wanted to escape the scene of his crime.

I tugged out of Fate's loose grip but only made it to the other side of the couch. I couldn't get up yet. I felt...weak.

The door closed softly behind Lars. My phone wasn't vibrating anymore.

Fate walked into the kitchen. He came back and placed a glass of iced tea in front of me. I ignored him.

"You'll feel weak for tonight, but it will go away," he said, as he stood looking down on me.

"How would *you* know? You're still connected." The anger churned inside of me and I didn't even know where to direct it anymore; at Fate for interfering, Lars for helping, Malokin and Luke? Myself, most of all, for letting all of this happen.

He sat down on the other side of the couch in the now eerily quiet room. My phone hadn't vibrated since Lars had started on the tattoo, confirming my fears. I didn't know how this changed me, my abilities or what I could do, but it changed enough that Malokin no longer wanted me. He'd have no need of Kitty.

"I might have been able to save her," I said, deciding I had enough anger right now to spread around. Why choose just one person to blame?

"You were becoming a shadow of yourself. You weren't saving Kitty; you were just giving him both of you." His voice sounded almost as tired as I felt.

I turned my head away from him, where I had it lying on the armrest and pulled my knees into my chest. I tried to hide the first couple of tears but once they started, I couldn't seem to stop them.

I was like a geyser that had been gathering pressure and finally erupted. The last month had been almost unbearable. I couldn't remember the last time I hadn't felt terrified. If it wasn't fear of what I had to do, it was fear of what was coming next.

I was relieved Fate had taken the choice out of my hands, and I was embarrassed because of it. I'd failed Kitty.

Fate's hand started rubbing my back, but I swatted

him away. It did nothing but make me feel more pathetic. He removed his hand but didn't leave.

"This isn't your fault." I could tell by the way he said it that he believed it, but I didn't.

I rubbed the back of my hand across my face, ashamed by my weakness. "Just tell me what happens now? I'm an outcast, like your guys?" I asked, not even caring but looking to change the subject to anything else. I watched him through lids that were becoming heavier and heavier.

"No. You've got another option," he said. I would've questioned him, but I couldn't stay awake anymore.

Chapter 32

Damage Control

I woke up in Fate's bed—again. It was becoming a bad habit. This time didn't bode any better than the previous times. Thinking back to last night's events had me closing my eyes and sinking deeper under the covers.

I was truly cut off. I could feel it, like an amputee felt a missing limb. It had been a connection so intrinsic to me that I hadn't even realized its presence until it was severed. And what were the ramifications of this? I wasn't sure, but common sense told me it probably wouldn't be good.

But nothing felt worse than when I thought about Kitty. I needed to find out what this meant for her. Was there a chance Malokin would keep her alive? She might already be gone. If she was, I hoped it had been quick. If Luke had been involved, I knew it wouldn't have been.

Images of her being tortured still haunted me daily.

What would they do when they no longer feared killing her? I rolled onto my left side, trying to quell the bile rising up from my stomach.

"Where is she?" It was Paddy's voice in the kitchen. *Now* he shows up? I could have used him a lot more last night; or last week, for that matter.

"She's in my room, sleeping," Fate replied, his deep voice carrying into the bedroom easily.

"I need to talk to her alone for a bit," Paddy said.

"That's a change," Fate barked at him. Why was he so angry? "You get fifteen."

I heard a single set of footsteps in the hallway, heading toward me. Paddy opened the door and his smile faltered as it met my stare. It wasn't his fault either, but that didn't stop the anger welling up in me. I had plenty to go around for everyone so step right up.

"Nice timing," I said. My words tasted like venom in my mouth, but I wanted to hurt him. He might not have verbally said he would be there for me, but his actions had. He'd never mentioned anything about bailing as soon as I needed him.

In spite of my tone, he came in anyway and perched on the side of the bed. "I know you're angry about what happened last night, but I'm partly to blame. Both Fate and I thought it was the only way."

"When did you two start chatting?" It seemed I couldn't talk without spewing anger.

"That's a long story and not important right now." He reached out his hand and placed it over mine. I was about to jerk out of his grasp until he said, "But I think I can fix this."

Those words had me staring back at him. What did

he know? The rage inside of me was still there, but something about the way he was looking at me gave me some hope. I wanted to tell him to get the hell out of here, but I couldn't; not if there was a chance to fix this. I squinted my eyes at him, not sure I believed it but desperate enough to listen. "How?"

"Let me give you a little explanation on what I think was going on, first. The working theory is Malokin tapped into your connection to the greater Universe when you were still human. When you died, being a transfer, you never completely shed that part of you. That's how he knew your whereabouts, what you did—"

"I've got that part, keep going." The damage of Malokin's wide-scale intrusion into every tiny detail of my life still burned. I didn't need a play-by-play of it.

He nodded and continued. "If you think of your connection in terms of a river, that mark on your hip was a sort of dam. It controlled and dampened the connection, but never cut you off completely, just slowed the water passing through. Malokin was, in essence, upstream of the dam, filtering everything through him first. By Fate and Lars finishing your tattoo, and cutting you off completely, they stopped the flow of information entirely. With nothing left to filter, Malokin lost his trace on you.

"It had to be done. If it hadn't, eventually, there would have been no connection anyway. Only what was channeled through him. At that point, I don't know myself what might have become of you." His hand, still resting on mine, squeezed my fingers.

"Why didn't you tell me? Why didn't you come to

me?" His disappearance had felt like a betrayal, another wound that I was struggling to heal.

He looked down at the floor when he spoke. "I couldn't. Understand, I do care for you greatly, but I couldn't chance any more contact with you until we figured out what was happening. I wasn't sure what his capabilities were." All traces of his kidding nature had been eradicated, until he almost took on the appearance of a stranger. "If they were to get me, it would be catastrophic. It can't happen."

Goosebumps spread down my arms. I still didn't know what he was, but I certainly didn't want to find out by Malokin getting a hold of him.

My eyes darted toward the door, thinking of Fate. He'd been in close contact with Malokin.

Paddy picked up on my train of thought and said, "He refused to cut you off, even after I warned him. But now we're pretty sure Malokin can't do it to anyone that isn't a transfer. However he did it, it was while you were still human."

Fate had refused to abandon me? My eyes watered but I held it back, but just. Why was that making me cry? Was I having a mental breakdown or something? Kitty might still be alive, and I couldn't waste time sitting here—an emotional basket case—because some guy who I had sex with a couple of times didn't abandon me along with everyone else. Time to get a grip.

"What about Kitty?"

"I've got a plan. If it works, we still might be able to save her, and you'll be able to go back to the office as well. You'll be as good as new, just a little different than the original version." Paddy had a way of talking, and minimizing things, the way only someone who'd seen a whole lot of ups and downs could.

And then I realized. "So you knew about the tattoos and how that worked the whole time?"

"Yes. I am the *recruiter*, after all." He stood up again and looked as if he were mentally preparing for something. "Now that we've cut off Malokin, I'm going to try and reconnect you."

I sat up; Paddy had my full attention. "You can do that?"

"Well, it's a bit unorthodox, and I haven't done it before, but yeah, I think I can swing it."

Thinks he can *swing it*? "How?" *Please, just once, could someone have a logical plan of action?*

He brought a finger in front of his mouth as one eye squinted. "That gets a little trickier to explain, but I'm going to connect you back, just through me instead...I think."

Nope, he had absolutely no logical plan. "Could this kill me?"

"No, no!" He shook his hands in the air, but paused suddenly, as if something occurred to him. "Okay, maybe there's a point one percent chance, but that's trivial."

"Fuck it. Let's do it." Then I thought of Harold. He'd already sensed something amiss. "Won't everyone know something's different about me?"

Paddy looked down at his watch. "You haven't been off the grid long enough to raise any flags yet. It's only been about five hours. As far as being different, you've always been a little off. Just pretend

257

everything's normal and they'll go along with it." Paddy did that shrug again, like who cared if they had doubts. Maybe I'd feel the same way in a couple of thousand years too, but I had less than a few decades under my belt.

"I'm your only shot." He smiled in a mischievous way that made me a bit nervous.

"And you feel good about this?"

He was rubbing his hands together. "I really think I can pull this off. I haven't gotten to try anything this cool in at least an eon." He patted my shoulder. "It'll be okay."

"But you've never done this?" He was awfully excited, in contrast to how I felt about it.

"No, but in theory it'll work." When I didn't look confident, he kept talking, "Hey, it's this or hanging out at Lars's tattoo shop." He leaned closer. "Pick your poison carefully."

Was hanging out with the guys that bad? Maybe not, but was it what I wanted to do for the rest of eternity? Hell no. I took a deep breath and said, "Okay," before I could change my mind.

He tiptoed over to the door and closed it very carefully, as to not make a noise. "Show me the tattoo and then close your eyes."

My fingers stalled at the edge of the sweatpants I wore. How was I wearing Fate's sweatpants anyway? Why did Fate keep dressing me in my sleep?

Paddy cleared his throat when I didn't move, bringing me back to the problem at hand. "Why can't I watch?"

"You can, but it might be a bit bright on your

eyes." He looked at me and then rolled up his shirtsleeve.

He examined his arm, looking at it this way and that. "Ah, what the hell, it doesn't matter." He took his forefinger and thumb and pinched some skin near the inside of his elbow and then ripped it off.

A light, brighter than the morning sun, shot out of where he'd ripped away a chunk of his skin, and the piece that had been torn was glowing in his other hand.

"I told you to shut your eyes, but you young kids don't listen to anyone." He neared me, still glowing from multiple areas, and I backed up until I hit the headboard. "Yes, that's a better position," he said, as if I'd done it intentionally to help.

I slid the side of my pants down while keeping my eyes tightly shut. "Is this going to hurt?"

"Possibly," he said, as if that were neither here nor there.

My eyes, squinting and barely open, looked down at where he was trying to force the piece of *flesh* he'd ripped off himself into me.

I expected a slimy feeling to touch my skin, but it was nothing like that. It was wonderfully warm and actually felt soothing against the still raw tattoo.

Whatever he was trying to accomplish didn't look promising. Paddy started applying more and more pressure.

"Go. In!" He was now bent over me, pressing more weight into my body than I thought he was capable of. If he kept it up, I was going to end up with a fractured hip.

"You sure this is going to work?" Before he

answered, something happened. My body was absorbing the light and flesh he'd been trying to force. It slowly sank into where the tattoo was. Paddy was propelled away from me, colliding with the door, and at the same time I felt like I'd been punched in the gut.

The door crashed open a second later and sent Paddy sprawling in the opposite direction.

Fate stood in the doorway, looking ominous. His eyes ran the length of me and then he stepped closer, as if he saw something of interest. "Why are you glowing?"

My eyes shot to Paddy first, thinking it was him, but the spot on his arm was already healed. If it wasn't him...

I looked down. I wasn't actually glowing, my tattoo was. It looked like there was a flashlight from underneath my skin, pointing outward.

"What did you do to her?" Fate towered over Paddy, who was holding his ground pretty admirably.

"I only did what we discussed." Nothing, not even Fate's glowering expression or being banged about the room, seemed to dim Paddy's satisfaction. "That's just a little after effect. It'll probably wear off," Paddy said. "Maybe."

Fate walked closer and ran his fingers over the ying yang tattoo. "It tingles when I touch it." He dropped his hand. "She's reconnected?"

"Through me," Paddy explained.

"Is that the same thing?" I asked. I trusted Paddy for no real reason other than an overwhelming gut urge. I mean, let's face it, the guy had screwed me out of moving on. Yet here I was, still letting him do crazy shit to me, but it was just one of those things I couldn't explain. I knew people, even if they weren't actually human. Paddy was one of the good guys.

"No, but I think it'll be pretty close."

I *think* and my *theory*; there was a lot of guess work going on here from Paddy, and I hoped he wasn't going to let me down again. I didn't want to think he'd turned me into a nightlight for nothing. I tugged up the corner of the sweat pants to cover it.

"You're going to have to do more than that." Fate was scowling slightly. Looking down, the light shining through the tattoo easily penetrated the cotton. "We'll find something for you."

"Do you think it will dull?" I asked Paddy, as I moved my palm over the tattoo.

"Recent events are causing me to step out of the box a bit. You can't expect me to know everything. I'm not God."

"And what exactly are you?" I had a piece of him literally pulsing in my body; I could feel it, and I still didn't know what he was.

"And here we go with the twenty questions again. You give them an inch and they want a foot! We have other more pressing issues. Must we get bogged down with the trivialities of name calling?" He walked out of the room, yelling he'd be waiting in the living room.

Left alone, Fate turned to me. "Are you okay?"

He didn't mean physically.

"I don't know what I am anymore." I had too many emotions roiling within me to be able to claim just one.

He shut the door and then paused a minute before he spoke again. "Are *we* okay?"

261

I nodded. All my words about hating him last night came rushing back to me. If anything, I hated myself, because as I stood there, the strongest emotion I felt about what he'd done last night was relief. That relief boomeranged back at me in self-disgust.

Fate, sensing the downturn of my emotions said, "No matter how you feel, it's not your fault."

"I can't…" I turned away from him. My tenuous grip on my composure didn't leave a lot of room for introspection. The mixture of pity and compassion in his eyes alone was enough to unravel me if I looked too long.

"I'm fine," I said, and would've sworn to the lie just to get that look out of his eyes. "I don't need your pity."

"It's not pity." His arms came around me, pulling me to him, even when I would've walked away. It felt good, and I could've fallen apart right then, but I managed to hold it together until he spoke. "I forced last night on you. If Kitty doesn't make it, it's my fault."

He was trying to shoulder the weight of her death again, and it undid me.

In life, I'd become jaded. After being an attorney for a while, I'd started to develop opinions of people in fairly short order. I'd title them and file them away as this or that. Everything they did was then filtered through that title, whether it was accurate or not. But once in a very rare while, something would happen; a word or action caught me off guard and made me reassess, but nothing ever this dramatic.

Fate's file had been clearly labeled arrogant,

egotistical and selfish, in big bold letters, written in a permanent, thick black marker. And in less than twenty-four hours, he'd blown apart that file into tiny shreds.

I'd assessed every action of his by a miscalculation on my part, and now I didn't know what to do with him. I didn't know how to label him anymore, and his file had turned out to be completely wrong. But then again, maybe that was the whole problem. Maybe I never should've labeled him to begin with. People very rarely ever live up to their titles anyway.

Pulling myself together, I took a step back from him, but needed a minute before I could meet his stare.

"You know, Paddy could be the devil for all we know." He was joking with me, lightening the mood because he knew I needed it. I knew he didn't think anything of the sort.

"True." I nodded but didn't believe it either.

"And yet…I trust him." Fate looked how I was feeling. Bewildered.

"Yeah, me too."

I started to walk out, but his arm snaked across my front, pulling me back against his chest. His other hand shut the door in front of me and then wrapped around my shoulders, pulling me even tighter. His chin rested on the top of my head.

My body tensed, and not because it didn't feel good, but because I didn't know what this was. It wasn't to comfort me.

Then he was letting me go, pushing me out the door toward the living room.

Chapter 33

Who did you say you were?

Paddy was relaxing on the couch with a cocktail when we entered the living room. He lifted his glass toward us and motioned for us to take a seat on the other couch, as if it were his home. We did.

He took a sip and then placed the drink on the table between us. Leaning back and looking more serious than normal, he settled in and began to talk. "I think we've all come to the same determination. We've got a problem." He pointed to me, "You've tried to deny it was a problem." There was no defense against that statement, so I sat and played with the string on my borrowed sweatpants instead.

He looked to Fate. "You've feared it was a problem but couldn't stop it." He paused and then leaned forward, picked up his glass again and finished off the remainder in one swig. "I've known it's a problem."

Uncurling my legs out from the corner of the couch

I'd tucked myself into, I got up and walked over to the wet bar. If Paddy needed a drink, it might be a good idea to join him.

My hand went to the Cutty Sark when I couldn't find my preferred brand. "Where's the Maker's Mark?" I knew he had some, and I was having a bad day. I needed *my* drink. My head swung to where Fate sat on the couch.

"I don't know." Fate wasn't looking at me when he spoke.

I shifted some bottles around and lifted a few up to peek behind them. "There was a full bottle and I'm the only one who drinks it. Where did it go?" I wasn't crazy. He'd given me a glass not that long ago.

"Drink the Cutty Sark," he said curtly, as if he had no interest in addressing the missing bottle.

"I don't *want* Cutty Sark." I plunked down another bottle a bit harder than I meant to. "I thought we were in a good place?"

"Darling," Paddy said, in his older and slightly raspy voice. I immediately looked at him, wondering what was up. He'd never, ever, called me darling. He wasn't that type of guy.

"Yes?"

"We've got bigger problems." He didn't raise his voice and delivered it in a teasing manner.

He didn't get it. That's exactly why I needed my Maker's Mark. You can't throw my life into turmoil and then screw me out of my bourbon, too. I didn't say any of that, though. I shut up and poured the Cutty Sark into the glass. I still couldn't stop my internal rant from leaking out in some shape. I walked back over to sit on the same couch as Fate and narrowed my eyes.

He looked at me briefly, turned away as if debating whether to engage or not and then spat it out anyway. "What? Just say it."

He didn't have to ask me twice. "Why would you throw out only my stuff?"

Fate scowled. "I didn't throw it out. If you must know, it broke."

"How?"

"Because that's just what happens to bottles when they get slammed against walls." He shrugged and leaned against the back of the couch with a shrug. His face said, *sue me if you have a problem with it.*

I was aghast at the sad ending for a perfectly healthy bottle. "You couldn't have thrown the Cutty?"

"No. I didn't want to throw the Cutty. I wasn't upset about the Cutty." He leaned forward, his body moving slightly in my direction, along with his hands before he clasped them together. "The Cutty didn't make me angry."

"I'm just saying, it was a brand new bottle and now I've got to drink Cutty Sark." I held up the glass to him, showing him what he'd done to me. My hand was shaking slightly as I did, and it hit me that I was still an emotional mess. It seemed like I was losing it over something as simple as what I was drinking, but that wasn't true. Dwelling on the Maker's Mark was easier than thinking of anything else, or remembering what I'd let Malokin and Luke do to me. What I'd been reduced to, and all for nothing.

Fate's eyes rested on my hand and then his palm was over mine, steadying it. "I'll get another bottle tomorrow," he said in a softer voice.

Paddy cleared his throat. "Are we done figuring out your drink?"

We both nodded.

"I need to find out if Kitty is still alive." I tucked my legs back up underneath me.

"We will," Fate said, with the same soft voice he'd used before.

"I'm okay." I wasn't, but the more he looked at me like I was on the verge of falling apart, the more I felt like I would.

He didn't believe me though, and I could see it in the way he watched me.

Unable to sit still another second under his watchful eye, I stood and started to pace the living room. This wasn't the person I was going to let myself become, the basket case that others needed to worry about.

"Paddy, what exactly do you know about them? I want answers." My voice sounded stronger than I actually was, faking emotional control until I hopefully got my feet back under me. I'd never been the weak link in my life, and I wasn't looking to linger in the position.

"Time to put your cards on the table," Fate said, in a show of solidarity.

Paddy sat silent for a moment, then one side of his mouth ticked upward. "Okay."

That hadn't been too bad. Probably should have put his feet to the fire a long time ago.

Paddy lifted his empty glass. "Have any more of that Johnny Blue?"

Fate walked around and poured him a generous measure. His eyes shifted to where I was pacing; that same look of concern made me force myself to stop and sit on the couch. Fate settled down next to me, this time sitting close enough that our sides were touching. What happened to the normal Fate that tried to bully me into what he wanted? Him I could handle. This new one, the guy who hovered, was making me feel more incompetent than ever.

I leaned forward, elbows resting on my knees. "Well?" I asked Paddy, avoiding Fate's concerned glances and trying to assert myself as anything other than how his looks made me feel.

"Something is going wrong." Paddy held up his glass and took another sip.

I put my face in my hands before I dragged them through my hair. "I hope you've got more than that."

He cleared his throat. "I do. As you know, there are certain positions in your office. All of them were created by us."

"Who's us?" I asked.

"The four. We are a part of the Universe, but not in the way you are. The forces you see swirling in the air, tweaking things here and there; we were once just a part of that larger energy. At some point, we developed a conscious sense of ourselves. A self-awareness, shall we say." He leaned forward and waved his hands over himself. "The four were born."

"So are you in charge of everything?" I'd known he was something more than just a recruiter, as he liked to describe himself. But I couldn't get my head around what he might be.

"No. We are just a conscious part of the whole. The Universe is way too vast for us to be in charge of containing all of it. Most of it is on autopilot, constantly seeking its own balance. We're more along the lines of a maintenance crew, so to speak." He waved a hand as he said the last line, again downplaying what his role probably was.

"A maintenance crew? You glow like the sun." The skepticism was thick in my voice and expression as I looked at Fate to measure his reaction. There was none. How could that be possible after what Paddy had just said? "You already knew about this," I said to Fate. It was a hunch, and if I hadn't seen the slight narrowing of his eyes, I would've thought I was being absurd to even think it.

"No, I didn't," he denied.

"Actually, come to think of it, how did you two even get in touch?" I pressed, as I looked at both of them.

Paddy took another sip of his drink, never breaking eye contact with Fate. "It was purely coincidence," he said.

Neither of them spoke as they watched the other. What did they both know? Whatever it was, I could see they were arriving at some unspoken truce, which left me in the dark.

"You know what, guys? Keep your secrets. I've got enough problems." And I meant it. I'd had enough lights flipped on for the time being.

Their silent truce in place, and me not pursuing it—at least for now—Paddy continued on with his explanation. "So, you have the positions that were intentional. But somehow, other forces that never should have existed are forming on their own."

"Just creating themselves?" Fate asked.

I felt a little better that Fate asked. At least he didn't know everything. Nobody likes a know-it-all, especially when they're looking at you the way he was me.

"Yes, and they're getting a firmer presence in our reality every day. They're already shifting the natural balance of things." Paddy looked older as he spoke, if that were possible.

My mind went back to my job in Montreal, how crowded the streets had been with people who were off balance. That was the first time it had hit me how out of whack things really seemed.

"Do you know what positions they're forming? What they're after?" Fate asked.

"The one man you've met, Luke, is Envy. We're not sure what Malokin is, or any of the others, but there are others. I think he's recruiting. You'd probably recognize several." He shot me a look, as if to imply I'd know exactly what he meant.

I didn't, not right away. It took me a moment before it clicked.

"My saves," I moaned, and put my head in my hands. "He kills them eventually but not until the right moment when he can swoop in and recruit." My mind started recounting the past weeks, mentally making a list of who I'd helped him with and the damage that would need to be undone. Looked like I might be giving Death a run for his money soon with helping people pass.

Paddy stood and walked over to the kitchen, still in view over the island. He stuck his head in the fridge and then popped it back out. Paddy looked directly at Fate. "We're going to need two things: your men, and take out. I can't believe all the healthy food you've got in this place. How do you expect me to eat this crap?"

"You want my guys?" Fate asked, ignoring the food comment completely. "They don't even know you are aware of them, and they aren't going to like finding out."

"I don't *want* them. We need them."

"We need to worry about Kitty, first. I'm not leaving her." I stood, ready to chase Paddy out of the kitchen if necessary to get our priorities back on track.

Paddy nodded. "That's what they're for. You need to set up a meeting with Malokin. Tell him what happened. Tell him everything but what I did. The more you tell him, the more likely it is he'll believe you. The last thing he knows is that you were fighting Fate."

"No, She's not going anywhere near him. I'll set up a meeting," Fate said.

"Won't work. He'll never meet with you again. He knows you double crossed him." Paddy walked over and laid a hand on my shoulder. "She, on the other hand, fought the whole time. He might still be willing to meet with her."

Fate physically removed Paddy's hand from my shoulder. "She's not doing it."

"Yes. I am."

Chapter 34

Out of Stock

Hours had passed since I'd called Malokin, and he'd agreed to meet with me tomorrow. Since then, Fate's new softer side had disappeared completely. He'd barely spoken to me since we'd argued about the new plan, and I was relieved we had company.

Half of Fate's living room was filled with his guys, called over by Fate in preparation for tomorrow. Paddy occupied the other half of the room.

Fate's guys couldn't stop staring at him. Although they tried to do it discreetly, they weren't fooling anyone. It made sense. They'd thought they knew it all and had seen it all, which was a reasonable expectation, considering their collective history.

But then there was Paddy. He looked like he had a foot in the grave, and yet he had as much presence in a room as Fate. Paddy seemed quite unperturbed by the attention and was making himself very comfortable at the bar.

"This stuff is really great!" He lifted yet another bottle. He must have made it halfway through Fate's alcohol stash by now, but it seemed to have no effect on him at all. Since I'd changed, my tolerance was twice, maybe three times that of a normal mortal. Paddy was a bottomless pit.

"Karma!" he bellowed across the room, to where I stood in the kitchen. "Does Fate have any more of this," he paused, holding the bottle up to read the label, "Chivas Regal?"

I wanted to yell back, *why are you asking me where he keeps his stuff*? The guys were speculating on my familiarity with Fate's home as their eyes watched me, waiting for my response. The craziest thing was, I actually did know where he kept the liquor backups. I'd walked past the stuff in his garage enough to know right where the extras were. In the end, I'd decided it would be easier to just get the bottle for him as opposed to dragging out the subject.

"Yeah, he's got a few spares in the garage. I'll get you one." I headed toward the door off the hallway, relieved to have a few minutes by myself. The coming respite was stolen when Fate appeared behind me, following me toward the garage door.

"Oh good, you can get it," I said, not looking for the confrontation I knew was bound to be coming.

His arm wrapped around my waist, steering me along with him anyway. I took a few steps away from him, farther into the garage, preparing myself for the fight to come. He shut the door and then stood there, blocking it.

I spun, my hands on my hips, as I said, "You know,

just once you could *ask* me to do something you wanted."

He paced halfway into the garage. "I asked you this morning. Look how well that worked out."

Fate had actually asked me several times to not call Malokin, and I'd done it anyway. I'd taken advantage of the fact that he'd been handling me with kid gloves to avoid a full-blown war. Since then, hour-by-hour, I'd watched his frustration build and knew I wasn't out of the woods yet.

He closed the distance between us. "You aren't going tomorrow. It's a bad idea, and I shouldn't have let it get this far." His voice was firm. I wondered if I was going to have a fight to leave the garage when another possible motive for his actions slammed into me.

I wasn't sure I wanted to know, but I asked anyway. "Is it tomorrow? Is that why you don't want me to go? Am I going to die?" What if he said yes? Could I still do this? The question made my knees go weak and I grabbed onto the shelf, refusing to sit even though I wanted to. Because, as far as I was concerned, the question wasn't about going or not, but what would happen when I did.

"I don't know when it'll happen." He rubbed a hand on the back of his neck as he looked down.

I grabbed a bottle of Chivas off the shelf, relieved to be ignorant of the exact moment of my death. Just because I'd asked didn't mean I wanted to know. It would make it easier to go into tomorrow without being certain I wouldn't come back.

"Eventually, we all die," I said, staring off into

space.

"Humans do. Not us. We can live for eternity, if we want." His hand gripped my shoulder, turning me toward him. "And you won't die; you'll just disappear."

When he looked at me, I could see in his eyes that he still didn't understand. The way his head tilted toward me and he watched my expression, as if he expected me to come to my senses at any moment.

I knew the possibilities. I wasn't in denial. It just changed nothing.

"You know how I feel. I can't have this fight again." I needed everything I had to keep going. Why couldn't he understand that this wasn't some sort of death wish but something I had to do?

"If you won't listen to reason, you give me no choice." He dropped his hand from my shoulder and straightened up to his full height.

"You could stop me, but you won't. Because that would cross a line, and you know it."

"I forced the other issue." He looked down at where my tattoo was.

"That was different, and we both know it." I laid a hand over my hip, which had been wrapped and taped with gauze until there wasn't a trace of light showing through any longer. I still felt the odd warmth there. "I understand this. I was losing myself. I wasn't thinking rationally anymore, I was in a constant state of desperation, trying to hold the pieces together, even as they were ripping apart. But you know this is different. I couldn't live with myself if I didn't do this, and I couldn't live with you." I leaned my hip against the shelf.

275

"What if I stop you anyway?"

There was a look in his eyes that made me think it was a very real possibility. He came closer, crowding my space. There was no denying it. I was an emotional mess, and it would feel so good to just let him shoulder all of this.

His eyes settled on my lips when he was mere inches from me. His fingers trailed my jawline and then urged my chin up. His thumb gently rubbed over my lower lip, parting it slightly as his head leaned forward. His lips touched mine and his tongue teasingly darted in my mouth, daring me to respond.

It was the first kiss we'd ever had that hadn't been coerced by Cupid. That's what made it so alarming when my senses seemed to be drowning in the taste and feel of him, no less acute than before. Pressed along me as he was now, I had that same overwhelming urge to get as close as possible. My hands wrapped around him as he pulled my hips snug to his.

His one hand cupped my ass and his other wrapped around my back, he surrounded me. That special sort of energy that was uniquely him was on full blast and overwhelming me, and I didn't want to fight it.

Then his lips broke contact with mine. "Say you won't go."

He wasn't going to give me a chance to answer, but his words yanked me sharply back into reality. I turned my head before he could kiss me again. Putting both palms on his chest, I pushed away from him.

"Please, don't ask me to do something I can't." I eyed him, wondering what the true purpose of the kiss had even been.

My eyes went back to the shelves, where the bottles of liquor sat. He had a backup of everything except Maker's Mark. I doubted he even did his own shopping, most of the time. He probably just made a list.

"Who stocks you up? Do you do your own shopping?" I asked.

His eyes went to the bottles. If there was one thing Fate was not, it was stupid.

"I told you, I'll get you more Maker's Mark." His arms crossed in front of his chest.

"Do you have a list you give someone?"

He shrugged, which I interpreted as a silent yes.

I scanned the extensive inventory until I laid eyes on the brand of wine Crow drank. It was maybe five dollars a bottle, but he loved it. Would drink nothing else.

"How often does Crow come by?" I asked, but he shrugged off the question. I knew why he wouldn't answer. I'd never seen him even talk to Crow since I'd been at the office and yet there was his wine.

It was the birthday party all over again. I couldn't have a slice of cake then, and I couldn't have a drink now.

I hadn't made the most basic list in his life, let alone the important ones. He'd stood by me last night; he'd gone against Malokin, an unknown risk, but yet, on some instinctive level, he was still resisting having me around.

"Why do you care? You don't want me to go, but you certainly don't want me to stay, either." He didn't answer, and that's when it really hit me. I was waiting for him to tell me he cared about me. I wanted him to deny what I was saying was true, but he wasn't saying anything. He couldn't answer.

I shook my head and went to leave the garage, but his arm went across my shoulders and stopped me. I didn't fight against him, but my pride kept me from looking at him.

"Just because I think you'd be better off away from here doesn't mean anything." His words were stiff, as if he were fighting to get them out. "It has nothing to do with what I want. It's just what's best, considering the situation."

"This conversation is over."

He didn't move his arm, but I broke his grasp easily as I moved toward the door. I'd finally found one confrontation that Fate wasn't prepared to have.

Chapter 35

You make my blood boil.

The building Malokin had agreed to meet me at was a high-rise in the middle of Los Angeles. The street was busy with cars, and I waited for an opening to cross. I knew two distinctly different audiences, both with differing goals in mind, were watching every step I took.

Paddy, Fate, and his men, were stationed all around. They had eyes trained on the windows of the suite Malokin was in, from every possible angle. Once I had knowledge of Kitty's presence, I'd stand in front of those windows and signal. If I didn't within fifteen minutes, they'd come anyway. That was the plan.

It was pretty simple; not too many things that could go wrong. Unless you thought about the fact that a cut across the carotid artery would incapacitate me in less than a minute, and kill me in under three.

"Miss?" the doorman asked, holding the door—which might very well lead to my death—open.

I nodded and stepped forward. "Thank you."

The lobby was a blur, and I only had eyes for the elevator, waiting at the far end of the grand entrance. He was on the top floor, but I would've known that without being told. Nothing but the penthouse suite would do for Malokin to vent his sadistic nature. Malokin hid his nature better than Luke, but it was there just the same.

Every step felt like I was waiting for a trap. The elevator doors slid shut and I expected it to plummet. When they opened, I waited for someone to be there with a gun to shoot me as I stepped toward the suite. Encountering no one wasn't doing much for my unease. If anything, it might have heightened it. I was prepared for a fight, with all the accompanying adrenaline, but had yet to find my target.

I rapped once on the suite door, and Malokin's voice called for me to come in. Not bothering to rise, he was seated by the large windows, smoking a cigar in the beautiful baroque-style room, completely alone.

As I walked toward him, I surveyed the place with the image of my death in mind. It was pristine, and had a plush carpet to lie upon, if I did end up upon it. As far as places to die went—or floors, in this case—it wasn't the worst.

My possible murderer's eyes didn't leave me as I made my way closer to him. All the dread I'd felt on my way here was becoming secondary to a certain strange satisfaction. This was the first time I'd met with him in recent times that he didn't know my every movement of the last twenty-four hours. He didn't have every word catalogued, along with other more personal situations no one had a right to eavesdrop on. If this was to be my last day, at least it was a free one.

"Have a seat," he said, motioning to the set of chairs I'd stopped behind.

"No. I'll stand."

It was such a simple statement but not between us. The act of refusing to sit was claiming my independence back. It was a polite "fuck you," and he knew it, evidenced by the twitch in his eye.

"I would've had you." After he spoke, his jaw shifted slightly to the right and then back. This was the most agitated I'd ever seen him. Actually, I wasn't sure I'd seen him riled until this moment, and it was another salve to my agitation. Was my possible death worth the admission? No, probably not. But I wasn't dead yet.

I placed my hands on the back of the chair in front of me and leaned forward slightly. "But you don't have me," I said, in a voice just above a whisper but in no ways weak.

"If you weren't helped, I would've been able to do anything I wanted to you, eventually. You were pathetic." He puffed on his cigar as he stood.

"Am I supposed to feel shame about that? Just so we're clear, I don't." It was one of the few things that didn't bother me. In fact, the only thing that was running through my mind was, if I got the opportunity, was I physically capable of killing him right now? If Kitty was dead, I wasn't walking out of here without trying. His life would end today, if I had any say in the matter.

"Nothing's changed. I still have her." His eyes were glued to me as I tried to remain stoic after this revelation. Malokin knew what those words did to me. Making me cling to hope. I couldn't turn back the clock and undo the things she and I had both seen and been put through, but sometimes just surviving had to be enough. Still, there was no going back. I felt it in myself and I saw it in Malokin.

"And yet...I think it has. How long would you like to play this game? Why are you really meeting me? Whatever you want to call this sick relationship we had between us, we both know it's over." I could repeat those words a thousand more times and not feel tired of them.

I choked on the smoke from the cigar he puffed on as he took a moment. Not because he needed time, I was sure, but because he wanted to toy with me.

His eyes roved over me and not in appreciation. "However they managed to cut you off, they were thorough."

"So you thought you could undo what was done?" I was more conscious than ever of the warmth that still radiated out from the tattoo.

"Yes. Perhaps. Now I see this was a waste of time." He shrugged, as if it weren't any real loss, even though I suspected he felt otherwise. After all, he'd hunted me for generations for a reason.

"What about Kitty?" he had no need to keep her alive now, let alone allow me to see her.

"She's right in there." He nodded to the double doors that looked like they led to a bedroom.

"What's the catch?" My hands gripped the chair, forcing myself to not burst toward her direction.

He set his cigar down on the ashtray and turned so

he stood facing me directly. "You've got two options. You can take your shot at me, or you can leave with her."

I stepped away from the chair in front of me. Face to face, we appraised each other like two duelists preparing for battle. I didn't believe for a minute he'd just let me stroll in there and get her. "You're going to let me and her just walk out of here? That's it?"

"Yes. That's right. But you have to walk away from your shot at taking me down. I know how badly you want to." Malokin smiled and waited.

"Want" was a humongous understatement. The thought of ripping into him had me salivating, and my nails were digging into the skin of my palms. My pulse picked up as I thirsted for revenge.

Palms up, he said, "Her or me. That's your choice. You won't get a chance at both."

He was baiting me. He knew exactly what I wanted to do, and it's what he wanted as well. Why, though? Was it a trap of some sort? If it was just my life, I might be willing to take the chance, but it wasn't.

My head turned toward the bedroom doors. I believed she was in there, too. I made my move closer to the window and made the gesture that would bring reinforcements. "I choose her," I said to him, hoping I'd still get both.

He was disappointed. He waved toward the door leading to the bedroom, slightly deflated. "Go get her."

I didn't move, but my eyes jumped to the door again. When I turned back he was gone. I'd let him out of my sight for less than a few seconds.

I ran and opened the double doors, expecting to be

attacked at any moment. Kitty was there, as he'd claimed. She was lying tied up and unconscious on the bed. Her chest moved up and down. She was still with us.

"Kitty?" I grabbed one of the knives holstered at my ankle and started to cut through the ropes that bound her. "Kitty," I yelled a bit louder. "You've got to get up."

Her eyes opened and the breath caught in my throat. Her eyes focused on me, but she didn't look like Kitty anymore. They must have given her something. I hoped that was all it was.

"You've got to get up. Do you hear me?" I was practically shouting in her face now.

She simply lay there. Her clothes—the same ones she'd had on when I'd seen her last—were filthy. Her hands...I couldn't look at them. They'd clearly started to heal in the broken position they'd been left in.

Pity wasn't something I had time for, right now. All I could focus on was getting us both out of there. I looped her frail arm around my shoulders and grabbed her about the waist. She was lighter than she used to be, or I wouldn't have been able to get her out of there on my own.

As it was, the stairway—if I could find it—wasn't an option if I had to carry her. The elevator was asking for trouble. If those doors opened to the wrong people, it would be like shooting fish in a barrel.

"Kitty." I squeezed her waist, trying to make her more alert. "I need you to try and walk."

She didn't even acknowledge I'd spoken.

Struggling, I made it into the other room, her feet

dragging the entire time. They'd said as soon as I'd signaled, they'd be here in less than five minutes. Where were they? Fate and the guys should've been storming in by now.

I'd have to choose. I'd never make it down all those stairs but wasn't willing to wait here for them, either. Fate had said I'd die by my neck being slit. If that were true, I wasn't going to get shot full of holes in an elevator. Choice made. I rearranged Kitty onto my back, holding her on with her arms in front of me and dragged her into the hallway.

I hit the down button and looked upward. "You got me involved in this mess. You'd better get me out!"

The doors opened seconds later. I propped Kitty up under the floor buttons, so she wouldn't take any bullets if the doors opened to fire. I leaned slightly over her and hit the lobby button.

It was the longest elevator ride of my entire life. Malokin wouldn't make it this easy. I looked at the walls of the elevator and I wondered if instead of saving her, I'd dragged Kitty into a metal coffin. It occurred to me now that I knew the means of my death, not hers.

Three floors.

Two floors.

The doors started to open to the lobby without gunfire, and I felt a glimmer of hope that we were going to get out of there. Relief started to bloom inside of me, and I let out half a cry from the excitement that not only did I have Kitty, but we were both alive.

"Kitty, you gotta help me and get up." I'd deal with the lobby people, but it would be easier if I wasn't dragging her the entire way. And where was my backup? Could they have missed my signal?

Either way, it didn't matter now. Kitty wasn't budging, and I needed to get moving. She wasn't going to make this easy on me. "Hey, cat girl, get your ass moving!" I felt bad for screaming at her after everything she'd been through, but she needed to wake the hell up. We could both easily end up dead. Until we were miles from Malokin, I wasn't going to feel safe, lobby full of people or not.

She didn't even look at me. So much for tough love.

In my concentration on her, I hadn't bothered to assess anything beyond the lobby hallway, but now the smell of smoke drew my attention.

Where were the people in the lobby? Why didn't I hear them? I poked my head out of the door that was trying to close.

There was nobody there; no one behind the desk, even. But beyond it, on the street where I could see through the makeshift barred glass doors, was absolute mayhem.

The building across the street was a roaring fire, flames shooting ten feet out of the broken windows. People were running in every direction, with sticks and makeshift weapons in their hands. What the hell had happened?

I kneeled down in front of Kitty with a renewed sense of urgency. I grabbed her face between my hands. "Get. Up."

Her eyes, which I thought were deadened a while ago, now showed so much pain that it made me physically weak myself. A tear escaped and drifted down her cheek and I wiped it away, not wanting to see it there.

"Kill me."

My jaw dropped open, but I couldn't speak. What had they done to her that was so bad that even in the face of freedom, she preferred death?

"No. Do you hear me? You're getting up and coming with me. Neither of us are dying today." I yanked her arm around my shoulders again and dragged her slowly out of the elevator with me. "If you want to die, you do it by yourself. You aren't pulling that shit on me. You hear me?"

She didn't answer and I didn't care. I'd carry her all the way to South Carolina on my back, if that's what it took. Hopefully, it wouldn't.

Once I got us out of the elevator and behind the receptionist's counter, I dug my phone out of my pocket and scrolled down quickly to Fate and dialed. When it went straight to machine, three times in a row, my hand started shaking. The cell towers were down.

A banging sound drew my eyes to the glass doors, and I peeked out from our position. Men and women, from every walk of life, were starting to ram the doors. A metal garbage can smashed into the glass. A long crack appeared, but it was still intact, even if it wouldn't be for long.

I shoved the phone in my back pocket and shook out my hands. It was all me. There was no time for nerves now.

"Listen to me," I said to Kitty, as I kneeled down on the marble surface next to her. Her eyes flickered to my face. "I don't want to die here. Do you hear me?"

She nodded. "But I will not leave here without you. So if you want to die, you're going to kill me, too." The words were harsh, but I would've said worse to get her moving.

More tears started coming down her face but I couldn't let them affect me. "Stop crying and help me get out of here."

She shook her head then looked down at her legs. "I can't walk."

"What do you mean?" I looked down at her jean clad legs in confusion and then felt along them with my hands. I didn't need to search for the answer very long. Halfway up both shins, my hands ran across the reason for her claim. They were no longer straight bones, but each had an unnatural angle. They'd been broken intentionally, in the same place and the exact same way.

I forced my lips together to keep from crying out at what they'd done to her. I shouldn't have been shocked but was anyway. Who knew what else they'd put her through? Pity was what I felt, but I couldn't let it show. Pity could be a death sentence, right now.

Another crash against the door jarred me back into the immediacy of the moment. I leaned over to see what the status of the lobby doors were. There were five people, two women and three men, trying desperately to get in, and it wasn't to seek shelter. They seemed crazed.

Crawling underneath the counter, I dragged Kitty to the cramped place beside me. "There are people that are going to break in at any moment. We need to stay quiet."

Once they passed, I'd get us out. I needed to get to

288

the next block over. We had a contingency plan; if anything went wrong, we'd meet at a small diner there. I just hoped if we made it, the others would too.

Glass shattering on the marble proceeded feet trampling in, as three sets ran past and two ran right towards us.

I held a finger over my lips to Kitty, who nodded. A knife in hand, I was prepared to fight our way out of here, if necessary.

Two pairs of feet came to stand in front of us. When they paused, I had no choice but to jump out. I couldn't wait until they found us. With so little maneuvering room, we'd be sitting ducks.

It was two of the men, and they appeared even crazier up close. They both lunged at me at the same time. I didn't think they even knew what they were doing, but if it came to them or me, I wasn't planning on waiting until the bloodlust left their eyes to ask if they'd had a bad day.

It wasn't just me, either. The idea of what Kitty had been through enraged me, and I wasn't letting her die now, after all she'd been through. I used the rage I felt for her—for what they'd done to me—to make short work of the two threats. I lashed out at the one on my right, slicing his stomach open, and spun immediately to my left, opening up the other man's neck.

I turned back to Kitty. The woman who'd just been traumatized by monsters was looking at me like I was the scary one.

"Kitty, I had to kill them. I couldn't take the chance of not getting you out of here. If you'd seen their eyes, it was us or them." Standing in a puddle of my victims' blood as I spoke wasn't any great help toward calming her down. Everything I said was true, though. There had been something deadly when I'd met their stare.

"We've got to go," I continued, too nervous to reach for her yet.

When she reached out a hand to me, I choked up but tried to hide it. She was going to be okay. If I could get us out of here, she'd be the Kitty I knew again, one day.

With my help, she crawled out from under the desk, but she still couldn't stand. No one had come into the lobby in the last few minutes, but a steady stream of looters and people were passing by the door. It looked like a war zone out there. If they were all like the two I'd just encountered, I'd have to fight our way out of here, and I'd never be able to do it carrying her. I'd have to go alone and get help.

"It might be safer to hide you somewhere and come back."

"No," her grip, even as malformed as it was now, was tight on my arm. "Kill me then but don't leave me here."

Where Malokin might still be close by. I knew it was what she was thinking, but I didn't say it either.

"Okay. We'll go together." I should've probably said die together. It was the epitome of stupid to try and get us both out of here like this, but I couldn't leave her, either. "Wrap your arms around my neck and—"

"Hey, chickie! Looks like you need a little help." I heard Bobby and spun around to see the other two

Jinxes with him as well.

If I hadn't been so busy holding up Kitty, I would've kissed every little devilish face. "How—"

"We've been watching you," Billy offered. The three of them stood in front of us, skateboards in one hand and guns in the other.

"You've been watching me? Why? For how long?" And how did I never notice them there?

"Ever since we saw you with that loser," Bobby explained, as Billy and Buddy alternated between watching the entrance and taking in the situation inside.

"But why?"

"First we were just nosey, but man you've got some interesting shit going on. It's like your life was made to order for our own amusement." Bobby's little blond eyebrows hiked up his forehead. "I mean, that mental breakdown thing you did the other night? Whew, that was a real show. Oscar worthy, is all I can say."

"Yeah, your life is like our ultimate inspiration," Billy said. "You're so jinxed, and we didn't even touch you. Really, you're like textbook screwed, these days."

"Whoa," Buddy said, from where he'd stopped to stand near Bobby. "Kitty, you look like shit. If this is what retirement looks like, fuck that."

She was leaning against my back so I couldn't see her face, but I felt the shudders go through her, shaking her too-thin frame. I started throwing the Jinxes the evil eye, but then I heard her laughter. The sound had me torn between laughing and crying in relief, to hear something other than despair coming from her.

"Come on," Bobby said. "Let's get the hell out of

291

here. Buddy, you take Kitty's legs and…"

When Bobby's voice trailed off, I looked up to see what was wrong, but it was something right. Fate was walking into the building with his men. Their clothes were black and sooty, like they'd just walked through the fires of hell.

Fate didn't stop until he was less than a foot from me, his eyes roving every inch of my frame until they settled on mine again. His hand reached out and smoothed a piece of hair away from my forehead, and then dropped quickly, as if he was surprised he'd done it.

"You look okay," he said.

"I am. What happened?" I asked.

"Malokin bombed half the buildings within a two mile radius, including the one we were in," Fate explained, as he lifted Kitty from my grasp and handed her to Lars, who was next to him.

I caught a glimpse of Lars's gloriously long black hair, now partially singed.

Noticing where my attention had gone, he said like the diva I hadn't known he had in him, "Don't ask. I'm not ready to talk about it, yet." Then he bestowed the brightest smile I'd ever seen on Kitty.

"I thought you retired?" Kitty asked, once in Lars's arms.

I'd forgotten that they might know each other. Lars, Bic, Angus and Cutty had all once been employees. If we got out of here, I was going to have to pick Kitty's brain. Maybe I'd get to finally find out what they'd done in their previous employment.

"You ready?" Fate asked me.

"To get the hell away from here? You have no idea." I scanned the lobby, but one face was missing. "Where's Paddy?"

"When it started going bad, we made him leave, just in case."

I nodded.

"Everyone ready?" Fate called to the group and received various acknowledgements.

When he moved to the front of the group, preparing to head into the fray, I stepped up beside him. Fate's hand tugged me backward, pulling me behind him, instead.

"What are you doing?" I pulled my hand out of his grasp and moved forward again.

"I want you to stay behind me, in the center." His hand darted out to push me backward again.

I jumped out of his reach. "Did you notice the dead bodies? I'm perfectly capable."

I thought he was going to fight me, but he didn't even look upset when he said, "Promise to stay by my side?"

"Promise," I replied quickly, thinking this was too easy. Maybe he was trying to fight his controlling ways.

"Cutty, you're taking the lead," Fate said, then looked at me. "Don't forget, you promised."

"You tricked me!" The knife in my hand wasn't going to see much action, buffered on every side as I was.

"In my defense, you do make it easy." It was hard to stay mad when he smiled at me like that.

We all started moving forward, and even the most crazed people moved out of our path when they saw us coming. The guys said the police had set up barricades around the perimeter of the rioting and bombing. Fate knew exactly which way to go to leave the area without the police or media seeing us.

Twenty minutes later, I stood in between Fate and a recently arrived Paddy. We stood on the outskirts of a larger group of onlookers, behind a police barricade. People from all over had amassed at the edge of the scene. Black plumes spread out into grey clouds before becoming a dingy horizon. Reporters questioned police officers about what was happening but only received "no comment" responses.

Lars had already left, offering to get Kitty situated. The other guys had insisted on helping. I kept forgetting they'd all worked with her and had probably missed her. Watching the four guys gather around her, wanting to care for her, was endearing. When they left, I knew she was in good hands.

"I think I just figured out who—or what—Malokin is," Paddy said, turning to look at the two of us. "He's Wrath."

"Wrath, as in anger? Is that even a thing or position?" I asked.

Paddy nodded. "Theoretically, anything that has enough energy in the Universe can take form."

When I thought back to the hotel room, it made sense. "When I was up there with him, he was trying to goad me into attacking him. I couldn't understand what purpose it served."

"He probably feeds off it," Paddy said.

"But why let me go?" I asked. "He didn't even try and kill me." That might have been the most nerve-wracking question I had. What else was Malokin planning?

"He's gone. For now, anyway," Paddy said.

A stray wad of ash hit me square in the forehead, and I immediately looked for the Jinxes. They were further off to the side, and Bobby lifted his chin and nodded me over to where he was standing, away from the crowd. I obliged, still reeling from the latest revelation and embracing a reason to get some space.

Bobby's eyes scanned the crowd I'd left by the barricade and lingered on Fate who, even though he hadn't followed, was paying apt attention nonetheless.

"You know your loser?" He did a single nod of his head as he asked.

There wasn't a doubt he was referring to Luke. "He's not mine, but yes. What about him?"

He pulled a scrap of paper out of his back pocket and shoved it into my hand. I smoothed out the crumples and saw the address of the building Luke had occasionally used. One particular time would never leave my mind.

"He's there." His finger tapped the paper.

I looked at the three devious little faces that always seemed in mid-smirk. "How do you know?"

"We've got a tracker on his car," Billy said. "Let's just call it a bottle of Johnny Blue once a week and we're even."

They sold themselves short, but I didn't tell them. I would've bought them a case every day for the chance to get my hands on Luke.

Bobby dug into the pocket of his hoodie and dug out a set of keys, which he thrust at me. "Here are your keys. If you call the guards for a door back, it's parked at the old arcade."

They were at the arcade, too? These guys were turning out to be worse than Malokin. "How did my car get there?" I looked at the keychain with a naked girl and looked back at him. "These aren't mine."

"I'm lending you my set. What, do you think we skateboard everywhere?" Bobby rolled his eyes and the other two laughed.

They had their own set of keys to my car? "You're the reason I constantly have no gas? I thought I had a leak!"

"Hey, you can't blame it all on us. That thing is a gas-guzzler. We can't be filling it up all the time."

I stuck the keys in my pocket before I spoke. "You aren't getting these back. No more taking my Honda."

"Sure, of course not," Bobby said, taking and then patting my hand.

Shaking my head, I realized how stupid I was. "You have more sets, don't you?"

They all shrugged and shook their heads as a murmur of, "No, of course not," and "We wouldn't do that," spewed from their lying little lips.

It wasn't important, right now. I knew where Luke was. I looked back over my shoulder and saw Paddy nod once. He already knew something was afoot. Fate was walking toward me.

"You had to expect that," Bobby said. "You *are* his girlfriend."

"No, I'm not."

"Whatever."

I walked a few feet away, with Fate heading

toward me, and dug out my phone to call for a door.

Chapter 36

Your Turn

"He's in there." I stood on a hill above the building Luke had sometimes used. It wasn't Malokin, but he would do. In some ways, I wanted Luke's blood most of all. Malokin might have been the mastermind, but it had been Luke who had screwed with my body and mind on a daily basis.

"He's mine," I said to Fate, who stood beside me.

Doubt flashed across his face, and I didn't have to ask why. "I know what I look like, but you need to trust me. I can handle this."

"You've said that to me before." His voice held no hint of teasing now.

His words stabbed deep into my psyche, and the self-doubt that plagued me returned. It felt like a condemnation, even though I didn't think he'd said it with malicious intent.

His worries were justified. How could he feel confident when I was still trying to patch all the pieces that were once me back together? It was exactly why I had to be the one to take him down.

"This fight is mine. It has to be. He stole…" My mind flitted over how to describe what he'd taken, until it finally settled on the simplest explanation, and yet the most accurate. "Me. He stole *me*. Who I was; who I'd spent a lifetime becoming. I need this."

He nodded in understanding, even though I knew he couldn't possibly fathom what I was feeling. "I know you want him, but I can't let him—"

"You aren't going to have to."

His eyes roved over me and landed on my left side, where I was resting all my weight to ease my knee, an older injury still plaguing me, made worse by dragging Kitty around. They then traveled to the rip in my shirt, and the bloody gouge peeking through, my newest addition.

"Even if I only had one last breath in my body, I could do this. You could tell me this was the moment you saw in your vision and I'd still go in there. He needs to die, and I need to be the one who kills him. Because if I don't, I'm not sure I can get me back."

He sighed as he turned to me. "Killing him isn't going to do what you think."

He believed what he was saying, but I didn't want to. I was clinging to the idea that this would fix part of what had been broken.

He looked like he might give me a fight, but then he simply nodded.

"I'm going in alone."

"You'll have your space," he said, not technically agreeing, but I could live with that. As long as Luke died by my hand, nothing else really mattered. I headed toward the building alone, just the way I wanted.

The room was dark when I opened the door. Luke sat at a desk, just staring at the wall. The door slammed closed behind me but he still didn't turn around.

"Are you going to get to your feet, or sit there like a coward?" Anger and disgust dripped from my words.

He laughed, his voice bouncing off the walls. "Not at all. I'd prefer death to what would come at the hands of Malokin." He got to his feet finally and turned. He slipped off his suit jacket and laid it over the chair he'd abandoned. His tie was tugged off and placed on top of it. "You couldn't think I'd make it that easy."

"Wouldn't want you to. Where would be the fun in that?" I kneeled down and slid one of the knives I was carrying over to him, proving just how much I was looking for a true fight.

He picked it up with a look of disgust. "You'll never learn."

"To be like you and Malokin? No. I won't." I circled him, and he moved along with me.

He ran his fingers along the edge of the knife and smiled. "I told Malokin you weren't for us."

"Did you, now."

"Yes. He thought there was some potential in you. He had big plans for you. He blames me for losing you." He shrugged. "Malokin thought he was smarter than me, but I knew you better. I saw what you were, and he only saw his plans. You were never going to bend. Break, yes. Bend, never. You would've ended up a shell of yourself but never would have been useful to him. I didn't care though, because I enjoyed breaking you. I almost had you, too. Broken, that is. The cracks had started to show."

I wanted to deny it, but he was right. I'd started to break. And even though my physical form might not show the marks after I healed, I'd have the scars forever. And right now, I really didn't believe I'd be the stronger for it in the long run. I felt like I was barely holding the pieces together.

All of my anger was wrapped up in one target at the moment. Luke—standing in front of me, smug as ever—was the inflictor of so much hurt, and it taunted me.

I looked in his eyes, the way he was staring at me, and couldn't get past the degradation. His very existence was a reminder of what I'd become. What I'd *let* him take from me. And that was how it felt. I'd allowed him do this to me, even though I knew it wasn't true in a logical sense.

"Before I'm done, I'll hear you beg," I said.

He cracked his knuckles. "Like your friend Kitty did? I understand. It's quite enjoyable."

Rage burst inside of me and I lunged at him, knife fisted in my hand. I caught the flesh on his chest but was deflected by his ribs. He, in turn, caught me with a slice to my forearm.

The new pain focused me. I spun around, out of reach of him now. No more stupid moves made in anger. I could feel Fate's eyes on me. He was close by, even if I couldn't see him. If this got messy, I knew he'd step in, and I couldn't have that.

"You'll see. Malokin will win, in the end. You have no idea what's coming," Luke said, trying to throw me off my game again.

"No, I might not know what's coming, but I know where you're going."

I swung my leg back and kicked him in the head. I heard the crack of his neck breaking. It wasn't the tortured death I'd longed for, but it was still by my hand.

He fell instantly. I stared down at him, but I felt nothing but numbness. I should've felt better. This was supposed to make me whole. This was going to make me okay, or something closer to it than I felt right now.

It didn't.

He was dead, and so was part of me, still.

Fate walked up and stood beside me, to where Luke lay dead at my feet.

I stared down, wondering if I could somehow breathe life into him and kill him again. If I did it slower this time, would I feel better? If I had dragged it out, would that have made a difference?

"Doesn't feel like you hoped." He wasn't gloating.

I looked at Fate. "No. That obvious?"

"It's all over your face."

I looked at Luke's body. My kick had been so strong, so filled with rage, it hadn't just broken his neck but ripped it partially from his body. Still, as my hands lay by my side, stained with some of his blood, I felt he'd been lucky. He'd died quickly. He'd deserved much worse. "I must be a monster, because I wish I could do it again."

"No. You aren't." Fate sighed loudly, as if he were as weary as I felt. "I doubt that's an option anyway, but it wouldn't matter. Sometimes people take things from you that you can't get back, no matter how hard you try."

When he spoke, he sounded like he was intimately acquainted with loss. I waited to see if he'd expand on it, but he didn't. I wasn't going to press for details just to ease my own pain.

I stared at my dead nemesis. Even if this did make me a monster, so be it. I might have regrets in life, but not about this. Not even a speck.

This hadn't made me feel better, but perhaps it had helped in other ways. "Did today change anything else? Do you know if I'll still die like you saw?" When he didn't answer immediately, I bit my lip and looked at him.

He turned his head toward me, and all I saw in his face were the words he didn't want to speak. Nothing had changed.

"I wish I hadn't asked."

"We'll figure something out," he said, and his arm wrapped around my shoulders, pulling me in to him.

I replied with the obligatory, "I know," but we were both full of it.

When Cutty walked in it was a welcome distraction. I wasn't surprised to see him, either. I would've been more shocked if some of the guys weren't lingering around.

"Whoa!" He said as he came to stand on my other side. "Dude, that's some fucked up shit. Who did the honors?" Cutty made a circular motion over the killing wound with his finger.

"That would be me."

"Hardcore."

303

"Thanks, I guess."

Chapter 37

Reorganizing

Kitty's desk sat in the corner of the office, papers still scattered about, bags of cat treats piled up along the perimeter. No one had touched it, not even Harold.

As people walked in and out, their eyes would dart over to it, pause a moment and look away. Everyone knew she wasn't retired anymore. That something bad had happened, but no one openly discussed it. A lot of things were being whispered lately, almost all of them true.

"Karma!" Harold yelled from the door of his office.

I closed the manual I was still working on and left it on the table. It was there, out in the open, for anyone to see, as I moseyed over to his office. Things needed to change here, and the manual was my shot across the bow. Either get on board or it would be a hostile takeover. With what might be coming, things were going to have to come out into the open.

Harold was already seated behind his desk again by time I walked in. He motioned for me to shut the door. I obliged.

His eyes perused me. He sensed it. Everyone did. There was something different about me, and it went beyond just the regular transfer stuff. But like Paddy had guessed, they couldn't quite figure out what exactly it was they were picking up on.

"What's different about you now?" Most didn't come right out and ask, though.

"Didn't we cover this stuff like a week or two ago?" Messing with Harold was becoming one of my favorite pastimes.

"Just because I don't know, doesn't mean I won't figure it out. When I do…" he waved a pencil in my face.

"You're going to stab me in the eye with the tiniest stake ever?" I made a fake gasp and put my hand over my mouth.

"You think this is a joke?"

"No. I'm sure it would be quite painful."

His face became almost as red as his hair, and I stood and walked to the door. I knew Harold well enough to know when the interrogation was complete.

"And stop working on that manual!" he yelled as I walked out.

"Sure, I will," I shouted back, though we both knew I was full of it.

Grabbing the manual from the table I'd been sitting at, I walked out of the office. I passed some of the gardeners on my way out and could feel their eyes on my back. It had been like this all week, and I didn't think it was going to be changing anytime soon. No one said anything, but they all sensed it, not just Harold.

Something was different about me, but no one asked. I was glad; I had no explanation for them. Whatever Paddy had done was changing me, but I didn't know how. Neither did he, for that matter; I'd asked him.

But it was happening. Sometimes at night, when I was very still, I thought I could feel it churning and spreading within me. Whatever it was—whatever he'd done—it was slowly growing, reaching out its tendrils within me. Every day it wound itself a bit deeper, weaving a little tighter into the very essence of what I was. Soon, it might be so much a part of me I might not feel it at all.

Maybe I should have been frightened. A year ago, I wouldn't have known enough to be scared. A week ago, I'd been too numb to be frightened. Now I knew that something was going on, but I just accepted it, just as I accepted a lot of things.

I walked out the door and left my car in the lot, deciding to get some air instead. Or so it appeared.

But I had another purpose, besides a little exercise. I could feel *them* watching. Malokin and whoever he had recruited now. It had started the very evening after the hotel incident, when we'd rescued Kitty. I'd felt their eyes on me every day since. They were always watching.

They were there when I left my condo in the morning, and they were there when I returned for the evening. I'd even taken to leaving the outside light on for them, a silent invitation that still hadn't been accepted.

I hadn't taken more than a few steps when Fate fell into step beside me, not saying a word. He joined me often enough for my walks now that I'd come to expect it.

He watched me as well, but that didn't bother me. I'd finally accepted that we were on the same side of this fight, and I needed comrades, or whatever we were to each other. He knew they were out there too, and he knew they were watching me.

"Shit, I'll be right back," he said.

I paused to see what had aggravated him. He made his way over to a car, the driver in the process of taking a box out of its trunk.

"It's supposed to go to my house, not here," I heard him say to the guy.

I glanced toward the writing on the case he was holding. I could've sworn it said Maker's Mark on the side.

The driver nodded and reloaded his trunk. He pulled out of the lot as Fate walked back toward where I was waiting.

"What was that about?" I asked, already having a good idea.

"Just someone who runs errands for me." He shrugged it off as nothing. "Feel like coming by for a drink one night?"

"I'm pretty picky about the establishments I frequent. I'll have to think about it." I turned my face away so he couldn't see my smile and looked out in the distance to the far off tree line.

I could sense them in there. I couldn't pinpoint the

spot, but I felt the disturbance. On a fluke, I tried to let the thing I'd sensed growing inside of me leak into my stare. The disruption that was there was suddenly retreated from the periphery of my senses.

That's right. You better run from me because I'll be coming for you, and I won't be alone this time.

Epilogue

"Do you have anything you'd like to share with me?" Paddy leaned a hip against the column next to him. In his opinion, there were too many columns in this place, but he wasn't surprised. He knew the decorator, and modern wasn't his deal.

"Yes, why are you leaning like that?" Farah, one of the three forms sitting on the dais, asked.

An image of Fate sprung to his mind. He'd been watching him so often, he must have picked up the habit from him.

"It's actually quite comfortable."

"It looks awfully pedestrian and undignified," Farah said.

Paddy smiled, completely content with his posture. "Would you care to talk about what you are truly upset about?"

He eyed the three sitting there. They weren't bad, but he wouldn't go as far as saying they were good, either. Like so many things in this world, they just simply were.

He wasn't sure when he'd moved past the state of being that they were in, to actually rooting for someone or something. He didn't want Karma to succeed, just to keep the peace and order. He wanted it on some deeper level he had yet to understand. He cared, now.

"I'm not upset about anything."

Paddy pushed off the column and strolled around the enormous space. "She did well, did she not?"

"I must admit, I agree with Paddy. I was quite impressed with her," Fia said.

The other man, Fith, nodded his head, as if Farah speaking out on Karma's behalf emboldened him. "I have to agree, as well."

"You both just want to agree with Paddy," Farah said, throwing accusatory looks at them.

"Farah, you must admit, you might be wrong about her," Fith continued.

Farah's lips pursed in a tense line until they finally relaxed and she spoke. "We don't know anything for sure, but perhaps."

"I'm inclined to think she's the one." Fith leaned back in his chair, looking more comfortable with the idea by the second.

"I agree," Fia said.

Farah remained silent, and Paddy slowly walked closer to the dais, where they sat upon their chairs. One chair—his—remained empty, and it would remain that way. "So?"

"Aye," Fith said.

"Aye," Fia said.

They all looked at Farah.

"We can't proceed without a unanimous decision,"

Paddy reminded her. They didn't have these votes often, but he knew she hadn't forgotten. Farah never forgot anything. Ever. Even the smallest slight.

"Not until I speak to her," Farah said.

"Then you'll have to come to Earth, but you never do that," Paddy said, stating the obvious.

"No. She'll come here."

Paddy was shocked, but he didn't show it. The other two were a different story.

"What are you saying, Farah! No one comes here. You know what could happen," Fith said.

"If she's so special, why not?" Farah countered.

Fia leaned forward to look past Fith, who sat in the middle. "No. If she's the one, we can't jeopardize her like that."

"I won't agree if she doesn't come here." Farah leaned back, looking smug. "Well, Paddy?"

"I guess we'll be having company," Paddy said. It would be the first guest they'd had in eternity.

Fated, Karma Series Book Three, Coming Soon!

Visit me on the web at www.donnaaugustine.com.

Made in the USA
San Bernardino, CA
06 February 2018